FADE TO BLACK

NOLON KING

STERLING & STONE

FADE TO BLACK

FADE TO BLACK

Chapter One

Sloane

How DO pedophiles live with the brutal truth of what they've done?

How do survivors like Sloane Alexander live without it?

Sloane had no fucking clue.

Those thoughts, and the harsh reality of what happened to her twenty years ago, had been driving her life in one way or another ever since. At least now they were finally taking her somewhere.

She should be looking at the dailies, but she couldn't tear her eyes away from the nanny-cam, showing her the inside of what her daughter, Jolie, kept calling the "babysitting trailer." The life she had longed for was finally here. Not just for her, but for Jolie. Sloane's baby girl had never looked happier, and despite the day one footage still awaiting her review — more specifically, a *yay* or *nay* on her accent — she wanted to soak up her daughter's wide smile while she could.

"Sloane?" Lila asked. "Are you okay?"

She looked over at her assistant director and smiled. "Yeah, great. Sorry. I guess I just got lost for a second there."

"Your kid is playing with Orson Beck's kid." Lila smiled back. "Who could blame you?"

Sloane did have a big job to do, but Lila had an indisputable point. Orson Beck was one of the world's biggest movie stars. Right now his son, Connor, had an arm around her daughter while the two of them were sharing a book and taking turns flipping the pages.

Adorable for sure, but work beckoned. She turned her attention from the nanny-cam to the scene in question. "Can you play it back without sound this time?"

"Without sound? Doesn't that defeat the purpose."

Sloane shook her head. "I want to see if her expression bothers me if I can't hear the accent."

"Ah. Got it." Lila dragged a finger back across the footage before pressing *Play*.

Though watching the scene, she wasn't paying attention. Too many emotions warred inside her. This was the first day of her dream come true. She wanted to soak it all in, take none of the wonder for granted. But her will was competing with the need to get the job done, on if not ahead of schedule.

Still, her new reality deserved a moment of reverence. Sloane had worked long and hard to make this happen. She was finally back in the states, filming a script she had written. Poured her heart and soul into, really. The film had a cast and crew that was better than anything she could have ever assembled on her own. Thanks to Dominic and Melinda, of course.

She owed the Shellys everything, same as she always had.

West Hollywood Sunset hadn't been shot yet, and it was

already a movie full of miracles. Sloane hadn't even told the Shellys she'd been working on a draft because she didn't want them to see it as her indulging a hobby or airing her diary in the guise of a potential indie darling. She didn't breathe a word about the potential film until the script was finished, at which point she sent a hard copy across the pond without preamble. Even the subject line had been a whisper.

Check it out and let me know what you think!

They loved *West Hollywood Sunset,* both as a story and as a mission. Neither Dominic nor Melinda ever made promises they couldn't keep, so when the Shellys vowed to both support the movie and "fully back its potential," Sloane knew the results could be explosive.

Of course, they had their reasons. But still, Orson Beck?

He was only taking a supporting role, playing a young version of Dominic Shelly. Despite Dominic adoring the casting for obvious reasons, the role was far enough below Orson's industry status to render his casting impossible. His involvement in the film smelled like a favor to Sloane. That wouldn't surprise her in the least — it seemed like half of Hollywood owed the Shellys something.

While the other half were indebted to her enemy.

Any other producers would have required, or at least requested, that Sloane cast a known actress in the lead. But that was the opposite of what Sloane wanted for *West Hollywood Sunset,* and the Shellys not only respected her wishes but encouraged her vision.

That's why Cassidy Cavalli had been cast as the stand-in for Sloane Alexander's pre-adolescent self. The thirteen-year-old actress had been in a few BBC productions but was unknown in America. An unproven lead, one of the biggest movies stars in the world taking a small part at scale, and still the Shellys were willing to let her hire Miles Dupont for sixty-percent of his typically handsome fee.

Miles would have been happy to also work at scale, of course. He and Sloane shared a daughter, but the Shellys saw anything less than sixty-percent as either an insult or a potential negative for their director. Hiring a world-renowned cinematographer — and Jolie's father — was yet another example of how hard the producers had worked to make their newest director fall in love with everything about working on the project from pre-production on.

The footage ended.

Lila turned and looked at Sloane expectantly. "So?"

"Can you play it one more time?" She really hadn't been paying attention.

"Sure thing."

Sloane's life was finally coming together. The Shellys were going to make this film a hit. But even better than any potential box office or streaming success, she was eager for the vindication. Dominic and Melinda had always been her saviors, even back then, when few people were even willing to hear her accusations, when doing so was considered an indulgence.

But not only did the Shellys listen to Sloane, they *believed* her. Encouraged Sloane to speak her truth, aloud and at the top of her lungs if need be, despite the expense to themselves.

Not that it had mattered. The Shellys couldn't really do anything for her back then.

Thanks to Nicole Everett denying every word. Maybe Sloane should never have—

No. She needed to stop that.

Return to the present. Keep her eyes and mind on the footage. This was *now*, not *then*.

She didn't need to be thinking about how vicious Wentz had been in his attempts to discredit her.

Dominic and Melinda had been there for her then, and they were here for her now. They had helped her to steer clear of his vengeance by negotiating the breaking of her contracts with minimal penalties and helping her move to London.

Now they were funding Sloane's revenge against the man who had ruined her life.

Yes, *West Hollywood Sunset* would help her break back into Hollywood, but the producers were also designing her film as a dirty bomb, destined to obliterate one of the world's worst destroyers of childhoods.

She had no interest in making a documentary, since documentaries were the broccoli of film, nor was she pitching her movie as the truth. Still, Hollywood was familiar with her story, and once word got out that the Shellys were making a movie written and directed by Sloane Alexander about a sexual predator preying on a pair of underage actresses, feathers would be ruffled, then war declared.

But like what Tarantino did with *Once Upon a Time in Hollywood* or *Inglorious Basterds*, Sloane would be revising history to give both herself and Nicole a happier ending. The sexual predator would be destroyed, and the young girl who accuses her could finally save her friend she had lost.

Maybe there was a parallel universe where good things had happened, and Sloane didn't have to spend so much time wondering how Nicole was doing. She landed a few more roles after the scandal, but the transition from child actor to adult roles was always rough. Not everyone could make it, regardless of promises made by people at the top. Nicole wasn't one of them, and since her old friend wasn't on LiveLyfe or any other social platform, Sloane didn't have any means in which she could easily cyberstalk her.

The footage ended again.

"Did you get it that time?" Lila asked.

Her assistant had to know she was spacing it. "Last time. I promise."

Lila was already reaching for the screen, ready to rewind it yet again.

This time, Sloane really did watch.

Onscreen, Cassidy's character, Daisy, was trying to convince her friend and fellow actress, Jennifer, to tell a grownup about how Oliver, their producer, kept inappropriately touching her. It was a tough scene, but Sloane wanted to tackle it on day one because she believed it would anchor Cassidy's emotions and make her character easier to access for the rest of the shoot.

Despite Cassidy's earnest delivery, Sloane couldn't help but feel that there was something off about the scene. Cassidy's British accent was peeking through the dialogue, and Sloane thought that might be diluting the performance. She wanted to watch her face sans audio to see if the accent still bothered her. After three months with a dialect coach, it shouldn't be.

Sloane leaned ever so slightly forward as the scene neared its conclusion. She loved everything, right up until that final moment.

"You can do it," said Cassidy, onscreen as Daisy, speaking to her good friend. The sound was still down, so Sloane read her lips. Not that she needed to; she knew the script by heart, because hers was the open wound that birthed it. "You just can't do it alone."

Daisy's eyes went glassy as she took a pregnant breath and let the moment steep before she finished her thought. "We'll go together."

"We'll go together," Jennifer repeated.

And scene.

"Now with sound."

Lila complied, starting the scene at the beginning for the fourth time, now with Cassidy's hint of an accent perfectly audible.

Her expressions and posture were perfect, as was the emotion in her delivery. But the word *together* sounded like it came from someone who was born and raised in Manchester, England before moving to Southern California. If Cassidy was doing an impression of thirty-two-year-old Sloane, it worked. But as twelve-year-old Daisy, it didn't.

She hated that the last line needed a reshoot, especially since everything else was so perfect. But that was a director's job, and Sloane felt grateful she was getting the chance to do it.

Sloane looked over and saw that Lila was studying her face.

"You don't hear it?"

Lila shrugged. "Seriously, I bet you're the only one who will ever hear it."

"Maybe. Can we watch it again?"

"You're the boss." Lila scrubbed back and pressed *Play*.

Perhaps it wasn't the footage bothering her.

Could be the memories that felt like a falling piano.

Her eyes were burning. She kept blinking, but they watered anyway. Beads of sweat popped out on her forehead. No, it was *covered* in sweat. Same for her palms and her wrists, and — *what the hell?* — the nooks of her elbows. Her mouth was dry, and her spine suddenly felt like someone might snap it like a twig underfoot. She felt agitated for no reason, and wanted to lash out at Lila. Yell at the poor girl for something she didn't even do. Or better,

Sloane could get out of here, hit the nearest bar, and drink herself stupid. Jolie could keep on playing with Connor. She needed to be alone. Just like she'd been—

"Are you okay?" Lila cut off her memory.

"Yeah, I'm—" She screamed as a crash interrupted her.

But at least that time Sloane wasn't alone.

Lila had yelped a little, too, and looked wildly around until her gaze settled on something not too far away.

"What was it?" Sloane was thinking a hundred uncomfortable thoughts, both connected and wildly askew.

"Looks like a light kit fell over." Lila pointed.

"Do you think anyone was hurt?" Sloane worried about anyone who might have been injured but also considered what the accident might mean for her insurance. That was followed immediately by guilt for having what she supposed might be a mercenary thought.

"I'll go see." Lila left Sloane wringing her hands.

Turned out she didn't need an assistant to play the footage. She watched it without paying much attention another two times. At the end of the second viewing, Sloane decided there wasn't anything wrong with Cassidy's delivery and the scene could stay as-is.

"Anyone hurt?" Sloane asked when she saw Lila approaching.

A light nod. "Sasha got sprayed with a few shards of glass and has a couple of superficial cuts. Abel is taking care of her."

Sloane nodded, distracted.

"Just a scare," Lila said.

Sloane kept nodding, not wanting to believe this was what she suddenly thought it might be. An omen at the very least; her worst fears, coming true ahead of schedule.

No. She was just being silly. She was a bit shook before

the lights fell, was all. It would be foolish to let the old delusions get the best of her.

But paranoia made a powerful argument.

"I'm going to take a look around, anyway," Sloane said.

Chapter Two

Sloane

SLOANE INTENDED to investigate the crash immediately, but she ran to the restroom instead.

It was dumb, letting all the stupid paranoia swallow her up like that, but curbing those biological responses had always been hard. Given the reality of her work, of course the old emotions would return to haunt her. She did manage to keep herself from vomiting, sitting on the toilet lid while working to control her breath, slowly inhaling and exhaling enough times for things to start feeling almost regular again.

Shooting had *just* started. It would be a big mistake to let her worst fears start driving her emotions or her behavior. And an even bigger mistake to allow the cast or crew to see their director at anything less than her best.

She washed her face, glancing in the mirror and anticipating the battery of questions Lila would surely be asking her. The AD was probably waiting on the other side of the bathroom door.

Once she was satisfied with her appearance, she left the bathroom. As expected, her AD was waiting for her. She walked past Lila without a glance and, anticipating the question, said, "I'm fine."

"Someone should tell your face."

Sloane stopped walking and looked at her. That had been a bold thing to say, and she would have normally appreciated the candor, but right now she was frazzled and agitated, in that order. The first emotion came courtesy of that fallen light kit, and the second was a direct result of the accident.

"It was just one of those things," Lila added. "They happen all the time."

"I know." Sloane was already walking again. "And I'm not worried. I was just deep in thought when it fell, so the accident startled me more than it should have."

"Good to hear." Lila clearly didn't believe her. "Tomosino and Becky are looking into it right now."

Sloane didn't reply, thinking hard while simultaneously trying to not get lost in her thoughts and hoping her AD wasn't judging her.

Tomosino and Becky were both terrific production assistants. Everyone who worked for Shellter Productions was a high performer at the top of his or her respective game. Dominic and Melinda each had a sixth sense for spotting raw talent. Sloane had been watching them operate for most of her life, enjoying a front row seat for the last twenty years as they went from the husband and wife team representing a small cadre of Hollywood up-and-comers to the power couple now staining the indus-try's lips.

Still, it didn't matter how excellent Tomosino and Becky might be. They were production assistants, not lighting techs … or investigators.

Except Sloane didn't need an investigator.

And she really needed to bar such thoughts from assaulting her mind.

There was no longer any scene of the crime by the time Sloane and Lila arrived in tandem. The glass was all gone from the ground. Abel got a couple of cuts while helping Sasha, but his were even more superficial than hers, and both were ready to work. Still, the accident had the feel of a narrow miss. A little to the left or right, and that fallen light kit might have led to a brutal injury. Perhaps even death.

That wasn't a constructive thought, and right now the production was waiting on Sloane, but she wasn't ready to do anything beyond studying a scene that was no longer there.

She turned to Lila. "I'm glad it's cleaned up, but shouldn't we be investigating?"

"Investigating what?"

Sloane didn't want to say it.

"Are you suggesting that Christian didn't properly do his job?" Lila asked into her silence. "Or are you suggesting that there might be sabotage on our set?"

"No, I'm not suggesting that at all." But that was exactly what she was suggesting. "Where is Christian? Why isn't he here? Shouldn't he be setting everything back up?"

Sasha, Abel, Tomosino, Becky, and a mess of people whose names Sloane couldn't rattle off the top of her head right now were all watching her while pretending not to.

Lila said, "Christian's on his way in right now. I called him a few minutes ago."

"Why wasn't he here?"

"Dominic has him working next door."

"Oh." She nodded. "Of course."

Maybe it was arrogant to think the Shellys would give Sloane an entire crew all to herself.

Christian entered the scene on cue, having just caught the wiggling caboose of their conversation. He glanced at the broken light kit, now in a pile off to the side. His face twitched with annoyance and worse. "I told Dominic I could flip back and forth between projects. Sorry about that. So, what happened?"

Lily gave him the lowdown as he nodded.

"Any idea how that might have happened?" Sloane asked. Then, because she was the director, she said, "Is it possible that you made a mistake?"

"Of course it's possible." Christian shook his head. "Do you have any idea how many times I've done this? Thirty-two years now. And I still triple check my work every time. So yes, it's possible. But not likely."

Christian didn't sound defensive at all. His voice had the tone of a man reading facts.

"What would cause the kit to fall?" Sloane asked.

"It could have been anything." Christian shrugged. "For instance—"

"In your opinion, could whatever happened to cause the crash been done without someone tampering—"

"In my opinion, no." He gave her an emphatic shake of his head.

Lila cleared her throat. "I'm not sure that—"

"We need to call the Shellys," Sloane said.

She looked like she wanted to argue. Instead, she nodded. "I'll call them right now."

Maybe this was nothing. It was *probably nothing*. But Sloane knew herself well enough to cut her paranoia off at the pass. She needed to look this situation in its beady little eyes and acknowledge that her worst fears could possibly be true — the monster who tried to destroy her was now sabotaging her movie.

Yes, of course there were an infinite number of alternative explanations. But that one lived and writhed in her gut enough that she couldn't ignore it.

Waiting was hard. The Shellys were always busy, and it wasn't reasonable for Sloane to expect them to drop everything. Day one and they were already behind schedule. Seemed like everyone on set was ready to work except for her.

But Sloane was the director. If her head wasn't in it, how could she be expected to make magic?

The doubt kept creeping through her, gaining strength and waging war on her confidence.

Dominic would be pissed.

Melinda would have to soothe him.

Sloane should really be working right now.

And she shouldn't have had Lila call but rather should have called them herself.

She could do that now, tell them never mind, sorry to bother them.

Or maybe Sloane could call the police. They would look into things, maybe ask a few questions. Then it would be in someone else's hands, and she could get back to work.

She had her phone out and was deciding on who to call first, the police or Melinda. The law made more sense. Sloane could more easily tell Melinda not to worry about it if the cops were on their way.

"Lila?"

Her AD was talking to Abel, the two of them standing several feet away. Lila paused her conversation and turned to Sloane.

"Can you please call the police and report—"

"I really don't think that's necessary." Lila tried to smile, but the expression seemed so uncertain on her face. "There was an accident. This sort of thing happens on set."

"Lila's right," boomed a voice from somewhere behind her.

Sloane turned to see Dominic walking in-stride with his wife, their expressions neutral.

"I'm glad you guys are here." But Sloane wasn't so sure about that. "It's probably nothing, but—"

"Lila's already caught us up," Dominic said.

"Why don't we take a little walk." Melinda gave her a kind smile, but there was no question mark at the end of that sentence.

Sloane followed the Shellys, same as she always did — this time to the edge of her set where any potential eavesdroppers scattered like leaves in the wind.

Dominic, direct as always, started right in. "There won't be any way for you to prove this was sabotage."

"There's also no way to prove it was only an accident." Her blurted words sounded sharper than she intended.

"Publicity would be bad for this project," Melinda said in her perfectly even tone. "Especially now."

"I thought there was no such thing as bad publicity. Isn't that what you guys always say?"

Dominic shook his head. "Not exactly."

Melinda clarified. "You're mistaking our expressions. The quote, 'There's no such thing as bad publicity' belongs to P.T. Barnum. We prefer Oscar Wilde's, 'There is only one thing in the world worse than being talked about, and that is not being talked about.' But the story being told *does* matter."

"Story is everything," Dominic added. "You can only affect your reality, but you can always change the narrative. The better you are at that, the better you are at winning life."

Melinda stared at her. "So, what's our story?"

Sloane knew some approximation of what she was supposed to say, but it wasn't fair. She offered the Shellys a shrug instead of her answer. "I don't know."

"Do we want law enforcement to be a character in this particular narrative?" Dominic asked.

She shook her head.

"Calling the police right now is a losing move," Melinda said. "I have no doubt Christian and his crew did their jobs effectively. The police will draw the wrong kind of attention. If the sabotage is coming from inside, then Dominic and I are more equipped to handle the situation. If it's not, then the police won't be any help anyway. Our resources will still be more devoted and potentially less corrupted. You're worried this is related to Wentz, and we both know he has friends on the force. It's better for everyone if you let Dominic handle this by talking to the union."

Sloane was dying to look at the floor, but needed to shove past her discomfort and accept what her producers were saying. The Shellys always had her back, and they always knew best.

"You're right." Sloane nodded. "We've lost enough time already."

"That's our girl."

Melinda put a hand on her shoulder. "What can we do to make sure you're still able to meet your obligations for tomorrow morning?"

Dammit.

She kept wanting to forget about that.

Melinda wasn't referring to the shoot — Sloane had agreed to meet with John and Vicky Treadwell, a hotshot writing team the Shellys had hired as part of the overall deal for *West Hollywood Sunset*. There would be a memoir to accompany her movie, and the Treadwells — despite being blockbuster authors themselves — would be ghosting it.

"I don't need anything." Sloane delivered her very best smile. "I'm ready, and I've got this. I'll finish today's shoot, have an awesome night with Jolie, and be prepared for my first interview with the Treadwells tomorrow."

But really, Sloane could not have been less excited about this obligatory part of her project. Of course she wanted to take the predator down for what he had done to her and Nicole all those years ago, and of course she wanted to finally be heard, but there was a big difference between the art of catharsis she found in spinning fiction around her trauma and reliving the nightmare through an unending battery of questions.

The memoir would tell the story of what happened.

Yet, Sloane was much more interested in the narrative of what *could have* or perhaps even *should have* happened. She and the Shellys had the same goals — to get her career started off right with the best possible movie, while damaging if not altogether destroying the monster's reputation in the process. Her memoir would tell the true story that inspired *West Hollywood Sunset*. The two projects would each feed the other.

Sloane had no doubt the Shellys were right, but that didn't make it any easier to do.

"We're already here." Melinda squeezed her shoulder. "Would you like us to stay?"

She shook her head. "I'm sure you have better things to do."

Dominic's phone buzzed in his hand. He glanced at the

screen, then at Melinda before turning to them both. "I'm sorry. I have to take this."

And with a nod he was off.

"I've got it," she reassured Melinda. "Promise."

But even before the words were gone from her lips, they sounded to Sloane like a lie.

Chapter Three

Dominic

DOMINIC HAD BEEN on the phone with Bryant Nash for fifteen minutes now, and he could feel the conversation continuing to slip away from him more and more by the moment.

But it wasn't his turn to speak. Right now, he needed to pretend Bryant was being perfectly reasonable and wasn't a cowardly pile of shit.

"That makes sense." It didn't, but Dominic nodded along with the words anyway. Bryant couldn't see him, but that didn't matter to Dominic in the least. He poured his whole self into the posturing, visible or not.

Bryant kept milking his bullshit excuse as Dominic walked the lot. He sounded desperate for Dominic to say something that might make him feel better. But there was no mystery around what was happening right now or who was pulling their former investor's strings.

"So, you do understand?" Bryant asked once finished.

Dominic offered him a long moment to marinate in his

cowardice before responding. "You want to pull funding from *West Hollywood Sunset* without any warning or reason, despite your numerous commitments, *after* filming has already started. Seems easy enough to understand. Did I miss anything?"

"I'm sorry about the lack of warning, but I did give you a reason."

"Oh. Is that what you call it? 'Things are a bit tight for me right now' sounds a lot more like an excuse to me." Dominic sighed then waited a few seconds to see if Bryant might interject, knowing he wouldn't. "I don't want to insult you by saying, or even implying, that you haven't given this enough thought … but really, Mr. Nash, *have you given this enough thought?*"

"Come on, Dominic. Don't do that."

"What am I doing?"

"*Mr. Nash?* We've known each other for more than a decade."

And how long have you known Wentz? But instead, he agreed. "Yes, we have."

"And you haven't last-named me since the day we met."

"I remember that day. Park City. You approached me at the Montage, said you were starting to invest in a few projects and were dying to do business with the Shellys. Is that right?"

"Sure, and haven't I—"

"You were with your wife, right?"

"Yes. Why are you asking me that, Dominic?"

"That wasn't your wife in Cabo, though." No question mark on that one.

Or any response from Bryant.

"What about Ibiza? I don't remember seeing her there, either."

Still no reply.

"One might think it was only when traveling internationally that you need a replacement for Allie. Maybe she doesn't like all the jet lag ... but I do remember that redhead in Napa, and that awfully young-looking brunette in Carmel."

Bryant finally found his balls. "Are you seriously blackmailing me right now?"

You mean, after Wentz already got to you? "Not at all. This is just the threat of blackmail."

"You can't do that to me."

"I think you mean, *You don't* want *to do that to me.* I would agree, Mr. Nash. That's the last thing I want to do."

"You don't have pictures, you don't have proof, and you're not dumb enough to ruin one of the best investor relationships you have."

Bryant was right. Dominic just wanted the guy to talk. "What is the relationship worth if the investor is no longer investing?"

"It's just this project," Bryant said.

"You mean, just the one about about the Hollywood producer preying on children. You mean, just the movie that's not even been officially announced. Do I have that right, Mr. Nash?"

Another long and uncomfortable silence.

Melinda was walking his way, but still Dominic said nothing, letting Bryant stew in the uneasiness and hopefully wonder if he'd made a massive mistake, choosing to align with the wrong mogul.

He finally cleared his throat. "It's just not a good time."

"Give me a call when you change your mind." Dominic yanked the last word from their conversation, killed the call, dropped the phone into his pocket, then smiled at his wife.

"Shall I start guessing, or are you going to tell me what that was all about?" Melinda said.

"It was Nash. He needs to back out."

"Needs to, or wants to?"

"Needs to. If he doesn't want Wentz to ruin him."

Melinda raised her eyebrows. "He said that?"

"Of course not." Dominic shook his head.

"Did you push back?"

"That wouldn't have helped." He shook his head again. "This is a long play."

Melinda was quiet, obviously thinking.

"What is it?" Dominic asked.

"Did you mention his extracurriculars in Cabo?"

Dominic nodded. "I mentioned all the ones he knows we'd be aware of but kept the rest to myself."

"Why? Wouldn't he—"

"Three girls, five girls, a hundred girls — the number of infidelities won't make a bit of difference. Wentz obviously has something much worse on the guy."

"Maybe not," Melinda said.

"You think it's a pipeline issue."

"I do." She nodded. "It's not that Wentz can ruin his reputation or his marriage, he can get Nash blacklisted in Hollywood, where he's been making most of his money for the last—"

"Thanks to us! We're the ones who—"

"That doesn't matter." Melinda put a hand on her husband's shoulder. "Wentz has been at this longer, and people are allegiant to him. There's a reason why nothing ever sticks."

"Nearly thirty years in the business, he knows where all the bodies are buried. I'm sure he has something on Nash. And the shit we've seen …" Another shake of his head. "Nothing would surprise me. But you're right; this might be as simple as following the money. Nash could have his funds tied up in any number of projects. Maybe Wentz threatened to stir up a scandal or fire the lead in some project where Nash will lose a lot more than the relative pittance he's invested in *Sunset*."

"You said he wasn't going to be a problem."

"I didn't think he would be." Dominic shook his head.

Melinda sighed as she looked at her watch.

"Don't even think about it," Dominic warned her.

"I can be in Napa by——"

"No, Melinda. Paying Nash a personal visit right now isn't going to change anything. This particular problem is bigger than your powers of persuasion, formidable though they are."

"He's fifteen-percent of our budget, Dominic."

"If we do our jobs and this movie does what we both know it's going to do, then that money-grubbing fuck will have plenty of egg on his face by the time this is over. So, he's out. Who cares? Nash has lost the chance to make a shitheap with us. Someone else will be happy to——"

"We're already shooting. And again, *it's fifteen-percent of our budget*."

"We can cover the money ourselves if we——"

"That's not how it works. Remember the model, Dominic. *Other people's money*."

Dominic offered his hand to Melinda.

She took it, then they started walking off the lot.

"I have something to tell you," he said.

But Melinda already knew. "Someone else dropped out, didn't they? Who was it?"

"Fairfax."

"Why didn't you tell me?"

"I took his call on the way over here, but we came in together, and then I had to deal with Nash."

"So, now I'm caught up. And we both know Sloane's worst fear is being realized."

Dominic said, "We just started shooting, and that's three hits in one day. We could rationalize any one of those events on their own, but the three of them together tell a story that's hard to refute."

"This film is Wentz's worst nightmare, and there's probably nothing he won't do to stop it."

"So long as he knows he won't get caught."

"We need a plan."

"We have a plan, Melinda. Hundreds of them."

And they did. Hollywood was one of the most ambitious places in the world, and the Shellys put much of the industry's drive and vision to shame. Dominic and Melinda had been steadily amassing their empire for twenty years now and had plans on top of plans on top of plans. They were creating a new and unprecedented platform and had quietly built the content, relationships, and infrastructure to cement their place in the streaming wars with an immediate and lasting foothold.

The Shellys had made an awful lot of noise on their way to the top and were now entering battle with a few enemies eager to see them dead. Not just the biggest players who didn't want to face their stiff breed of competition, but men like Liam Wentz. The uber producer had been holding a grudge against them, standing in the way of their success in obvious yet invisible ways for two decades, ever since they intervened to help Sloane when the press was rolling her in tar and feathers for accusing the predator of making advances on her and Nicole.

They stopped in front of their twin Teslas, parked side by side. Melinda's was white and Dominic's was black, but his was backed in so the driver's side doors were next to each other.

"We have to strike hard," Melinda said.

"I don't disagree in principle. But we need to be careful. We don't know how much Wentz knows."

"I'm not afraid of him. You shouldn't be, either."

Dominic shook his head. "I'm not afraid of Wentz at all, but I'm not willing to lose everything we've built here."

"Do you believe the light kit could have been an accident?"

"Of course not," he said.

"Do you believe either of our investors pulling out is a coincidence?"

Dominic looked at Melinda, not needing to dignify her question with a response.

She finished her thesis. "If we know all of those things, then we have to do something."

"Yes. Absolutely. But at the moment, that *something* should be keeping an eye on things. We sharpen the axe now, knowing we'll need to chop the tree later. For the time being, our focus should be on Sloane and making sure she's safe."

"Do you think he would be bold enough for a direct attack?"

"If Wentz thinks he has no other choice?" Dominic shrugged. "Sure, I do. And so do you."

Melinda nodded.

"We'll beef up security around the set and assign her a detail."

"She can't know. Not until the last scene is shot."

"Of course not," Dominic agreed.

But something inside him insisted that the situation might already be out of their—

Chapter Four

Sloane

CONTROL.

That's what Sloane needed most right now but couldn't seem to get.

She was already feeling disappointed for letting it slip away from her so soon into the production. That chagrin led to shame and guilt, which then dragged her down into a spiral she had to claw her way out of.

So, no surprise, the rest of her day on set was a bust.

She tried to resurrect the situation, and Lila did her best to help, but Sloane's head wasn't in it and she kept making dumb but obvious mistakes. Cassie and Orson separately gave her a timid "You sure?" for things they shouldn't have had to question. She felt ashamed of wasting everyone's time, but that guilt was still better than knowing she might be ruining her movie.

Eventually she called it quits without having to call it a day, declaring that Cassandra and Gina — the actress playing Jennifer — needed some extra rehearsal time. An excuse for sure, but not exactly a lie. The girls were happy to run their lines, and Sloane could go over the dailies again if she needed to.

But she didn't.

And thinking about what she actually did need, Sloane knew she should get away and regroup before losing her shit in front of everyone. Right now, it felt like she was location-scouting an upcoming nightmare. She wanted to grab Jolie and hit the road. Too many harsh memories were suddenly assaulting her, and a Hollywood backlot was the last place in the world she wanted to be.

"You sure you want to go right now?" Lila asked.

It was an annoying question, and Sloane worked to keep herself from snapping back. Losing face was the last thing she wanted to do. *Of course* she wasn't sure, *of course* she already felt like a failure, and *of course* she was already doubting whether she really had what it took to be a director on a film of this scale — so much bigger and bolder than the trio of indie releases she'd nailed on her own.

"Trust me," Sloane replied, mustering confidence she didn't come close to feeling, drawing from the same well of malleable emotion that had put her on the shortlist of up-and-coming child actors two decades ago, before she opened her mouth and ruined it all. "It's not just me. This day is off the rails already. Let's all get a good night's sleep, and we'll catch up tomorrow."

Lila looked at her watch then nodded. "You're the boss."

But that didn't make Sloane feel better at all.

She went to the trailer where Jolie was still playing with Connor. She knocked once then entered the room with a smile that was hard to wear and even harder to keep on her face.

"Mommy!" Jolie looked up at her, beaming.

"Hi, Sloane." Connor gave her a sheepish smile.

Tiffany didn't say anything, but at least she wasn't on her phone and appeared to have been engaged with the children before Sloane even entered.

"Hello, Jolie. Hello, Connor." She found herself smiling back and meaning it, glad Connor had used her first name instead of calling her Miss Alexander like he had been. "Grab your stuff, sweetie. It's time to go."

Jolie scrunched her face. "I thought we were going to be here until after dinner."

That inspired Sloane with an idea. "We were going to be. But I thought you might want to go out for a *special dinner* instead."

"I love special dinners!"

"I know you do," Sloane said.

The trailer door opened and everyone turned. Orson entered with a friendly wave. "I heard a rumor we were done for the day. Is that right?"

Sloane nodded.

"Where are we going for our special dinner?" Then before her mother could answer, Jolie offered a suggestion. "How about Pirate Pizza?"

Sloane hated everything about that dump. "Sure. We can go to Pirate Pizza."

"Yay!" Jolie started clapping.

But that didn't keep Sloane from feeling suddenly embarrassed, realizing that she'd just admitted to taking her daughter to a place that made Chuck-E-Cheese look like it deserved a Michelin star, and she'd done it in front of a Hollywood legend in the making.

"Can we go to Pirate Pizza, too?" Connor asked his father, sounding absurdly excited.

Orson laughed then turned to Sloane and Tiffany, explaining the obvious. "He loves Pirate Pizza."

Tiffany shrugged. "I think it's like the law when you're little."

"I'm not little." Connor crossed his arms.

"Me neither." Jolie followed his lead.

She was little enough to still like a dump like Pirate Pizza, but Sloane wasn't about to push the point. Her stomach was churning and a migraine was surely on its way.

"Are you ready?" she asked Jolie.

"Can Connor come with us?"

"If he wants to," Sloane replied, only feeling the full weight of her embarrassment once the words were all out of her mouth.

"PIRATE PIZZA!" Connor yelled.

"Sounds fun." Orson smiled, surprising the hell out of Sloane.

Tiffany shot her a barely perceptible look. Might have been jealousy.

"You don't want to do that." Sloane shook her head.

Orson Beck was a movie star, and on this particular set, she was his boss.

"Nonsense. I imagine you'll want to head home right afterward, so we can take separate cars. Which one do you guys go to? The one on San Fernando?"

"That works for me." If it had to.

Sloane couldn't believe that Orson Beck had ever been to the Pirate Pizza on San Fernando Blvd. The place felt more like a public restroom with a ball pit and a couple of arcade cabinets than any place a movie star would want to spend so much as a second of their time.

Tiffany got paid the same whether they quit early or

not, so she was thrilled with the new development. Sloane agreed to meet Orson and Connor at Pirate Pizza, then she held hands with a giddy Jolie all the way to their rental car — a RAV4 she expected to hate but was warming up to fast.

Jolie talked nonstop until her mom was pulling into the parking lot. She talked about how much fun she had with Connor, about all the games she was going to play and all the prizes she was going to win at Pirate Pizza, and about how she and Connor had both decided that they might want to be actors, just like their parents. It wasn't the first mention, and each one was making her feel increasingly uncomfortable.

"I'm not an actor," Sloane reminded her.

"But you were," Jolie argued, without sounding argumentative. "*Remaking Christmas* is my favorite holiday movie."

"That's only because your mom was in it."

"We're here!" Jolie jabbed her finger at the window.

Sloane parked, feeling like an idiot and seriously second-guessing herself. What was she thinking, inviting Orson Beck to their Pirate Pizza excursion?

Where was he? And what if he didn't show? She shouldn't have been in such a hurry to get in line. Now they were next, but Orson and Connor had yet to arrive.

"What are we going to order, Mommy?"

Sloane looked at the menu, wondering what the hell she'd been thinking. The pizza here was a joke. Salty and greasy, it sat like a rubber tire in her stomach every time. But that's what Jolie always wanted. A burger and fries would surely be terrible, but it had to be better than the pizza.

"I'm going to get a burger and—"

"But we *always* order pizza."

"Why did you ask me if there was only one right

answer?" Sloane looked at Jolie for a long moment before she finally finished her thought. "Like I was saying, I'm going to order a burger and fries. You can join me, or you can have a pizza all to yourself."

"I want a pizza all to myself!"

"Pepperoni?"

"Next," called the cashier.

There was an explosion of noise from somewhere behind them. Pirate Pizza was undiluted chaos, with every kid indulging in bedlam, animatronics singing cringey sea shanties and telling jokes that even toddlers considered stupid, and colored strobing lights that seemed designed to inspire seizures.

Sloane and Jolie moved to the front of the line.

"Ahoy, matey," the eyepatch-wearing cashier said with an illegal degree of enthusiasm. "Welcome to Pirate Pizza. Would you like to order a Davy Jones Locker, now with twice the cheese?"

"YES!" Jolie yelled.

"I guess so." Sloane smiled at the cashier. "Can you please tell us what comes with that?"

"Of course!" She beamed, hard enough to lift her eyepatch just a little. "It's a large one-topping pizza with twice the cheese, a drink, and fruit cocktail."

"Fruit cocktail?" That sounded like a terrible idea.

"What's fruit cocktail, Mommy?" Jolie asked.

"It's the hot dogs of fruit, honey."

Jolie made a face.

"Exactly," Sloane said.

"So, no fruit cocktail?" Then, as if it might influence her decision, the cashier added, "It's not extra."

"Are there any substitutions?" Sloane asked as though she cared.

"No, ma'am."

Annoyed, Sloane said, "Fine. We still don't want the fruit cocktail, but I'd like an order of onion rings."

"I don't want onion rings — why is fruit cocktail like hot dogs, Mommy?"

The fried onions weren't for Jolie. "Hot dogs are made from leftover meat. Fruit cocktail is made from leftover fruit, drowned in syrup."

"I like syrup."

"Not on your fruit, honey." Sloane could feel irritation from the people behind her, though the cashier appeared perfectly patient, looking back at them expectantly, waiting for a firm *yes* or *no* on that fruit cocktail.

"What would you like for your drink with the Davy Jones Locker?" the cashier redirected them.

"Lemonade!" Jolie told her.

"Would you like to make your drink Buried Treasure?"

That meant super-sizing it. "Sure. I'd also like a cheeseburger and an order fries — actually, can you make that a double cheeseburger?" She turned to Jolie. "Do you want fries instead of fruit cocktail?"

"I want to try the fruit cocktail."

"Can you make that two orders of fries?" Sloane asked the cashier.

"Plus the fruit cocktail?"

"No fruit cocktail," Sloane corrected her.

"What about Connor?"

Sloane glanced at the entrance. Still no Orson. "They're not here yet."

"We should order for them."

"We don't know what they want."

"They want pizza," Jolie said.

Sloane gave the cashier an apologetic glance, but she was still just looking back with one eye covered, her smile as wide as it could be.

"I'm sure Connor's father will want to order himself." He was probably only allowed chicken breast and kale, seeing as today was one of those days ending in Y.

"But then they'll have to stand in the line."

Jolie was right. The line was a lot longer now, and they were helping to lengthen it.

"Can we get another Davy Jones, please? And another order of fries ... do you have salads? Never mind." She shook her head. "I can imagine your salads. Let's get another burger. And two more drinks."

"Is that three or four?" asked the cashier.

Someone groaned behind them.

"Do you have any hard liquor?" Sloane laughed.

The cashier failed to return her mirth. "No ma'am."

"Just water for me, please."

"So I have three drinks and a water, two Davy Jones with extra cheese — no fruit cocktail — three orders of fries, and one order of onion rings. Would you like all the drinks to be Buried Treasure?"

This place kept pissing her off. Why couldn't they just say *large?*

That was a lot of food, especially considering one of the grownups almost for sure wouldn't be allowed to eat.

"Sure. Supersize everything. And can you please add another order of fries, and another order of onion rings." Just in case, she didn't want to get this wrong. "And another pepperoni pizza."

"Who's that for?" Jolie asked.

"In case Connor doesn't like extra cheese."

"What if he doesn't like pepperoni?"

"I don't know, Jolie."

Sloane could feel the stares, and hear the grumbling behind her.

She was ordering like a glutton, and even before the

cashier delivered her total Sloane knew what she was *actually* doing, finding an excuse to shove a bunch of garbage into her gullet, because that might make her feel the weensiest bit better for a few fleeting seconds.

Until she was back to feeling terrible.

But even knowing the hangover was a sure thing didn't curb her desire to drown in salt, sugar, and fat.

"Connor probably wants his fruit cocktail," Jolie argued on his behalf.

She glanced at the door again. Dammit Orson. "Fine. One fruit cocktail."

The cashier nodded.

Jolie said, "I want my fruit cocktail!"

Sloane was all out of fight. She also didn't want to get murdered by the people behind her. "You can go ahead and give us all the fruit cocktails." She smiled, hating this moment and its location.

She paid, after adding four ice creams to her bounty of garbage, feeling safe to do so after seeing that the desserts looked like they needed an hour to thaw.

She and Jolie shuffled off to the side and waited for their order. Every second Sloane spent standing there dragged her deeper into doubt. She was a hog who couldn't control stop herself from ordering a trough full of slop.

Their number was called. She collected their trays with Jolie's help, looking down at the smorgasbord of terrible choices, suddenly horrified of Orson walking through the door.

Just as she was adjusting the three trays packed with trash, and figuring out how she could get to the tables in a single trip, he did.

Chapter Five

Sloane

IN NO PARTICULAR ORDER, Sloane wanted to laugh, vomit, and disappear into nothing.

She and Jolie were sitting across from Orson Beck and his son. Weirder still, the four of them were having a great time. *So far.*

That should have been enough for Sloane, but the day's events had her spiraling. And like usual, the spiral had her questioning every little thing she did. Over ordering was bad enough, but now she wasn't even eating. Sloane was afraid to put a single fry in her mouth, now that she felt him watching.

"You're not eating." Orson looked from the spread to Sloane.

No, she wasn't. And not for lack of wanting. She longed to shove handfuls of onion rings into her mouth. She wanted to inhale the burger, crappy as she knew it would be. Jolie suggested that they start their feast with the fruit cocktails first. It wasn't a novelty for Connor since his

35

mom — former movie star Alexis Belle — brought them to Pirate Pizza all the time. He loved fruit cocktail and was thrilled to follow Jolie's lead, despite being the elder between them. At first, Sloane played off like she was being polite, waiting for the children to finish their appetizers before they all dug into the banquet together. Now she was abstaining for no apparent reason.

"I'm not hungry." That wasn't technically a lie. Sloane wanted to eat, but that didn't mean she was hungry.

Orson eyed the spread with an actor's mock disbelief. "Really?"

He took a fry, popped it into his mouth, offered her a performative smile, then followed that first fry with a proper handful, obnoxiously chewing while their children both laughed.

She wanted to join him. Few things would soothe her fraying nerves better than fast food. Specifically fries and ice cream — both on the table and waiting for her gluttonous attention. She wasn't delusional. Years of therapy had left Sloane with plenty of insight about how her own bullshit factory operated. But sometimes she needed the thing that got her from here to there, and fast food was better than a bottle of wine. Or pills.

Orson started in on one of the burgers.

Sloane picked up the other one, unwrapping the trash as her heart began to beat faster.

"Dominic and Melinda never let me eat like this." Orson shook his head, laughing, already halfway through his burger and reaching for an onion ring.

"Are you going to get in trouble?" Sloane asked.

Orson pulled a face.

She assumed he meant *Are you kidding me?* and raised her eyebrows.

He put the burger down and wiped his mouth. It was a

two-napkin job. "It's not like it used to be for me with them."

"You mean now that everyone thinks you'll be the first actor to break the thirty-million mark?"

"The fact that there's a conversation around it, sure. But that's not going to happen. I'm not worth thirty-million. It's a waste of money, and I can't see me ever accepting it."

"What?" Sloane was shocked. The kids were oblivious, arguing over who would win in a battle between Batman and Wonder Woman, with each child fighting for the opposite gender. "Why wouldn't you take it?"

"Because the kind of project that would pay me that kind of money would be the kind of project I wouldn't want to make."

"You mean something with a budget massive enough to cover a payday that big?"

"Exactly," Orson said. "A movie like that is a product."

"Aren't all movies?"

"Yes. Of course. But a movie like that is *mostly a product.*" He shrugged. "What's the difference between a million and thirty-million?"

The burger stopped halfway to her mouth. "The second one is thirty times more than the first. *Exactly.*"

"I already have more money than I can ever spend. More money than Connor or his great grandchildren can spend, even given some very long lives. I've made my string of romcoms and super hero epics. I'm absurdly proud of the work I've done, but now I can afford to make what I want to for the rest of my life."

"Aren't you a little young to pull a Bill Murray?"

Orson smiled and shook his head. "I don't think you're ever too young to pull a Bill Murray."

"Maybe not." She smiled back, wondering if he was stuffing his face just to make her feel better.

"I know you think I agreed to do *West Hollywood Sunset* as a favor to Dominic and Melinda, but that's not true."

"It's not?" That's exactly what she had thought.

"They can think it …" Another shrug. "But I would have done this for free."

"That's not true."

"I love the script, I love the story, and I loved you in—"

"Don't say it."

"A Prayer for Alice Tremble."

"Oh." Sloane didn't know what else to say.

"You expected me to say *Remaking Christmas?*" Orson asked.

"Everyone says *Remaking Christmas.*" She felt her cheeks flushing, a direct result of her yearning to disappear. Sloane swallowed and looked over at Jolie and Connor, now discussing the hierarchy of ice cream flavors. "No one ever says *A Prayer for Alice Tremble.*"

"Sounds like the theme of that movie." He smiled.

She smiled back, hard.

Sloane was the director. This was a perfectly appropriate conversation to have with one of her actors. They were even with their children.

But … they were even with their children.

"That was my favorite film I've ever worked on," Sloane admitted.

"I can tell."

Her phone rang. Glad for the distraction, she pulled it out, looked at the screen, made a face and scanned the message before returning the phone to her pocket.

"Bad news?" Orson asked.

"Not at all." She shook her head. "Just something I don't want to do."

"Something the Shellys have assured you will be a great move for your career?"

She gave him a knowing smile. It was a salve to feel so understood. "Something like that."

"You've known them a lot longer than I have." He shrugged. "I imagine you've seen some stuff."

Sloane nodded, glancing again at the children, too enraptured by magical anecdotes to invest in what the adults were saying.

"Anything you want to talk about?" Orson asked.

She looked back at him, considering. It was a good offer — an understanding ear on a day when she needed it most. But wanting the conversation made her feel week.

Sloane retreated, wishing she could sink into her booth.

Orson wasn't prying. He seemed genuinely happy to listen, or not, whatever was best for her.

"You know the Treadwells?" she asked.

"Sure. John and Vicky do a lot of work with the Shellys. They're ghosting your memoir, right?"

"Oh, that's right. Of course you would know." Sloane felt herself flush again. "Melinda showed me the final cut of *Close to Home*. It's amazing."

"That's what they're best at." Orson shook his head in apparent adoration. "They're always pairing artists with material that's perfect for them. Selena Nash is an excellent example. She knocked it out of the park and had the Shellys' full support to make it happen. I'm sure John and Vicky will get the best out of you and deliver a book you'll be proud of."

"Even if I didn't write it," Sloane said, still hating the idea. She changed the subject, sort of. "That was Vicky, messaging me with a list of topics they'd like to cover."

"The satanic panic from the 80s?" Orson looked at her seriously.

"No." She laughed. "I wish."

"Anything's better than the bullshit you want to bury, right?" Another knowing smile.

Orson was gorgeous. And that was a perfectly appropriate thought, seeing as she was his director.

She looked down at what remained of their spread and took inventory of their collective gluttony. It was hard to say who had eaten what. The shoveling had been a constant once she finally acquiesced and began stuffing her face along with everyone else.

Sloane grabbed another handful of fries. "It's just a lot of talking about myself, and I don't want to hear anything I have to say."

"I doubt that." Orson shook his head and went for the last of the onion rings. "You're just sick of people only pretending to listen. You won't get that from John and Vicky. They're good people."

"Was *The Secrets We Keep* really based on them?"

He nodded. "Far as I know, yeah. True story, more or less."

"Wow." She shook her head. "That's nuts."

Orson shrugged, maybe he was just more used to it. "Same for *Close to Home.* I figure it's only a matter of time before they make a biopic about me. It doesn't matter that I'm barely marching toward forty. I'm sure they'll want to make a movie about the dark side of my rise to stardom. Can't you see it? *Red Carpet Black.*"

She could. That was exactly the kind of thing the Shellys would do.

He changed the subject. Sort of. "It was hard enough in my twenties. I can't imagine what it was like for you as a kid."

"Probably exactly like you can imagine." Sloane glanced at Jolie, then felt embarrassed by her involuntary reaction, as if she had broadcast her worst fears in neon to Orson.

"It's a crazy business."

"Marylin Monroe nailed it," Sloane said.

"How's that?"

"You know the quote?" Maybe he didn't. "'Hollywood is a place where they'll pay you a thousand dollars for a kiss and fifty cents for your soul.'"

"Ouch." Orson swallowed. "But also, *yeah.*"

Now they even had their silence in common.

She grabbed one of the few remaining fries, now cold and nowhere close to good. But it turned out, she didn't order too much.

"I have the nanny deal with some of Connor's friends' moms. They just …"

"Won't stop throwing themselves at you?"

"Something like that," Orson said.

"Everyone is always in love with him!" Connor paused his conversation with Jolie to interject.

Then Jolie said, "Every time we go to Provisions, someone asks my mom if she's the little girl from *Remaking Christmas* all grown up, no matter how she wears her hair."

Sloane drowned in another wave of embarrassment.

Connor and Jolie returned to their rat-a-tat conversation.

Orson nodded at Connor and mouthed his next words to Sloane more than actually saying them. She strained to hear. "*I worry about his skewed reality.*"

She took a second to decode what he'd said, then replied too loudly. "I know exactly what you mean. I can't stop worrying about it." Then she leaned across the table and spoke in a much softer voice. "Jolie just started talking about wanting to be an actress, and I can't stand the idea of letting her go through anything close to what I did. But I also don't want to …"

"I know." Orson nodded. "Same for me."

Sloane couldn't remember another conversation where there had been so much both said and unsaid. In their moment of relative silence — the children were still yapping away, and the sounds of pre-adolescence at its loudest caromed against the Pirate Pizza walls — she decided to ask something that had been on her mind ever since Orson Beck had agreed to a bit part in her stupid little movie.

Your art of catharsis, Dominic redirected in her memory and mind.

"Why did you say yes to *West Hollywood Sunset,* if it wasn't a favor?"

"I already told you. I loved the script and the story. It was something I wanted to be a part of as soon as—"

"I get scaling down from tentpole projects, but you're still a lead, and Casper is a supporting role. Why would you take that?"

"You know what my favorite Tom Cruise performance is?" Orson asked.

"You're going to say *Magnolia.*"

"Because it's his best?"

"No. Because it's his smallest, and therefore the one that will prove your point right now."

Orson shook his head. "That would be Les Grossman in *Tropic Thunder.* But Frank T.J. Mackey in *Magnolia* feels like a real person. That's how I felt about Casper. Honestly, when I saw the offer, I wondered what you would see in a 'movie star' like me."

"Are you kidding?" Sloane laughed. "I've been in love with your work ever since that interview you did with *Hollywood Hunted.*"

"Oh. That."

"Don't wave it away, Orson. That was one hell of a show of honesty and integrity."

And it was. That right there made Sloane wonder whether she wanted Orson for his acting ability, marquee status, or ability to light her up in numerous ways. He was a man's man who followed his passion and erred on the side of art.

The perfect actor for Casper — Sloane couldn't allow herself to see Orson as anything more than that. It didn't matter that he was calm and down to Earth and grounded in a way that a world-famous actor who might someday command thirty-million a film and was the favorite to front the rebooted *Fatal Attraction.*

Orson still hadn't responded.

Again, she looked at the remains of their gluttony to give herself an excuse for breaking their gaze. The food was embarrassingly all gone and the natives were now getting restless.

He finally spoke. "This is going to be my *A Prayer for Alice Tremble.*"

"You mean a box office footnote that Roger Ebert called, 'A Hallmark card with none of the subtlety.'?"

"I mean, 'my favorite movie making experience.'"

"That's a lot to live up to," Sloane said.

"You can do it." Orson grinned then slapped his hands on the table and addressed the children. "Let's eat these ice creams, play some skee-ball, then get a good night's sleep. Tomorrow's going to be a great day."

Orson might be right, if Sloane could find a way to escape her appointment with—

Chapter Six

Sloane

JOHN AND VICKY were perfectly kind, but Sloane still wanted to be anywhere else in the world other than in her trailer with the Treadwells for their interrogation.

"So, you were eleven years old when your innocence was stolen from you?"

Instead of answering Vicky's question, Sloane looked down at her phone then back up at them. "Do you mind I if take this?"

John and Vicky nodded in tandem.

Sloane pretended to answer the call, feeling like an idiot, and kind of an asshole. It hadn't even been ringing. Her phone had buzzed with a text, which was enough to prompt her into the charade. Anything was better than answering these questions. She felt done, and they had barely started.

"Uh-huh …" Sloane nodded, talking to no one. "Whatever you think."

She pretended to listen, looking at her interviewers with a captive expression.

Of course they knew what she was doing.

"Tell them I'm on it." Sloane sighed. "After my interview is over, of course."

She nodded at nothing while smiling at the Treadwells then ended her imaginary call.

"All taken care of?" John asked.

"All taken care of," Sloane repeated, then explained something irrelevant but true to cover her lie. "Yesterday was sort of a disaster, for a few reasons. We need to reshoot one scene because Cassidy's accent is noticeable enough to throw it off. We have her working with a dialogue coach this morning while I'm in here with you."

"We appreciate the attention." John nodded and queued up his wife.

"But would you mind turning that off for the rest of the interview?" Vicky nodded at Sloane's phone. "We understand you're busy, but we can get most of what we need to frame the basics if you're really with us."

"I understand." Sloane smiled and shut off her phone.

Of course, Vicky was right. She wasn't trying to be disrespectful, but the interview was only just starting and yet it already felt acutely uncomfortable.

"So, you were saying?" she asked Vicky.

"I was asking about your age when all of this started. You were eleven years old, right?"

Sloane nodded. "A few weeks from turning twelve. Liam used to tell me I looked like 'quite the little teenager.'"

Vicky nodded. John wrote something down.

Sloane wished for something to eat. Cheetos would be nice. A jumbo bag, the biggest they made. Right about now, she would love to shove as much artificial cheese into her mouth as she possibly could. She needed the orange dust narcotic — or anything similar — to deal with these questions.

The Treadwells weren't trying to be invasive or dredge up old and painful memories, at least not any more than they needed to do their jobs. But that's exactly what was happening, and their queries might have been easier to answer if they *were* being hostile. Maybe then Sloane could tap into her rage instead of floating in this salty sea of unrelenting vulnerability.

"A few weeks from turning twelve," Vicky repeated.

"And how old was Nicole?" John asked.

"She's two months older than me. Couldn't you get that off of her IMDb page?"

"Of course." John gave Sloane the kind of smile that would have made her feel sure he had a daughter, even if she didn't already know that part of his story. "But the more we hear from you, the better our context and understanding."

"Okay, sure," Sloane said.

"You're doing great," Vicky told her.

"Liam was the producer of the movie, right?" John asked.

"Yes." One-word responses were fair when they already knew the answers.

"Did you audition for the role?"

Sloane turned from John to Vicky. "Everyone auditions, but Nicole and I were personally selected for the movie. He told us both that we were 'perfect by ourselves' and 'even more perfect together.'"

John scribbled something else on his tablet.

"Did that make you uncomfortable?" Vicky asked. "Or did you like the attention."

"Initially, I liked the attention," Sloane admitted. "But

only because I didn't know any better. He was really nice at first, even insisting that I call him by his first name. He always had treats for me. After he found out that I really liked Japanese candy, he usually had something in his pocket. I was little and didn't know any better. So of course I trusted him."

"I notice you never use his name," Vicky said.

"You both know who I'm talking about."

"How quickly did it go from candy to touching?" John asked.

"That happened fast." Sloane swallowed, hating the question. "The touching wasn't too bad when it began, but it did make me uncomfortable, and it started happening right away."

"What kind of touching was it, at first?" Vicky asked, compassion in her eyes.

"Small things. He would start rubbing my shoulder or try to hold my hand. But I didn't like any of it, and either nobody noticed or they pretended not to."

"Do you mean the crew?" John tried to clarify.

"I mean everyone." That part especially hurt. "The cast, the crew, my mom. Everyone."

Vicky nodded. "How about Nicole? When did the two of you start discussing this?"

"Right away. Or at least I tried. But she never wanted to talk about it."

John said, "So, the cast and crew, your mom, *and* the only other person who could have understood how you felt."

"Right," Sloane agreed. "Nicole liked all the extra attention. She thought it made her special. And my mom …"

"Go ahead," Vicky prompted. "Finish the thought."

"There's nothing to say. I was her paycheck until I

wasn't. Things between us progressively deteriorated after that. These days, we don't talk."

Vicky nodded, understanding that Sloane didn't wanted to discuss her mother even less than she wanted to talk about *him,* so she leaned forward, and the slight movement somehow matched the compassion Sloane could still see in her eyes. "Can you tell us about the day with the necklace?"

Sloane nodded. She hated talking about that day. "There isn't much to say. We were about a month into shooting the movie and—"

"It was a two-month shoot?" John interrupted.

"That's right." Sloane nodded again. "So about halfway through. He wasn't on set all the time, or even every day, but it was noticeable whenever he was. On that particular day he invited me inside his trailer, right after we broke for lunch. I actually didn't think anything of it at the time, even though I'd never been alone with him in his trailer before. I still feel bad for going, even though I know it wasn't my fault, and no one was around to stop or even warn me away from what I was about to do. But that's the thing about being a child actor. You spend so much of your time alone, you just …"

She didn't finish her thought, instead rewinding back to the more relevant reply the Treadwells were waiting for her to deliver.

"We were sitting on his couch, and he gave me a piece of jewelry … a necklace."

"What did it look like?"

She wanted to hate John for asking. But this wasn't his fault. So she shook her anger away. "It was white gold, both the chain and the letters."

"And what did it say?" Vicky asked, but she knew, too.

"*Big girl.*" She shoved the words out of her mouth, then

finished that part of the story. "He put it around my neck and told me I was years past my age. Then he said I had an 'unbelievable career ahead of me' and felt 'especially proud to be giving the world such an extraordinary talent.'"

Sloane chewed her bottom lip to keep from crying. After a long moment, she continued. "That's when he started touching me."

"Where was he touching you?" Vicky's tone was feather light.

"Everywhere." Her voice cracked. "He went under my shirt … but it wasn't like I … then he tried going down my pants … but I …"

Sloane stopped. She couldn't get the words out for several long seconds. Then she drew a deep breath and finished. "I freaked out and ran away from him."

"Did you tell anyone what had happened?" John asked.

Sloane hated admitting this part, but she shook her head like she always did when responding to that ugly little question. "He yelled at me as I was running out of the trailer that I was in big trouble if I breathed a word about what happened in there to anyone."

"And you believed him?" Another unnecessary question from Vicky.

"Of course I believed him!" She needed to calm down, so her next words came softer. "He could even be scary when he was trying to be nice. But when he issued an overt threat? I've never seen anyone so menacing. His yelling has given me nightmares for twenty years."

"I'm sorry to hear that," John said, sounding like he meant it. "Can you tell us what happened the following day?"

"We broke at lunch like we always did, but this time he

took Nicole into his trailer. I knew what he was going to do, so—"

"You *knew*, or you *imagined*?" Then Vicky crammed a qualifying explanation into the end of her thought. "I don't doubt your instincts at all, we're just looking for a timeline."

Whatever her reason, Sloane still resented the question. "Then I guess I *imagined it* when she went in and *knew it* when she came out."

"Fair enough." Vicky nodded.

"What did you know when you came out?" John asked.

"I tried warning Nicole before she even went into his trailer, but she didn't want to talk about it. I told her what happened to me and said I thought he would probably do the same thing to her and make her do stuff she didn't want to — I think that's how I put it — but she just said something like, 'He told me I was his special girl.' She swore he'd never do anything to hurt her. But then, like an hour later, after she left his trailer, I knew he had."

"What happened next?" John asked, after another pregnant moment. "Is that when you went to the Shellys?"

She nodded. "I trusted them more than anyone else."

"Including your mom?" Vicky asked the question Sloane had answered so many times before.

The answer hurt every time. "She really wanted me to be famous. Mom was always saying, 'This is the dream!' And I was so afraid of killing her dream."

"*Her dream*," Vicky repeated.

"What happened when you told your story to the Shellys?"

Sloane said, "They were professional."

"In what way?" John pressed her.

"Melinda promised they would take care of it, then Dominic went and talked to … him. Of course he denied everything, so the Shellys filed a complaint, but they told me before they did that it would have little chance of going anywhere."

"Did they give you a reason?" Vicky asked.

"Not that I really understood at the time, though it makes sense now. Dominic and Melinda have always been honest with me, and as direct as they could be at the time."

"Tell us about the relationship between you and Nicole. What happened after you brought your concerns to the Shellys?"

"He—" She closed her eyes. Took a deep breath. Started again, this time mustering tremendous effort to get out that one vile word. "*Wentz* spoke to Nicole's mother and claimed I was trying to ruin my rival's career by tarnishing her reputation."

"And why would you do that?" Then probably because she could either see or sense Sloane's irritation, Vicky added, "I know it seems like we're asking a lot of obvious questions, but every little bit of insight will really help us with this book."

"It's fine." But really it wasn't. "That's what men like that do. He's a ruthless, sadistic sexual predator who likes his victims prepubescent and insists on their silence. He'll do whatever he can to make both of those things happen. I don't think Nicole's mother is a bad person. She just did the easy thing by crucifying me."

"And how did she do that?"

Sloane turned from Vicky to John. "She went to the tabloids and said whatever she could to discredit me."

"That must have really hurt."

She turned back to Vicky. "The Shellys shielded me from the worst of it, but I did see most of her comments years later, after therapy."

"In London?" John clarified.

"Yes, in London." Sloane nodded. "We moved right after filming wrapped."

"And whose idea was that?" Vicky asked.

"The Shellys talked my mom into it. They said that since Wentz had blackballed me, my career in the States was essentially over. We had two choices, so far as they were concerned — file a lawsuit that I almost for sure couldn't win and try to salvage a career that had little chance of surviving, or cut our losses and move to the UK where I could play an American adolescent for the remainder of my teenage years."

John wanted to know how her career played out on the other side of the pond.

"It fizzled. Almost immediately. I had a contract with the studio, and the Shellys managed to make sure they didn't demand the termination payment for getting out of it. Whether the blackball hit the BBC or I'd been convicted in the court of public opinion, I'll never know. But that was it, my career as an actress was over. The media hated me and most of my fans had turned against me overnight."

"Did you ever hear anything else from Wentz?" John asked.

"Once." She drew a deep breath and tried not to shudder. "I saw him at an awards show for *The Good Daughter.* I didn't want to go, but the Shellys said it was important and so did my mom. I was so afraid of running into him, but everyone promised me I wouldn't."

"But you did?" It sounded like Vicky really didn't know this part of the story.

Sloane nodded. "He cornered me and ..."

"It's okay," John reassured her. "Take your time."

She did. A long time. But eventually, she was composed enough to finish. "He said if I ever said anything bad about him again, he'd kill me."

The Treadwells traded a glance.

Then Vicky gave her a decisive nod and a change of subject. "Tell me about therapy."

"There was a lot of it." Sloane gave them an uncomfortable laugh. "I went a few times a week for years."

"Do you still go?" John asked.

"I'm okay now."

He nodded and scribbled.

Vicky said, "Did the therapy help?"

"Absolutely." Sloane sighed and reset herself, sitting up after realizing how deeply she had sunk down into the seat. "Retiring from the business did more than anything, but the talk therapy was what really made all the difference."

"What did it help with most?" John asked.

The answer left her like a reflex. "Dealing with the psychological aftermath of being hated and treated like a liar who would say anything to get what she wanted."

Vicky nodded. "Did you miss the business?"

"Yes, but not acting. I still loved film and ended up going to the London Film School where I got my MA in filmmaking."

"Is that where you met Miles?" he asked.

"It is." She nodded. "We loved each other right away, but neither of us wanted to get married. He's a wonderful father."

Vicky said, "You're friends?"

"Best friends, yeah."

She changed the subject. "So, what brings you back to the states?"

"*West Hollywood Sunset.*"

"How many movies did you make in Europe?" he asked.

"Three. But all together they had about the same budget as a day or so of *West Hollywood.*"

"Impressive." Vicky smiled.

"Hard," Sloane countered. "But worth it."

"Did you ever ask the Shellys to help you with any of those first three movies?" John asked.

"No." She shook her head.

Vicky looked surprised. "Why not?"

"I needed to prove myself first. Dominic and Melinda had done enough for me already."

She asked a follow-up question. "What made you change your mind?"

"I was ready to tell my story."

"You mean *West Hollywood Sunset,*" John said.

Sloane took a second to consider her wording. "The story about how a powerful man tried to rape me, and how there were no consequences for his actions."

A long silence was felt by all three of them. Sloane almost enjoyed it, instead, she chased the quiet away.

"The budget for *West Hollywood Sunset* is more than it should be, but that's because the Shellys expect great things."

"The film is autobiographical?" John prompted her.

"It's about a child star who successfully takes down a Hollywood producer. Does that sound autobiographical to you?"

Vicky answered. "It sounds like maybe you'd like for it to be."

"All that therapy has helped me move past my trauma. This movie is proof to myself and the world that I'm no longer a victim."

"Do you think it's your message or your storytelling voice that the Shellys are most interested in?" Vicky asked.

"Or do you think this is personal for Dominic and Melinda?" added John.

"Of course it's personal. And I think the Shellys are

interested in the message and my voice. They're not just investing in the film. They're making it high profile for their upcoming streaming platform."

"What's next?" John asked. "If the movie does what everyone wants it to, then you'll have a lot of open doors. But are you protected if it bombs?"

"I'm making a trilogy of films after we're finished shooting *Hollywood*."

Vicky raised her eyebrows. "About?"

"Whatever Dominic and Melinda want. We haven't discussed anything specific. They want me to focus only on *Hollywood* for now. There's also this."

"*This*," Vicky repeated.

"This interview. Your memoir." Sloane looked at them both.

"*Your* memoir," John corrected her.

"Sure. My memoir."

Vicky looked her straight in the eyes. "So, the memoir wasn't your idea and you don't want to do it, is that correct?"

"I'm fine with it," Sloane said.

"You sound uneasy." Vicky still hadn't blinked.

Sloane did. Then she looked away before turning back to meet Vicky's gaze again. "Yes, I'm uneasy about the memoir. But Dominic and Melinda both promise this is the best move. Especially Melinda. She really believes in it. So, I guess I do, too."

"But it sucks talking about it," John said flatly.

"The movie is great. I'm hoping it will open people's eyes to the ways people like him get away with the terrible shit they do and that my work will help future child actors while being an entertaining piece of art the Shellys are proud of. And good enough to help the Juke brand when they finally go public with it."

For the first time, Sloane wanted to talk. It felt good to be opening up and venting emotions. So, she kept right on going. "I'm happier behind the camera than I ever was in front of it. I'm in a great place, really. It's just that I've dealt with all of this trauma already, and the movie is my response. This feels like additional distress that I don't need or want to be dragged through. Especially while I'm shooting *Hollywood*."

"Maybe that's the point," John said.

"What do you mean?"

Vicky explained. "Don't the Shellys always have a way of—"

"Getting the best out of the people working for them, no matter the means," Sloane finished. "Yeah. They sure do."

"We appreciate your candor and promise you're in excellent hands," Vicky said.

She nodded. "I believe you."

John smiled at her. "Mind if we ask you a few more questions?"

"Whatever you need," she said.

But the Treadwells never got a chance. Someone pounded on the door.

"Sorry," Sloane said to the Treadwells before turning toward the door. "Who is it?"

The door opened. Lila entered the trailer looking panicked. "You better come outside. *Right now.*"

Sloane

Sloane felt like she had fallen off her water skis and was now being dragged behind a boat in its wake. Lila was marching three feet ahead of her, on the phone and yelling at someone who was apparently barking right back, loud enough for Sloane to hear, though no specific words.

She hung up and made a sort of growling sound before turning toward her boss with a heavy sigh and a forced but genuine smile.

"Where is everyone?" Sloane asked, looking around at a ghost town of her set. "Please don't tell me there's been a fire."

"The story tells itself outside." Lila clutched the phone in her white-knuckled fist. "I'll be right out there. I need to make another call before—"

"Can't you just take one minute to—"

"I've got it," said Miles, coming up behind them, apparently relieving Lila so she could douse another fire.

"Thank you!" Lila looked both grateful and relieved as she spun around and started marching back toward the trailers.

"Where is everyone?" Sloane repeated her question for a new set of ears and saw for the first time the sorrow in his eyes.

"Union strike," Miles said. "We can't film with all of our workers picketing outside."

"A strike?" She couldn't believe it. "*All of our workers?*"

She was already marching toward the door. Miles kept pace beside her.

She threw it open and yelped. Even knowing what she was about to see, the sight was still surprising. The picketing would have been hurtful under any circumstances, but seeing the line filled with people Sloane had been starting to think of as maybe friends just yesterday was like an acid rain on her heart.

But there they were, waving signs and shouting about the working conditions at Shellter Productions.

FOLLOW THE MONEY!

GOOD ENOUGH ISN'T!!
SHAME ON YOU, SHELLTER!!

"What are they bitching about? Those signs aren't even saying anything!" Sloane exclaimed.

This was infuriating. Not just that she had to be dealing with this, but that she had been yanked from an old trauma right into a new one, without so much as a second of rest between an emotional frying pan and a professional fire.

Miles put a hand on her shoulder. "I don't have the words for how hard this sucks, but I'm sorry."

"You speak four languages and you don't have the words?" Sloane tried to make a joke, but it fell flatter than a punctured tire. "Where's Jolie?"

"She's with Tiffany. I was waiting for Lila to get you."

"Not everyone is picketing. Where are—"

"We're done for the day, chérie." He squeezed her shoulder than pulled his hand away. "Everyone has gone home."

Sloane stared at the picket line, shaking her head. "I seriously can't believe this."

"I know." Miles sighed and looked at the ground.

"Can you please go and get Jolie?"

"Of course. What are you going to do?"

"I'm going to call Melinda."

Miles looked surprised. "Not Dominic? Isn't this more his domain?"

"And what domain is that?"

"Stomping it down," he explained.

"I'd rather understand it first. And for this, I'm betting that's Melinda's domain."

He nodded. "Good luck."

Miles made it two steps before Sloane was dialing Melinda.

"There's a picket line outside of the studio right now," she said one-and-a-half rings later.

Melinda sighed. "Of course there is."

"*Of course there is,* as in, *you already knew that?*"

"Yes. But something like this was also inevitable. You know who we're dealing with."

Sloane suddenly regretted not starting the call with video. Seeing Melinda's expression might make her indifference a bit easier to swallow. "So, you're saying this isn't a big deal."

"It isn't a surprise. We discussed this. Many times."

"It wasn't ever supposed to happen this early."

"You're right," Melinda agreed. "Wentz was obviously onto us early. We don't know how that happened, but it's our bad regardless, and we will get to the bottom of it. In the meantime, believe me when I tell you that things are under control."

"What am I supposed to do now?" Sloane looked around the empty set, her heart suddenly the weight of a two-handed melon.

"Enjoy a long weekend with Jolie. By the time you return to work, everything will be back on a schedule that has already accounted for an untold number of hiccups."

"I wish you sounded more concerned."

"No, you don't," Melinda told her. "Call if you need anything, but we both know you won't."

She hung up.

Sloane walked to the nearest chair and sat.

Then she stared at the ground for five long minutes thinking about all the places she could maybe take Jolie and feeling like a terrible mother for not wanting to do any of them.

She should be here, figuring whatever this was out. Not running to Santa Barbara or San Diego.

"How do you feel about omens?"

Sloane looked up to see the man behind the voice, already smiling because she knew who it was. "I tend to believe them more than I should."

Orson nodded, smiling back at her. "Me too. So, what does that say about our movie so far?"

"I like that you think of it as *our* movie."

"That's what it is, right?"

"I hope so. I would love for the eventual audience to see it that way."

"This was an omen of good things to come," Orson said. "The universe wants us to know each other better. Because that's how we'll make a great movie. The more you know me, the—"

"And how do you suppose we do that?"

"I just got off the phone with Elouise. A super nice lady who helped me rent a place in Malibu that I'm thinking of buying. Connor and I are staying there for the next few days while I consider it. I'd love a second opinion. Maybe you and Jolie would have a good time waiting this out at the beach with us."

Sloane felt many things at once.

Of course she was delighted by the invite. But she couldn't deny her attraction to Orson, nor avoid the inappropriate landmines looming ahead if she were to live in his place for a few days. Even if nothing happened — and nothing would — there was an air of impropriety about it. Sloane was the director, and thus had power over her actor's career.

Though who was she kidding? Orson Beck was bigger than anyone involved with the film. Except for the Shellys, and even that was becoming less true all the time.

Besides, Melinda's hand was obviously behind this invitation. He was being polite, keeping her distracted on the

Shelly's behalf. Orson was one of the few true movie stars left in the world, but only because they had the foresight to bet on him.

"So … do you and Jolie want to have a good time at the beach with me and Connor? Or would you rather stick around here and feel miserable for the next few days?"

Sloane was almost for sure making a blockbuster mistake.

But at least she'd be making it with a movie star.

She finally stood and looked Orson Beck right in the eyes. "I want to have a good time at the beach with you and Connor."

"How about a great one?" He smiled and started walking toward Tiffany's trailer.

Sloane followed. "Even better."

But something wasn't right.

And Malibu wouldn't be able to solve it.

Chapter Seven

Sloane

MALIBU WAS SOLVING EVERYTHING.

At least that was its promise, midway through what would surely be an unforgettable day.

Sloane didn't know if it was the handsome cottage, the constant crashing of waves, or the fact that she was enjoying it all while watching her daughter playing and talking to one of her favorite movie stars. Or more specifically, that one of her favorite movie stars seemed to be showing definite interest in her.

Orson glanced at Connor as his son added yet another level of sand to what was already an extremely top-heavy castle.

"Admiring his ambition?" Sloane asked.

"It's like he's trying to use the entire beach to build his estate."

"He must get that from his father."

"Hardly." Orson laughed.

"Are you kidding?" Sloane still didn't understand this

part of him. He acted so humble about everything, but for one of the planet's biggest stars, that *had* to be an act. "Are you trying to tell me that you're *not ambitious?*"

"I'm not saying that." He shook his head. "But I'm not nearly as ambitious as you think."

"Right. Because superstardom happens by accident."

"It happened to me because the Shellys *made it happen.*"

"Oh, because Dominic and Melinda are totally random about everything and they picked your name out of a hat."

"I'm not saying I have zero ambition. Of course I'm driven. I just think Connor gets the relentlessness from his mother."

Sloane didn't want her smile to show, so she grabbed her glass of Mexican lemonade — the adorable nickname Orson had given to their margaritas to make her feel better about drinking so early. She was dying to know more about his ex, especially since most of what she knew had come from either the tabloids, or throwaway comments made by the Shellys.

"Do the two of you still get along?"

"Me and Alexa?"

"Yeah." She nodded.

Alexis Belle was gorgeous and rich. Her dad owned a few Los Angeles restaurants, all of them famous, and her mom was a B-list actress. She played Orson's mom in his first role, a web series called *F the 90s* that had blown up about a decade ago.

He shrugged. "We actually get along great these days."

"*These days?*"

"We've had our moments for sure. But the last few years have been great. It helps that Alexa's remarried now, and that I'm not working at Provisions for a few bucks an hour above minimum wage, still living in The Brick, and constantly stressing about whether or not I'll be able to pay my child support."

"What's The Brick?"

"The shithole building where I was living when I made the Onyx List. Connor was five years old and we were fighting *all the time.*" Orson shook his head, obviously bothered by the memory. "About everything. These days we really only have one argument."

"And what's that?" Sloane asked.

Orson chewed on his thought, clearly considering his answer before speaking ill of his ex-wife. "We disagree about what it means to give our son a great childhood without spoiling him."

"Is that possible? For our children to grow up without being at least a little bit spoiled?" She was careful to say *our children,* because it wasn't just him.

"Well, sure. But we can still be aware." He drew a breath then explained. "Anyone growing up in the United States in the twentieth century is by definition a bit spoiled. And with access to a life like this" — Orson waved a hand to indicate the private beach and the long row of multi-million-dollar mansions — "the little things become even more important. That's the kind of stuff we argue about."

"Do you think Connor will be in the industry?"

"I hope not," Orson admitted with another shrug, eyes on his son who was still adding to the top of what appeared to be a very shaky sandcastle. "I mean, if that's what makes him happy, then of course I'll support him. But a lot of people get into this business for all the wrong reasons, and those reasons are already taken care of."

"What do you mean?"

"Money, fame, opportunity. Connor has those things already."

"*You* have those things already," she corrected him.

"What's mine is his."

Sloane shook her head. "Sorry, but it doesn't work that way. Connor's going to want his own accomplishments, and that means ones that have little or nothing to do with you."

"Of course. But I can still open the door for—"

"It's not the same thing." She laughed with another little shake of her head.

"So, he shouldn't have access to my hard-won advantages?"

"Sure he should, but not at the expense of his own growth," Sloane said, then explained. "It's like with the Shellys. I could have asked for their help a few years ago, but I never did. Yes, they would have been happy to open a few doors for me, even if they didn't fund my projects themselves, but I needed to prove myself first. Knowing I could make a movie without Dominic and Melinda gave me the confidence I needed to do it with them."

"I respect that, for sure. But I would argue that you could have asked for the Shellys help earlier, and that there wouldn't have been anything wrong with doing so. I don't want Connor to be spoiled with *things,* but I do want him to have a lot of great experiences and to appreciate what he has. My doors are his doors, especially when it comes to the Shellys. I imagine the same will be true for you."

"What makes you say that?"

"Look. Dominic and Melinda might as well be my family. They've done everything for me, and I really do love them. But part of our deal is that we're always honest with each other. That's my number one condition, and for the last five years, they've respected it."

"What happened before then?" Sloane asked, sensing a story that few people would understand. One Orson might want to tell.

He offered her a thoughtful smile but redirected their exchange. "Before then … I had to find my voice."

Sloane glanced at her daughter, happily playing with Orson's son, and took a chance. "You can do better than that. I'm sure we both have our Dominic and Melinda stories. I'll gladly tell you all of mine if you'll tell me the best one or two of yours."

He laughed then gave her a well-earned smile. "Do you remember Hadley Witt?"

She looked him square in the eyes as if about to ask a very serious question. "You do know we get tabloids in London, right? Or maybe you forgot that I've known Dominic and Melinda since I was ten years old."

"Sorry. Of course." Another laugh, this one sounding slightly embarrassed. "Well, Hadley and I were never *really* a couple."

"You sure looked like a couple."

"We absolutely did. The Shellys made sure of it."

"So, what? They made you go out with her?"

"Not exactly." Now he looked even more embarrassed than before. "But they definitely let me know it was in my best interests. Hadley was on the Onyx List a couple of years before me. The Shellys were … well, I suppose they were consolidating our career trajectories."

"Double dipping with their promotional opportunities," Sloane said, to prove her understanding.

"Yeah. Exactly."

"Was it just for the pictures … or did you actually have sex with her?"

Orson raised his eyebrows. "That's a bold question."

Her heart was beating a little too hard. "This is a bold conversation."

"They wanted Hadley to keep me in line. I didn't exactly know the score at first and was dumb enough to think she was genuinely into me. After seeing things for what they were, I felt entitled to my side of the transaction."

"That's fair," Sloane said, imagining Orson Beck in bed with Hadley Witt.

He didn't respond.

And she had to ask. "Have you been asked to handle me? Is that why we're here right now? This is you keeping me in line for the Shellys?"

Her question clearly bothered him, but the patience never left his face. "I might be one of the Shellys' properties, but I'm not *property* and I don't *work* for them like so many other people do. Our relationship is different. We're here right now because I want to help you."

She swallowed. "And how do you want to help me?"

"Your relationship with the Shellys is also different. You should never be afraid to use that."

"How so?"

"You've known them all your life. Since before Dominic and Melinda were *The Shellys*. Since before Shellter Productions. They're morally gray, but as loyal as they come." He shook his head. "I just don't want you to wrongly think that they have all the power in your relationship. You need to talk about things with them. Even if you just need a shoulder to cry on or lean on, or whatever, please know that I'm here."

His words were a symphony of warmth, but Sloane couldn't help but think that they sounded like some sort of a setup. "Why do you care?"

Orson took another moment to think before answering. "The last few years, it's gotten harder and harder to trust the people around me. In a way, that fake relationship with Hadley helped to open my eyes. It happened early and fast. Part of me can't help but think that was at least part of the point, that Dominic and Melinda did that on purpose to teach me. But then again, I might be giving them too much credit. Point is, I can trust you."

"But we barely know each other." Why was she arguing against him?

"I know that you have a long road ahead of you. And I also know a slightly more detailed version of the same story everyone knows about what happened to you after *The Good Daughter*."

"Which part?" She instantly regretted sounding so bitter.

"All of it. Specifically, how you supposedly tanked your own career by leveling false accusations against Liam Wentz while also trying to ruin your costar, Nicole Cavalli. But it's an open secret in Hollywood that Wentz is a sexual predator with a thing for child actors, even if the media has kept mum on that truth. I've seen the way this town works, and I know the Shellys well enough to have zero doubt that your story is true."

Orson hadn't even finished being kind and understanding, but she still found herself in the middle of an impossibly improper response.

Sloane didn't want to be talking about any of this. She didn't want to discuss the monster or Nicole or any of what had happened to her. Such conversations were for therapy, not Malibu. She wanted to go back inside Orson's little three-bedroom cottage that he was now "almost for sure" going to buy. A half hour ago her trip to the beach had felt like a godsend, but now that trauma she could never get rid of was back to drag her into its depths.

Orson had no right to be talking about any of this.

"I'm sorry," he said, obviously but belatedly catching her expression. "I didn't mean to upset you."

"I'm fine."

She could practically hear him thinking, *You sure don't sound like it.*

Why was this so hard?

Why couldn't the past stay where it belonged?

Why did she have to doubt herself, even when good things were happening?

Like right now, she couldn't stop wondering if Orson had only invited her to Malibu because he felt sorry for her. Or because he was trying to satisfy his curiosity and get the real story the media had missed.

Sloane was hot for him but kept feeling chills thinking he might only be feigning his attraction for reasons she didn't understand. Even if none of that was true and Orson really did *think* he liked her, the star would be wrong.

He couldn't really like Sloane because he didn't really know her.

The things he did know all came from the stories that made her want to scream.

They shared silence for nearly a minute. Sloane had cycled through a dozen things to maybe say, but they were all so thoroughly stupid that she spent the entire time chewing on her bottom lip instead of opening her mouth.

"Everything will be okay." Orson looked at her, his eyes still patient, his voice still kind, and his smile still there. "The movie and you."

She looked back, wanting to believe him, but still not knowing what to say.

"What are you most worried about?" Orson asked.

"Falling apart." The words left her mouth before she could stop them.

He nodded, appearing to appreciate her honesty. "What would help you the most right now?"

"Getting back to work," she answered immediately.

He gave her a knowing smile. "Then you have nothing to worry about."

"Why is that?"

Orson smiled wider. "Because I'm sure the Shellys have that handled. I can picture Dominic yelling at someone right this second. Can't you?"

She surprised herself with a smile of her own.

Because, yes, Sloane could picture that, too.

Chapter Eight

Dominic

DOMINIC FINISHED YELLING THEN HUNG up the phone.

He walked to his bar with a smile. Poured a half-glass of Artemis Tull Diamond into a glass, poured a second for Melinda, then left both whiskeys on the bar until she got there.

It had been a satisfying call. Dominic didn't exactly enjoy verbally slapping people around. Doing so frequently would be a bad idea. It could lead to seeking the behavior out. And that would make Dominic a bully instead of the kind of man who stood up for the underdog. But he was excellent at twisting an exchange to his favor and relished any victory he could share with Melinda.

Dominic headed to the set of chairs by the window overlooking the pool and their sprawling back lawn. He took out his phone, scrolled for a few mindless minutes before deciding there were much better ways to spend the silence, then placed his phone on the end table between the chairs and took in his view instead.

He was right to abandon the technology. Dominic had only been staring out the window for a few seconds before his brain began bouncing from one connection to the next. So many details to so many plans, finally coalescing after all these years.

Juke would change the world, then the world would change everything else.

He looked over just as Melinda drifted into the room.

She glanced at the bar, saw their drinks waiting, then went to retrieve them.

After handing one to Dominic, she sat next to him. "Your news is obviously good. Why don't you go first?"

"So, opposite of the way we usually do things?" He took a sip.

She took a long one of her own. "I'd like to hear something positive." Then followed it with another.

"The strike is over. Everyone will be back to work on Monday. Carlson will probably cry himself to sleep tonight."

"Carlson needs to cry himself to sleep." Melinda took a third swallow, set her tumbler on the end table, then stood. She wrapped her arms around Dominic's neck and slithered onto his lap. "Thank you for taking care of that for us." They kissed on the lips, not long but just enough. "I'm glad that you handled that mess, but we do have another problem."

"I gathered." Dominic glanced at their glasses. "Should we finish our drinks first?"

"Parvati says Juke development is falling seriously behind."

"And …" Because of course that was the start, not the end, of it.

"And it's definitely sabotage."

"Do we know this, or do we think this?"

72

"That is the question." Melinda sighed, still looking into her husband's eyes. "And one Parvati and her team have spent an awful lot of time on. Honestly, if we weren't on the lookout for bullshit from Wentz we could have — *would have* written this off as part of a difficult development. At least for a while."

"You said, 'definitely sabotage.' How do we know for sure?"

"We don't, really ... but then again, of course we do. Day one sabotage on-set? The strike? Hacking our code? Do you really think—"

"Honey," Dominic softly said as he set a gentle hand on each of her arms, "of course Wentz is behind this. But what do we *absolutely know? Why* is production lagging, and how behind are we?"

Melinda nodded. Then her posture reset along with her voice. "There's a worm."

"What kind of a worm? What is it doing?"

"Or at least, Parvati *thinks* it's a worm. That's the problem, Dominic. You're asking what we *know,* and the answer to that is 'practically nothing.' We might have been hacked with a worm. Wentz might have an insider introducing broken lines into the code, but random shit keeps breaking, and there are twice as many evident glitches today than yesterday. The problems keep getting worse, and each of them goes deep."

"So the entire dev room is distracted."

"Exactly," Melinda agreed. "Which points to *sabotage.*"

"How far behind are we?"

"You're not—"

Dominic's phone started playing Warren Zevon's *Lawyers, Guns and Money* — a ringtone that only played when their lawyer called. He only ever called from that number with an emergency. And not the sort he wanted to handle over the phone. "Hold that thought." He gave her a nod then grabbed and answered his phone with an order. "Hey, Solomon. Face-to-face."

Melinda climbed off his lap. Then Dominic hung up and aimed his phone at the nearest TV. Two seconds later it went bright with their lawyer's stoic face.

"What is it?" Melinda asked.

"We have a serious problem." Solomon swallowed.

This wasn't just serious. It was worse than expected.

"Someone broke their contract," Melinda guessed.

"No." Dominic shook his head, already ahead of her. "It's worse than that." Then to Tummel, he said, "How many contracts?"

"Three."

Melinda asked, "Who?"

Solomon swallowed again. "Hendrix, Boone, and Coleman."

Silence.

Dominic finally said, "This isn't unexpected."

"Three is unexpected." Melinda shook her head. "*They* are unexpected."

She was right on both counts. They expected Wentz to squeeze hard and hit them with a broken contract or two, but not with three, and certainly not so soon.

The number wasn't even the worst of it. Amaya Hendrix, Samantha Boone, and Noah Coleman — the trio was at the top of every industry list detailing Hollywood's up and coming stars. Because the Shellys had put them there. They weren't three of Shellters biggest names, but they would be.

"This is our fault," Dominic said. "Every one of us should have seen this on our own. There's no excuse for our collective failure. *Of course* that fucker went for the low hanging fruit. We expected Wentz to hit us in our profit centers, but he hit our investments instead. Not only will Wentz benefit from our money and work, his signing our people onto projects is leverage he can use to make others jump ship."

"There is some good news there." Solomon brightened. "The contracts were all bought out — 3.7 million for all three combined, wired by the end of business today."

"They're worth a hell of a lot more than that," Melinda said.

"Then it's our fault for not making the buyout amount higher," Dominic argued. "This is on us."

"You're right, honey." She turned to Solomon. "Don't go far. We'll be calling you soon."

A single nod then the lawyer was gone.

After the screen turned black, Melinda climbed back onto Dominic's lap.

He looked into her eyes. "I know what you're going to say."

"Of course you do." Melinda began grinding against him.

"So, this is war?"

"It was already war," she said, grinding harder. "Consider this genocide for his reputation."

"Then genocide it—"

But her mouth was on him.

Chapter Nine

Sloane

"Cut!" Sloane called.

"Was that better?" Orson asked her.

"It was perfect."

He nodded.

Three takes, and the first two were terrific. But she wouldn't get anything better than that third one and both of them knew it.

She was back on set, exactly where she wanted to be, and the production was finally moving.

When she let it.

Sloane was pissed at herself for a few things, but at least she was back in a place where she could more easily focus her energies. The strike was over, almost before it started, leaving Sloane yet another reason to roll her eyes at her own idiotic behavior.

Why had she ever doubted the Shellys? Of course they could and would take care of it. Melinda had been right; the whole thing had been an excuse to take a nice little vacation … right at the start of filming. She had permission to see things that way and still wasted the opportunity. She could have fully enjoyed her time with Orson instead of losing her shit like she had.

Good thing he was such a professional. Orson came to the set ready to work. If Sloane didn't already know better, she wouldn't have any idea that his director fell apart just yesterday. He wasn't treating her with pity, despite her behavior in Malibu.

"Fifteen minutes," she announced to the room.

Murmurs and shuffles as everyone went their separate ways, including Lila. Then Sloane found herself quite suddenly, and mercifully, alone.

She sat, wanting a moment to think, but also needing to prove that she could go five minutes without checking on the nanny-cam, which was just one of her two-thousand neuroses. Approximately. Though that number did seem to be multiplying fast.

After Sloane had checked the nanny-cam a half-dozen times in the first hour, Lila offered to do that for her in the future, so she could "stay focused on the work." It was hard to ignore the sarcasm when Lila vowed to keep her abreast of any important updates with completion of their current project — a thousand-piece puzzle of Oliver from Pixar's *Ratatouille*. Sloane had to steal her glances after that.

It's not like she enjoyed feeling this neurotic. She hated that she couldn't stop checking. Or thinking about checking. Things were going great, and yet something in her stupid lizard brain kept insisting that Jolie was in danger.

Or that something was about to go horribly, terribly wrong.

If it hadn't already.

But that was ridiculous. The day had been going great

so far. The only thing even remotely close to a problem was her.

Cassidy's accent was barely audible, though Sloane was still having to work at pretending she didn't hear it. They reshot her scene from the first day, and Sloane was thrilled with the result. Or at least she wanted to be, and probably would be by the end of the day.

Orson nailed his first scene, which delighted her, not just because she could put that one to rest in her mind, but because his performance made it easy to imagine how he might approach a few other scenes that she had questions about.

She caught Miles smiling several times throughout the morning and well into the afternoon.

Her boxes were all ticked. And yet for some reason, her teeth were still on edge.

Sloane stood and walked over to the nanny-cam. After making sure Jolie was still alive and preferably smiling, she chastised herself for giving into such base paranoia yet again.

She was the director and doing her production zero favors by expecting the shadow of disaster to lay in wait around each and every corner.

It was so infuriating, this thing she couldn't outrun. Past trauma kept turning her into a victim of present para-noia. Sloane saw potential danger everywhere.

She couldn't stop staring at the lighting rigs, waiting for one to fall. Or analyzing every gesture made by the crew, assuming each one might be a precursor to someone walking out. Cassidy had delivered her lines perfectly, and yet Sloane couldn't stop wondering if she was perhaps missing something obvious. Or if—

"Hey." She heard Miles behind her. "You got a minute?"

She turned around and her stomach sank. She knew the look on his face. And it didn't help that he had waited until no one was around before approaching her. "What? What did I do?"

"I didn't say you did anything, chérie. So please don't start out being defensive."

"You look like you're going to scold me."

"You always think that," he said.

"Your fault for being German. What did I do wrong?"

"I'm half-French and half-Belgian, and you didn't do anything *wrong*."

"Fine, Miles. What could I have done better?"

"There are a couple of things we could do to move faster."

"You seemed happy with the day so far," Sloane said. "What am I missing?"

"I am happy. But we're almost three days behind schedule now. We should—"

"The schedule has padding."

"That doesn't mean we can take that padding for granted."

"I'm not taking it for granted, Miles! I'm—"

"Perhaps overthinking a few things," he finished.

Which only infuriated her further. "I'm taking the time to get things right."

"You absolutely are. But you're also overthinking Cassidy's accent. She's got this, okay? And—"\"

"You act like I'm being picky without any reason!"

"I didn't say you were being picky ..."

"*But?*"

"But I do believe that we're slowed down a bit by your neuroses—"

"Screw you, Miles!"

He softly replied with a shake of his head. "Remember, we're not supposed to raise our voices at one another."

"*Remember*, I asked you to please not use that word."

"*Picky?*" Then, "Oh. Sorry. I didn't mean to—"

"It's fine, Miles." She already wished this was over. He was right and she didn't need the reminder. "I'll try harder, do better, whatever. I get it."

He looked at her, obviously wanting to say more — anything from an apology to another slew of unwanted advice. After a long pause, he said, "I guess I'll go and check in on Jolie, then."

"Thanks." The guilt felt terrible. "Sorry for being a jerk."

Miles gave her a forgiving smile. "You're not being a jerk. We knew this was going to be hard."

"Yeah, well …" She didn't have an end to that thought.

But Miles didn't need one and wasn't waiting around for it. He wasn't even gone from the set before she was second-guessing herself again, starting with a trip back to the nanny-cam.

Everything looked fine. Connor was no longer there, which meant Orson had probably gone home. No movie stars queued up to rescue her today.

An old voice returned to her mind, chastising her, same as it had for the last two decades.

"You're in over your head because you'll never be good enough."

The voice sounded like it always did, so Sloane needed a second to register the ugly reality that the voice wasn't stuck in her mind this time. It was coming from right behind her — the monster standing in a place he absolutely had no right to be.

She wheeled around and found the courage to stare her enemy in the eye. "How did you get in here?"

"That's funny." He gave her a long and patronizing smile. "I came to ask you the exact same thing. How did *you* get here?" His smile widened. "We both know you have no business being on a film set."

He let the weight of his oppressive words sink in, then watched her try and wade away from the insult.

"You should leave before you make a fool of yourself again. Or before someone gets hurt."

"You hurt people, not me." Sloane wanted to sound strong, but he was making her sound like a frightened little child. "You're the one who needs to go."

He casually looked around the empty space, his smile never wavering, proving he wasn't in a hurry. "You still don't understand … I can go anywhere in this town that I want to, and there's nothing you can do to stop me."

"For now." She didn't even know what that meant.

"Okay, then." The saccharine smile grew, followed by a condescending little pat on her shoulder. He allowed her little victory before claiming it as his. "There's nothing you can do to stop me *for now*."

The monster tied her tongue and he knew it.

There was a slurry of words inside her mind. She couldn't decide what to say, and the longer she stayed in this marsh of indecision, the deeper her verbal paralysis.

He added the insult of a wink to the injury of his predator's grin, then he turned around and left.

She remained frozen inside the papery skin of the little girl he ruined.

Sloane wasn't sure how long she stood there, assaulted by *what if?*s and acidic memories.

She had to get out of there. *Now.* She'd been right to worry and needed to regroup. The Shellys would have to reassure her with something better than, *don't worry about it* or whatever meaningless words they would use to try and convince Sloane that she nothing to fret about.

She straightened her shoulders and walked back to the nanny-cam, looking over with an almost lazy glance, expecting to see Jolie fitting pieces into her puzzle. But instead, Sloane saw something that caused her to gasp, clap a hand over her mouth, then dash to Jolie's trailer.

She threw open the door, but the monster was already gone.

And so was Tiffany.

"Hi, Mommy!" Jolie looked up from her puzzle, offered her mother an enthusiastic wave, then returned her attention to the mess of pieces scattered across the table.

Sloane crossed the trailer in a few purposeful strides and was kneeling next to Jolie two seconds later, examining her daughter without being obvious, trying not to scare her, despite being out-of-body terrified herself. She didn't see any tangible evidence, but Sloane also knew she wasn't likely to see any physical damage done in such an abbreviated length of time. If anything, Jolie seemed overjoyed, gleeful like she had been at the beach building a sandcastle with Connor.

"Where's your father? Was he here?"

Jolie nodded, not looking up. "Yeah. But he had to go."

Goddammit, Miles. "Where's Tiffany?"

She looked up from her puzzle again. "Miss Tiffany had a family emergency."

Heart pounding. "What kind of family emergency?"

She shrugged. "Mr. Auspicious gave her a note."

A cold chill. "*Mr. Auspicious.*"

"That's what the man said his name was."

Pure fury. "That's not his name."

"He told me that, too." Jolie gave her an emphatic nod.

"He said it meant lucky, and that good things happened around him, so it was sort of like a nickname."

With clenched fists, she said, "His name is Liam Wentz."

"Oh," Jolie replied with zero inflection.

The monster's name meant nothing to her, and that was Sloan's fault. "He's not a nice man."

She insulted her mother with a laugh. "That's not true, Mommy. He's really nice. *See.*"

Jolie presented Sloane with something that made her want to break down and cry. She was wearing a piece of costume jewelry — on her ring finger. Such a small and simple thing, but in the moment, Sloane couldn't have imagined anything that would have made her want to retch more.

"Give that to me right now." Sloane held out her hand.

Jolie surprised her with a severe shake of her head. "It's mine!"

"I understand that, but he is a terrible person, and you shouldn't be—"

"He's lucky, and now I have a ring that makes me lucky, too!" Jolie seemed so suddenly upset. "You can't—"

"I'm not arguing with you about this." Sloane presented her open palm again, now more insistent.

Jolie glared, then surprised her mother again. "He said you would try and take the ring away from me."

"I bet he did." She was furious, still waiting for Jolie to fill her hand with the ring. "You're never to speak with that man again. If he comes anywhere near you, I want you to run away and find me or the first adult you trust." She shook her head again, cycling through a list of people to yell at.

Jolie finally handed her mother the ring, but not without an ample amount of pouting.

She took her daughter's hand and led her out of the trailer.

Jolie could be pissed at her all she wanted. Sloane was doing her job as a mother.

But still, she had to do better.

Because right now, Jolie was in danger.

The monster had somehow orchestrated his access to the set. He could have done anything to her. The ring was proof of concept, a warning, irrefutable evidence that even after all these years, there weren't any doors to her life that the monster wouldn't know how to open.

Maybe she shouldn't be making this movie. Sloane would never forgive herself if Jolie got hurt because of her mother's need for vindication. Maybe she should have stayed in London and left her past alone. Maybe life would be better if she could just learn to forget.

She needed some fresh perspective, outside from what the Shellys, or even Orson, might say to her.

"Where are we going now?" Jolie asked, still sounding mad at her mother.

"To see your father."

Jolie didn't cheer, nor did she complain. But Sloane didn't care what she thought either way. Miles might help her see things more clearly, and hopefully feel better about all of this.

Miles would know exactly what to do.

Sloane

Miles had no idea what to do.

Even after loading up on sandwiches from crafts services and taking Jolie to the Liberty Park for a picnic and some playtime, then talking for the last twenty minutes with Miles, Sloane didn't see things any more clearly and felt better about nothing.

But she was trying, and so was he.

At first, she was furious with him for leaving Jolie alone. He was supposed to be there with her, but apparently Christian had a slew of questions and was sticking around the set hoping that Miles might be able to answer at least some of them. He was sorry all over the place after hearing what happened, and Sloane venting her frustrated anger wasn't fair to him.

Miles wasn't any more negligent by leaving his daughter with Tiffany than she had been. They were both doing their jobs, and working under the more than reasonable assumption — especially given the amount of money being spent on security — that the set was safe, and that the staff would remain aware and exercise sound judgment.

Most of Sloane's rage was reserved for Tiffany. And while Miles understood her ire, he'd still spent at least two-thirds of their twenty minutes so far trying to talk her off the ledge.

"I'm not defending her or making excuses for her. I'm trying to offer an alternative opinion, which is what I thought I was supposed to be doing here."

"Maybe later." She glanced at Jolie over by the swings to make sure their daughter was still safe. "Right now, I need you to hate her with me."

"Fine. Tiffany is a terrible human who deserves to be fired immediately."

"The second part of that sentence is enough, Miles. I'm not suggesting she's a terrible human, but she's clearly an idiot. Of all the people in the world — why would she leave our daughter alone with *him*? Does she not know what this movie is about?"

"Maybe not." Miles shrugged.

She looked at him, surprised by the answer. "How could she not know what it's about?"

"Has she seen a script?"

"Of course not. You know—"

"The Shellys had everyone sign non-disclosure agreements, and there's been an NSA-level of secrecy around the film. Tiffany isn't even part of the production, she's a glorified nanny. She thinks she's working on a movie called *Flamingo Summer*."

"So, she's never read the news? She has no idea about my history with that man?"

Miles sighed, obviously not wanting to argue the point and hoping to drop it just to let his baby mama have her way — exactly the sort of thing that made him maddening and wonderful in relatively equal measure. "She was what, four or five years old when all of that happened?"

"It's legendary Hollywood gossip, Miles."

"You're not the center of the universe, chérie." Then he finished his thought and redirected the conversation. "You're right. Elle a merdé, she should be fired. *But* ... can we agree that Tiffany isn't really what's upsetting you?"

"I'm glad you know me so well." Sloane's tone suggested sarcasm, but she meant every word. "What's really upsetting me? Is it that he's still alive?"

"That's obviously part of it." Miles nodded. "Yet I maintain your own self-doubt is upsetting you more than anything else."

"And what am I doubting?" Of course, she knew without him answering.

"Whether you should even be making this movie." He looked at her. "Does that sound about right?"

"Do *you* think I should be doing it?"

Miles shook his head. "It doesn't matter what I think."

He waited a beat. "Of course I believe in you making this movie. I wouldn't be involved if I didn't."

"You might. For me."

"You know I'd do just about anything to help you ... so long as it doesn't come at the expense of my art. I'm shooting this film because I believe in the picture, and because I believe in you. Am I happy with this turn of events? Absolutely not." Miles shook his head again. "But walking away from this film will be one of the biggest mistakes of your life, and you don't need me to tell you that."

"I feel guilty," she admitted.

"That's a natural response. Let's talk about how to deal with the guilt instead of running away, which only makes it feel like the emotion is chasing you instead."

"It's not the movie I'm questioning, so much as what to do with Jolie. I feel like she's vulnerable, no matter what I do. It was too easy for him to get on-set today, so he obviously has people inside. But isn't Jolie in even more danger somewhere else, where neither of us can keep an eye on her?"

"What's your biggest fear?" Miles asked. "Specifically, with regard to our daughter's safety. *What is the worst thing that can possibly happen?*"

Sloane had thought about the answer to that question plenty, but if felt dangerous to vent such worries aloud.

"Voicing your fears dilutes their power," Miles reminded her.

She knew it was true, but his honest nudge in the moment was still hard to accept. "I'm afraid of him inviting her into his trailer."

Miles shook his head. "Liam Wentz doesn't have a trailer on your set."

"*Trailer* is just a word. It could be any private space where he …"

"Where he what, chérie?"

She shook her head, not wanting to say it.

"You wanted to talk about this, so let's—"

"Where he can do what he did to Nicole," she finished her thought, then rushed on with another. "Or hurt her in a different way, to get back at me."

"We've already warned her about him—"

"We should have done that before starting the movie."

"Agreed. We made a mistake that we won't make again. I'd argue that he'll never get her alone again, no matter how many baubles he might try and buy or bribe her with. But even if he somehow does, Jolie is a lot more like her mom than Nicole. She'll scream, then we'll bring the guy down that way."

"ARE YOU SUGGESTING WE USE OUR DAUGTHER AS BAIT?"

"Keep your voice down!" Miles whisper yelled — Jolie was kicking sand on the swings, not too far away. "Of course not. I'm just saying that I don't believe our worst-case-scenarios are nearly as bad as what you're imagining."

That was fair, but it didn't make things easier. "So, what do you think I should do?"

He shrugged. "I don't have anything better for you than the obvious answer."

"You think I should call the Shellys."

"I don't understand why you haven't already," Miles said.

She didn't either. Not exactly. Sloane was avoiding the discussion in part because she didn't want to be told that everything would be okay, which Melinda and Dominic were both black belts at doing. But Sloane suspected that the real reason she didn't want to call the Shellys was that doing so would force her to live the experience over again, aloud and in front of others.

Discussing the issue with Miles was one thing, but a conversation with the Shellys felt like talking to her parents. Or it would, if she had any.

Sloane still hadn't responded.

Miles said, "Melinda always makes you feel better."

"Will you stay with me while I call?"

He looked at Jolie, then all around the park with a smile. "Where do you think I'm going to go?"

Sloane was already dialing.

"We shut down early again," Melinda answered.

"You already know?"

"Did you really think there was any chance that I wouldn't? Are you calling to explain or apologize?"

"You sound upset," Sloane said.

"I'm not upset, but production shut down one hour and eighteen minutes ago, yet we're only talking now."

"*An hour and eighteen minutes ago?*" And they pretended not to micromanage her. "How do you know that?"

"Because Lila called the time of death at 1:46 p.m."

"Isn't that a bit dramatic?" Sloane said.

Miles was looking at her with wondering eyes. She turned away from him to focus on the call and saw that Jolie had been waiting for Mommy to notice her. She gave Sloane a giant wave as she swung.

"It's not dramatic," Melinda replied. "It's *precise*. Losing another day is something that must be accounted for."

"So, you are mad?"

"You're better than this, Sloane. No, I'm not mad. But I would like to know what happened today, and I shouldn't have to call you or wait for more than an hour to find out."

"You're right. I'm sorry ... he showed up today."

"*He* meaning Wentz?" Melinda sounded genuinely

surprised, though that made sense since Sloane didn't give anyone a reason for their abbreviated day.

"Yes. He waltzed right onto set during a break."

"What did he say?"

"'What did he say?' How about, 'How the hell did he get on set?'"

"One question doesn't exclude the other. So, Sloane, *what did he say?*"

"That I'm a fraud who doesn't belong on a movie set. But that's not even the upsetting part, Melinda — he was alone with Jolie."

"WHAT?"

"He sent Tiffany home. Gave Jolie a toy wedding ring. He—" She stopped.

Melinda picked it up immediately. "I'm so sorry, Sloane. None of that should have ever happened. And you have my word that it won't happen again. This is all on us. Tiffany was my hire. She's obviously an imbecile, and security is clearly much weaker than either Dominic or I believed it to be. Wentz is ahead of us in ways we didn't anticipate, despite effectively forecasting for years. He probably has an insider, and that person will need to be rooted out. I'm not saying any of this to scare you, but the truth is you're already frightened and both of us know it. Hopefully, this is soothing. Yes?"

"Yes," Sloane agreed.

"This is our top priority. Expect to start shooting tomorrow with a new and improved Tiffany, much tighter security, and clear communication from us about what we know, along with a plan for our next best moves. If anything unusual happens, call one or both of us immediately."

"Thank you," Sloane said.

"I promise, we won't let him silence you again."

And then Melinda was gone.

"Are you okay?" Miles asked as she pocketed her phone then swiped at a tear.

"Much better." She tried on a smile and found that the fit wasn't too awkward.

Miles opened his mouth, but Jolie came running over before he could get anything out.

"You said twenty minutes, or 'no more than a half hour.' It's been a longer time than that. Now you have to push me or play hide and go seek." Jolie crossed her arms and awaited their reply.

Miles looked at his watch. "It's been eighteen minutes."

"And Germans are never wrong about the time," Sloane added.

"Your mom and I just need a few more minutes." Then to Sloane, he said, "Are you ever going to stop calling me German?"

"Okay, Daddy." Jolie gave them a loud sigh to make it clear she was granting them a big favor, then she scurried over to the slide.

Miles turned to her. "So?"

"We're getting a new Tiffany and tighter security. But more than that, the Shellys are on it."

"They've always been on it. What's different now?"

"I don't know exactly." She shrugged. "But there was definitely something in Melinda's voice."

"And what do you think that something is?"

Sloane had a theory. "He's obviously caught them off guard, and I can't think of many times when I've seen the Shellys surprised. Especially something they've plotted out so far ahead. Everything that's hit the production so far has to have come from somewhere inside. The accident on our first day, the strike, the contract problems, and him walking on the set."

"The Shellys are smart enough to expect sabotage from within. You told me they were anticipating that months ago."

"Sure. *Eventually.* The registered name for this project is *Flamingo Summer.* There is no public information whatsoever. And still he struck on day one."

"Exactly. Sabotage from within. Liam Wentz is one of the most powerful men in Hollywood, and Hollywood is an industry that's all about influence and power. *Of course* he has people."

"But it's more than that, Miles. Consider the number of hits. Don't you think there's more than one insider? How could the Shellys not take that personally, considering how diligently they've vetted everyone."

"How careful were they, though?" Miles looked unsure. "I mean … Tiffany?"

"Maybe Tiffany was great, and *he* just pays really well."

"Scheisse."

"Exactly," she agreed. Then, responding to his sudden change in expression. "What are you thinking? You're worried, aren't you?"

"Of course. But I think maybe I'm worried about a few different things than you are."

"Tell me. I think we still have like four minutes." She smiled.

He smiled back. "I just want to make sure Jolie comes first, before anything else."

"Obviously."

"Before our reputations. Before our professional goals. Before this film." Miles seemed to consider this next one, then went ahead and said it. "Before our romantic lives. *Before anything.* Nothing is more important than Jolie."

"Of course. To all of that."

She leaned against him, marveling at what the two of

them had accomplished together. Sloane had managed to date this man, have a remarkable child with him, and continue to nurture a constantly maturing friendship, while also being able to work alongside him as both collaborator and boss. Most people lived their entire lives with so much less than Sloane already had. She knew that and didn't want to take any of the good things in her life for granted. Especially Jolie.

But there was a boiling rage eating at the edges of her very self, burning blacker than she wanted to admit to anyone, including Miles. Or Dominic and Melinda.

Sloane had supposedly dealt with the trauma and left it all behind her. But the sequel was apparently here, leaving reminders like poison inside her. She had been too trusting, too naive, too willing to accept what was in front of her.

That particular sequence of thoughts once started always led to the most terrible one.

That maybe her life would have been better if he had actually raped her. Though most of Little Sloane couldn't really remember what was happening at the time, her screaming instincts staved off disaster.

But had they, really?

Because most times Sloane felt like she would have much of the same trauma she did now, but with proof of his monstrosity. Maybe then everyone wouldn't have called her a *liar, a needy little attention whore*, or *everything wrong with California* — as if an entire state's problems could be distilled to one little girl.

Maybe then she wouldn't have wanted to spend the next several years sleeping, or hoping for a coma or amnesia — anything to eliminate the whispering screams that relentlessly plagued her.

Even if he never penetrated her, the monster had still raped the innocence right out of her life.

And taught Sloane a hard lesson that she was forced to learn far too early. That women, or in her case, children, who accused powerful men of something dark were then shown their insignificance as a group.

Yes, of course Sloane would surrender the film if she had to.

But it was infuriating to imagine that he might force her to give up and let him get away with his evil again. She had to move across an ocean to stop him from finishing what he started and ruining the remainder of her childhood. Now she had weaponized her trauma to craft a piece of art that could serve as both sword and shield.

Yet the very day she donned her armor and stepped into battle, he was there to get inside her head, destroy her Hollywood debut, and erode her faith in the people around her.

A parasitic presence, feeding off of old hate and shame to become something grossly symbiotic. Sloane hated that her trauma fueled her, because she loathed its existence, knowing that the symbiote would only grow in size and strength once nourished with silence. That's why—

"That's all the minutes!"

Jolie's announcement yanked Sloane from her reverie. She sat up and straightened on the bench next to Miles. She was just guessing at the time, but Sloane had zero doubt that Jolie was right.

"It's time for the swings," she reminded them.

"*Or* … maybe we could get ice cream," Miles suggested.

"ICE CREAM!"

Miles stood and held out his hand.

Sloane grabbed Jolie's hand and offered Miles the other.

Then the three of them walked over to their picnic blanket and started putting everything away.

Sloane tried to focus on the good things.

And tried not to think about any of her many resentments.

Maybe Sloane needed to have a narcissistic mom who treated her like a meal ticket so she could be the best possible mother for Jolie and possibly change the world with her art. Maybe there was a good reason people preferred drama to the truth — not just the media and the world that consumed it, but the law who either listened to her, or didn't.

The truth of it all was so much harder to take.

The press would never help her. Nor would the cops. He had too many friends in both places.

So if the worst happened, what recourse would she have?

Even if Melinda was the only person in the world who could have made her such a promise, that still didn't mean she could keep it. He would do everything in his power to silence her, do anything to evade accountability. Attack her credibility and make sure no one would ever listen. From denial to rationalization, his arguments would be impressive and varied, sprinkled with apologies where necessary, all of them dripping with polished sincerity.

None of that ever — or could have ever have — happened.

To say Sloane Alexander is exaggerating is putting it kindly.

She is clearly a self-promoter, directing her Hollywood debut as a lie.

West Hollywood Sunset was supposed to be her revenge.

Instead, the film was giving her worst enemy the chance to ruin another life.

And this time, it was Jolie's.

Miles could surely feel her mood and did his best to

obscure it from their daughter, joking around and on their way to the car, fueling the mirth with funny words in different languages on their way to the Inside Scoop.

"Are you okay, Mommy?" Jolie asked when they got there.

"Just a little car sick," she lied. "Nothing a scoop of Mexican Vanilla won't cure."

"How are you really doing?" Miles whispered after Jolie was on the other side of the door.

"*Much better,*" she lied again.

But it was fine. Sloane could be sick today.

As long as she was fine tomorrow.

Chapter Ten

Sloane

SLOANE WOKE UP the next morning, sick as a dog.

She had no choice but to ignore it for now. She still wasn't over her nerves from yesterday, but *Sunset* was now several days behind schedule and Sloane wanted to prove that she could recover the lost time.

So she got out of bed, took two Advil before deciding to pop a third because *wow* was her head pounding. And a couple of Alka-Seltzers because something was seriously wrong with her stomach.

She turned the shower even hotter than she usually did, a degree away from hot lava, and let the water scald her scalp and rain fire onto her body.

After drying off, she still felt lousy but went downstairs and started on breakfast for Jolie in the well-appointed kitchen of their posh little rental. Five minutes into mixing batter for a fresh batch of waffles, Sloane decided she would pivot to pancakes instead. Flapjacks felt more manageable, considering her head and stomach were apparently planning some sort of mutiny inside her.

She almost bailed halfway through and turned to instant oatmeal, but if she couldn't make her daughter a short stack for breakfast, then she had no hope of a successful day directing.

"Good morning, Mommy!" Jolie announced, tromping into the kitchen, sounding even louder than she usually did while climbing onto the barstool. She slapped her notebook onto the counter. "Look, I drew a picture of Tiffany's family emergency."

Sloane looked at the picture. It was a house on fire. A woman that was almost for sure supposed to be Tiffany, though she was about two-thirds the size of the house, stood looking horrified beside it.

"Did her house burn down?" Sloane asked, frightened by her own question.

"I dunno," Jolie sang.

"Why did you draw a fire?"

She looked at her mother as though that were a perfectly silly question. "Because that would be a BAD emergency!"

BAD came out loud enough to feel like a nail in her skull.

"Can we go to the park again today?" Jolie asked.

"Sorry, kiddo. It's a workday."

"Yesterday was a workday, but we still went to the park."

"We weren't supposed to do that."

"Then why did we?"

"I think Miss Tiffany is still having her family emergency, so you're going to play with someone new today."

"She doesn't really play with us," Jolie said with a shake of her head. "Will Daddy be there today?"

"Daddy is shooting the movie, so he's there every day."

"Will Connor be there?"

"His father is on set today, so yes, I imagine he will be." Though what did she know? Maybe Connor was with his mom.

And maybe Orson was getting pissed at all the delays. There was a reason his scenes had all been scheduled first.

Sloane set Jolie's plate in front of her.

"Thank you for making pancakes for me, Mommy."

Eight simple words that did more for Sloane than the Advil, Seltzer, and shower combined.

"Of course, honey."

An hour later they were on their way to the set, and Sloane had half-convinced herself that she felt perfectly fine. Yes, she had a headache, but it wasn't a migraine. Her stomach was … unsettled, but nerves would do that, and at least she was getting her anxiety under control.

Everything would be fine. Or even better than that — things were about to be better than ever.

She pulled onto the lot and wasn't sure whether she felt soothed by the additional security or nervous thanks to the reminder that the beefed up measures were necessary.

Sloane submitted to an additional ID check and photograph at the gate, even though her laminated badge showed her as the director. An escort met her and Jolie at their assigned parking spot then walked them onto the set.

"Who is that man, Mommy?" Jolie whispered.

"He's kind of like a policeman. His job is to keep us safe."

She took her mother's hand, appearing to think. "Is this because of the man from yesterday … Mr. Auspicious?"

"Yes," Sloane answered, glad that Jolie had asked. "It is."

They went to the childcare trailer first. She knocked instead of just opening the door. A second later, Arnold Schwarzeneggeranswered. It wasn't really Arnie, but that was all Sloane could see when looking at him. Not the former governor of California, but Kindergarten Cop, specifically. Jolie's new sitter was six-something, with a square jaw, granite shoulders, and biceps that surely weighed more than she did.

"I'm Jake." He gave them a smile, his voice surprisingly light and friendly. "You must be Jolie."

Connor was already playing with a bunch of dinosaurs over in the corner.

"Both of our names start with J!" Jolie announced.

"They sure do," Jake agreed. "See how fast you can name five more words that start with J. *Go!*"

"Jellybeans!" Then, "Jammies … jokes …"

"Jewels," Sloane suggested.

"No helping!" Jolie declared. "Juggler … jam-packed!"

"Jam packed is two words," Sloane said, without knowing why.

"Nuh-uh. It's one word, Mommy. You always say our day is jam-packed, and you say it really fast."

"Sounds like it should count to me." Jake gave his compatriot a little wink.

"Super," Sloane said, already grateful for Jake, and the Shellys — probably Melinda — for putting him there. "That's five."

"We need one more," Jolie corrected her. "Jewels doesn't count."

"Oh, well in that case—"

"Judicious!" Jolie cried out. "Dad always uses that one."

"Great job." Sloane turned her smile on Tiffany 2.0. "Thank you so much for being here."

His smile was ever-present, calm and knowing. He gave her a light little bow of his head. "She's in great hands."

It was easy to believe. She pictured what the Shellys' Kindergarten Cop would do to the monster if he dared enter the "babysitting trailer" again.

Her nerves were soothed, but not entirely quelled. Sloane was glad for the nanny-cam, and would surely be checking it whenever she could, neurotically throughout the day. But so far, the monster had only struck in the most unexpected places. Some of her was still fixed on all the things he had done, but the rest of her couldn't stop wondering what would be coming next.

Because there was zero doubt that something was on its way.

She wanted to call Melinda and thank her. Like usual, everything had been taken care of exactly as promised. But she could do that later. After saying goodbye to Jolie and Connor, then thanking Jake again on her way out, she told herself that calling either one of the Shellys would only be another way for her to avoid thinking about all the things that were troubling her.

It wasn't just her head and her stomach. The set didn't feel empty, but surely it seemed emptier than it should have. Sloane could practically smell another something else, ready and waiting to go wrong.

"Miles!" Sloane called out when she saw him across the room.

He turned around and immediately put a smile on his face, but she could clearly see it was only there to protect her.

"What is it? Where is everybody?"

Miles sighed. "Half of the crew has called in sick."

"HALF OF THE CREW?" Sloane repeated. Several people looked over. She ignored them all, but then spoke in a much lower voice. "More sabotage? Another strike, a different day?"

"I don't think so." Miles shook his head and put a hand over his stomach. "I don't feel so well myself. Bad enough to stay home if my presence wouldn't have been missed. So yeah, if there is something going around then I can understand—"

"Something's not just 'going around,' Miles. Doesn't that seem awfully coincidental to you?"

"Well, that is how viruses work." He gave her a weak smile. "It doesn't mean that Wentz managed to sneak in here and poison us."

"Of course not. He would have paid someone to do it for him."

"Is it just crew? Or cast, too? Are we down any actors?" Connor had been in the childcare trailer, so Orson had to be around somewhere.

"Cassidy isn't here."

"Goddammit!" Sloane said before *here* had fully left his mouth.

"I know." Miles put a hand on her shoulder. "It sucks. But let's go over the shots, I'm sure there's something we can do."

If anything unusual happens, call one or both of us immediately

"Fine." Sloane tried to sound grateful instead of angry. "Just give me a minute. I'd like to call Melinda, even though she probably already knows about whatever this is. Considering yesterday and everything else, I should ask her if there's anything specific she thinks we should be doing."

He nodded. "Let me know what Melinda says after—"

"What Melinda says about what?" Dominic appeared from nowhere, surprising them both.

"Half of our crew has called in sick," Sloane explained. "I was just going to call Melinda and tell her."

Dominic nodded. "She's speaking to the Cavallis right now."

"About what?" Sloane asked, immediately suspicious.

She had good reason to question the motives of any parents with children scaling the ladder of celebrity, especially in a case such as Cassidy's, where they had her grabbing that bottom rung so they could push her little ass up the ladder before she could even talk.

"About the myriad of ways that this production has been breaking child-actor rules, even after only a few days of—"

"Are you kidding me?" Sloane threw both of her arms in the air, thoroughly livid. "*West Hollywood Sunset* is about the mistreatment of child actors. Of course I wouldn't mistreat one of my own, under any circumstances, or in any manner whatsoever."

"We know that." Dominic gave her a calm and patient smile. Sloane didn't know if his *we* was referring to him and Melinda, to Miles since he was standing right there listening to everything, or perhaps to everyone involved, since despite her integrity needing constant defense, Sloane's motives were never truly in question. "Melinda is handling it right now. You have nothing to worry about."

"Then why are you here?"

Another smile. "I'm here to make sure that we don't lose another day of shooting."

"We've lost half our crew and don't have Cassidy. What am I supposed to shoot?"

"We were just talking about this a few minutes ago," Miles interjected. "We can find something else to shoot."

"Take care of Orson," Dominic suggested. "Are there any scenes we can shoot off calendar that involve him but not Cassidy."

"Of course." Miles nodded.

"Excellent." Dominic turned to Sloane. "I'll be sticking around set today. Just direct me to wherever I'll be most out of the way."

She needed their help, and the production was slipping away from her. But Sloane didn't want to say any of what she was thinking.

"You're never in the way," she said instead.

Dominic went to find a quiet corner while she and Miles reconvened and decided to shoot the scene where Cassidy's character told her father what had happened to her. Sloane had wanted them both in frame, but Miles promised that the scene wouldn't lose any of its power if they shot some of it close in on each of the actors, starting with Orson today.

And of course, Orson was incredible. She asked for multiple takes several times, but only because raw nerves and a supremely upset stomach had her incessantly second-guessing herself. She would almost for sure run with his first attempt at every shot.

Despite their morning pivot, the production finished out an exemplary day. Their best yet, by far.

"You were brilliant," Sloane told Orson, trying not to gush, hoping she sounded like his director instead of a fangirl. "Especially since you weren't expecting those scenes — I'm beyond grateful."

"I've learned to expect anything in this business." Orson smiled. "It was no big deal."

She pointed toward the craft services table. "You want a coffee?"

"I'd rather have dinner?"

Sloane stopped. She didn't know what to say.

Of course, she *wanted* to say yes. But—

She couldn't even finish her thought.

Instead, Sloane raced to the restroom, hoping she wouldn't vomit before making it inside.

She burst through the door, ran right to the first open stall, fell to her knees, then barfed in the bowl, loudly and everywhere.

Sloane hoped that no one could hear her, especially Orson. But of course they could, and he was probably closest to the door right now.

A light knock, followed by his soft voice. "Are you okay in there?"

His asking only made things a million times worse.

"I think you should go," she told him through the door. "There's something going around. If you're not already sick, then you probably will be."

"I'll take my chances," he replied.

Sloane couldn't argue.

Instead, she kept vomiting. And wondering when the nightmare would end.

Chapter Eleven

Melinda

MELINDA LISTENED TO THE CAVALLIS, feigning sympathy and pretending to care.

They were in her office. Melinda had all the power but was showing them the courtesy of pretending not to. It was hard to take a word Cassidy's parents were saying seriously. But for now, the smartest thing was to stay all ears while they kept talking and getting the bullshit out of their system.

"Our daughter has rights," said Cassidy's mother.

"It doesn't matter how much she's getting paid — you can't just ignore her mistreatment," her father added.

Melinda let the moment sit for a few seconds, then only after she felt sure that their volley had officially paused, she spoke in her most patient and understanding voice. "I absolutely agree, Mrs. Cavalli—"

"Lisa."

"Cassidy has rights that must be respected. And to your point, Mr. Cavalli—"

"Walter."

"Your daughter in no way deserves to be mistreated."

Melinda let her consensus settle then finished her thought. "But I do have to disagree that Cassidy's rights have been disrespected, or that she has been abused in any way. I am happy to discuss any specifics in regard to your daughter or her treatment on set, but your accusations so far have felt more than a little vague and—"

"No one is accusing you of anything," Walter corrected. "We just have a few questions."

Lisa said, "Specifically, I'm not sure a director is supposed to be needling their actors about every tiny inflection."

"I assume you're referring to Cassidy's accent?"

"No." Walter shook his head. "She's referring to the ten-thousand takes she had to go through before it was good enough."

"I'm sorry, Mr. Cavalli." She wasn't. "From what I understand, the first take revealed your daughter's accent. And no disrespect intended, but from this side of the desk, that seems an awful lot like her failure to deliver what was promised as an actress."

"Now you just wait a minute—"

"No. *You* wait one moment, Mr. Cavalli—" Melinda raised her hand, palm out, waiting for him to back down. "You've been in this business a long time already, despite your daughter's youth. I'm confident you understand it's a director's job to encourage the best performance he or she can out of an actor. That includes reshoots. And in this particular instance, I believe those reshoots came after a bit of extra coaching."

Neither Cavalli responded.

"Serious question then," Melinda continued into their silence. "What should Sloane have done? Should she have pretended not to hear Cassidy's accent? Should the project have suffered in favor of protecting her feelings?"

Cassidy's parents sat across from her, quietly staring, surely wondering where exactly this whole thing had gone off the rails. This obviously wasn't what they'd expected. Whoever had put the pair of them up to this — and there was zero doubt in Melinda's mind that the Cavallis didn't get here on their own — didn't prepare them for the realities of their accusations. She would listen, and make them feel heard, but ultimately Melinda wasn't about to roll over for anyone. Especially not a matching set of superficial show parents like the Cavallis.

"We understand that Sloane is trying to make the best movie possible," Walter started.

"Which is why we signed up for the project," Lisa added.

"It's just that there are certain rules all productions are supposed to follow—"

"And we're concerned *West Hollywood Sunset* might be breaking some of those rules."

"You mean *Flamingo Summer*," Melinda corrected them.

They traded a glance, then Lisa said, "Of course, *Flamingo Summer*. But we all know the real name, right? Shouldn't we be using the real name?"

She looked at Melinda, waiting for her answer.

But Melinda held her tongue, staring back at them both, wanting the pair to squirm in the silence. It was an unwavering truth that she had consistently used to get her way in life. Given enough rope, people in the wrong would never fail to hang themselves. Melinda just needed to keep them talking. Eventually, they would say the wrong thing and provide her with the perfect onramp to redirect the conversation and squeeze them right out of it.

Walter picked up the ball. "We only want to talk about the rules. That's all."

"We have a production where the lead actor is a minor. Believe me, Mr. Cavalli, Shellter Productions is extremely concerned about the rules. Which of them do you feel we are breaking?"

He looked so unsure. Probably at least in part because he wanted to correct her again, remind Melinda that he was Walter and that his wife was Lisa, same as they'd been back in London when the Shellys were so excited about signing their daughter. But right now, she needed the Cavallis to realize that they had lost the luxury of a first-name-basis situation.

Lisa said, "The Labor Commissioner is supposed to issue permits to minors with required documentation from the appropriate school districts, but we haven't seen any of that yet."

Then, as if his wife's complaint made a lick of sense, Walter piled on. "There are supposed to be no more than five absences during the production."

Melinda laughed, loud and long, trying to unseat more than insult them, but thrilled to do both since the situation apparently called for it.

The most important part about casting a child was their talent and work ethic. But a good producer could never forget that the production was also casting that actor's parents.

Those parents could be a dream or they could be a nightmare for the producer. The only way to make sure that the house always won — the house in this instance being Shellter Productions — was to stay well ahead of the law.

The only thing the Cavallis had proved so far was that

they had no idea what they were talking about. Or who they were talking to.

"So, to be clear," Melinda said, "you have a problem with us not having supplied any documentation for Cassidy's schooling, and you're worried about compliance in regard to missing days, is that correct?"

"For starters." Walter gave her an emphatic nod, just seconds ahead of seriously regretting it.

"And it hasn't occurred to you that it's summer, and that Cassidy isn't in school right now?"

The Cavallis traded another glance.

"Even if she was in school, she's here on a visa for the summer, and compliance for her schooling is on the two of you, not us." Melinda leaned forward. "Would you like to know why you missed something so obvious? Why even though your protest doesn't make sense, you still felt like barging into my office to complain?"

Neither Cavalli answered, but they both clearly knew.

"It's clear that you have both been coached on what to say. You're not here because you thought something was wrong, you're here because someone specifically told you that there was."

"You don't know that." Lisa couldn't even get the sentence out without breaking at the end. The word *that* left her mouth with an extra syllable.

"Everything you've been told was either a lie or a misdirect," Melinda said.

"How do you know what we've been told?" Walter asked, arms crossed and defenses up.

"You've both told me plenty." Melinda indulged in another laugh before leaning back in her seat. "Do you know why Shellter Productions has been growing faster than any other studio for the last five years when measured on a per-project basis?"

She didn't wait for the answer, knowing that neither of the Cavallis was bold enough to open their mouths right now, despite their earlier bluster. "Because Dominic and I are excellent at what we do. That means having a firm grasp of details such as budgeting and scheduling, plus a firm grip on reality. But when it comes to working with minors, it also means a familiarity with the laws around child labor. So let me ask you, Mr. and Mrs. Cavalli, who do you think is more fluid in those rules and regulations — *me or you?*"

Still no answer from either of them, but Walter's animosity was now bleeding out of his pores.

Melinda continued. "History hasn't always been kind to child actors. Over time, laws have been built to protect children from mistreatment. As a result, some of these laws seem especially strict, complex, or perhaps even exhaustive. But it is all necessary. Am I correct in assuming that as parents of a child in the business, you have at least a cursory understanding of this?"

A pair of begrudging nods.

"So does whoever sent you in here. But they have no idea what's actually happening on set, so they provided you with weak yet universal arguments. Accusations to start a paper trail. That's all this is."

The Cavallis were shifting in their respective seats.

Melinda rounded the final base then brought her argument home. "Do you know how I can feel especially certain that Cassidy's needs are taken care of in this production?"

"How?" Lisa asked, loosening up more than her husband.

"Because Sloane Alexander is your director. I'm sure you know what that means, but since you failed to consider it before coming into my office today, I feel the need to offer a reminder. Thanks to her history in Hollywood, Sloane is deeply invested in following the rules. If anything, Cassidy is being treated better by her director than most child actors could ever hope for. Your daughter is being given more leeway, more care, and more opportunities to succeed by someone who sought her out specifically because she appreciated Cassidy's talent and will go to great lengths to preserve her innocence. So, would you care to amend anything we've discussed this morning?"

"We were contacted by a lawyer," Lisa admitted.

"A lawyer for whom?" Melinda asked.

"Someone auditing the production," Walter said. "They wanted to make sure that all the SAG rules were being followed. Apparently there've been a few reported incidents on Shellter productions prior to this one."

"There have been no such reports." Melinda shook her head. "Our record for the last several years is spotless."

She had no doubt the Cavallis had spoken to a real lawyer, but surely one that worked for Wentz.

Walter still looked like he was chewing nails.

But Lisa said, "We're really sorry. About all—"

"It's fine." Melinda cut her off, terse but smiling. "We have two choices right now. We're still in the first week of production. Replacing Cassidy will never be easier than it is right now. Sloane will be disappointed, of course, but she won't flinch if her producers believe it's the best move. And right now, given our conversation this morning, that might be our strongest argument."

"That's not what we want," Lisa insisted, sounding slightly panicked.

"Of course it's not. We're already invested in Cassidy and would prefer to see this through. But unfortunately, your daughter can only give us so much of her trust. The rest must come from you. Is that something I can count on?"

"Yes." Lisa nodded emphatically.

"And how about you?" Melinda turned to Walter.

"Yes," he said, sounding defeated. "You can count on us."

"It is important that you're happy," Melinda said, about to offer what would sound to the Cavallis like a concession but was really a request. "Even if school isn't in session, we could do a better job of making sure that Cassidy stays happy while not on the clock. We'll increase her overall play time."

Walter brightened. "We would appreciate that."

Melinda stood and started walking toward her office door.

The Cavallis followed a beat behind her.

She held the door open.

Lisa stepped through the threshold behind her husband but turned back on the other side. "I'm sorry about all of this. We do trust you and Dominic and Sloane ... thank you for everything."

"I understand. You were only looking out for your daughter's best interests."

Lisa gave her another appreciative smile, then Melinda closed the door.

She sat back at her desk and dialed Dominic.

"Did you finish putting them in their place?" he asked instead of saying hello.

"They won't be a problem."

"And Cassidy's weight?" Dominic asked.

"Andre has her on protein and no carbs. I told the Cavallis that we'd give her an extra hour of play time each day. We'll make sure she uses it to run around. Between those two things, the weight should stay off, and we can avoid the awkward body-image talk. Which is good, because I'm not sure Lisa would be able to handle it well." She took a breath. "How are things there?"

"You're not going to want to hear this, love. But Sloane is—"

Chapter Twelve

Sloane

SICK.

That's what she was — viciously, brutally sick.

Sloane had been telling herself that it was just nerves ever since she woke up this morning, but she'd flushed her vomit thrice already, making that little slice of self-deception that much harder to believe.

At least it felt like she was finally finished. Her last round was pure retching with not a drop of liquid. Her noises were humiliating, but at least it sounded like Orson had finally walked away, showing her a kindness by not lingering outside the bathroom door.

Sloane was the director. That meant being the leader and keeping everything under control.

But she had failed. Her production lived in the shadows of an ever-present threat, and all because of her. She was the reason for the film, and for its unending parade of frustrations.

She stood and flushed a final time, even though there

was only water in the bowl. She left the stall and went to the sink, inhaling deeply on her way, preferring the anti-septic scent of the bathroom to the sour reek that had colonized her nostrils.

She washed her hands and face, determined not to look in the mirror.

But after drying off, Sloane couldn't help herself. She wanted, maybe even needed, to see the damage. So she returned to the mirror and stared at her reflection. Her hair seemed too thin, the circles under her eyes looked dark enough to be a special effect, and her normally pale skin looked dressed in flour. A week ago she was thirty-two and looking twenty-seven. Right now, it looked like she was ready to club forty on the back of its head.

She took a deep breath, walked to the door, then pressed her ear against the wood to see if she could hear Orson on the other side.

She opened the door, hopeful that he wouldn't be waiting.

The hallway was empty. Orson was giving her space, and so was everyone else.

Tomosino was the first crew member she saw.

"Do you know where Miles is?" Sloane asked him.

"Sure do." He pointed. "He's in Daisy's bedroom."

She walked to set, still stunned that it looked haunt-ingly like a twelve-year-old version of her own room. The details were frighteningly similar down to the excess of cosmetics and body lotions on the dresser, the abundance of pillows on the bed, and even the Christina Aguilera poster on the wall.

"You okay?" she asked.

Miles was sprawled on the bed, doubled over and clutching his stomach. He sat up and looked at her. "Not at all. How about you?"

She shook her head and sat on the copy of her childhood bed and traced her finger over the green dots on the field of pink. "Remember Barcelona? The morning after that bad octopus?"

He nodded — who could ever forget?

"*That,*" Sloane finished.

"Me too." Miles finished nodding then started shaking his head. "With half the production hit, I think we can rule out anything viral. This is food poisoning, for sure."

"It should be easy enough to track. We can ask everyone who's sick if they ate from craft services yesterday, then ask what they ate. All three of us ate from catering because we swiped food for our little picnic, but Jolie isn't sick. We just have to figure out what we at that she didn't."

"When's the last time you saw her? Maybe it's just hitting her later than the rest of us."

"Maybe," she pretended to agree. "But not likely. She woke up extra chipper this morning. If anything, she seems more super-powered than sick."

"Then it's simple to pinpoint. We both had sandwiches, and she didn't."

"Are you sure?" Sloane asked.

"A hundred percent. She said that sandwiches are dumb and I asked why, but she didn't have an answer. I tried to make a joke, because you know how she'll forget her objections to just about anything once she's laughing, but that didn't work. I even told her a story about the Earl of Sandwich and still no dice. She had some of the fried rice, but barely. She gobbled it down then ran off to the swings."

"That's right," Sloane said, mostly to herself, nodding at the memory. "What was the joke?"

"Why? It wasn't funny."

"They never are."

"Not true," Miles argued.

"Fine. They *rarely* are. So, what was the joke?"

"I asked her if she was sure she didn't want a sandwich, seeing as they were part of the luxury lunch set. She asked what made the sandwiches fancy, and I told her they were 'pure breads.' Like I said, not funny. She rolled her eyes and went for the rice."

"Where was I during your little standup set?"

"Organizing the food on our blanket."

Sloane sighed, appreciative for her little conversational diversion with Miles, but knowing it was time to make the hard decision. "So, we shut down for the day again."

"I'm not sure we have another choice." He clutched his stomach. Involuntary or not it, punctuated his point.

"Can you find Lila and tell her to send everyone home? I'm going to find Dominic."

"Sure thing." He rolled onto his back, still clutching his stomach. "I just need another minute or two."

She left Miles to his misery then walked the set until she found Dominic a few minutes later, pacing in the distance and barking at someone on the phone.

He ended the call as she approached, turning to Sloane with a shift in his posture and warmth in his smile. "That was Spectacular Palate."

If Dominic was talking to the catering company, then he clearly already knew about the source of their latest disaster.

"What did they say?" she asked.

Dominic didn't answer. "We're paying the kill fee and cancelling the contract."

"What did they say?" Sloane repeated her question.

"It doesn't matter what they said." He waved a dismissive hand. "We—"

"Of course it matters!" She rarely ever talked back to

Dominic, but right now Sloane didn't feel like having her thoughts brushed aside as if they were irrelevant.

He looked at her, seeming to sense exactly what she was feeling — a rather remarkable trait that the Shellys both shared, and appeared to be better at than anyone she had ever met.

Dominic set a gentle hand on her arm. "I'm not saying *you* don't matter, Sloane. I'm saying that we're not going to get anywhere with whoever I talk to on the phone. It's tipping our hand."

"Isn't it tipping our hand to cancel the contract?"

"It's a response, sure," Dominic nodded, "but the less information we offer, the better."

"We do agree that this is his doing, right?" The fury had returned and was ready to burn her.

"This has Wentz written all over it. But getting into it with Spectacular Palate is a waste of time. And exactly what he would want us to do. At most, an investigation will turn up a low-level employee who was bribed to leave a jar of mayo out overnight. Unless that individual confesses, it will be impossible to prove it wasn't an honest blunder. We'll never catch Wentz that way, and it would be a mistake to waste our time trying."

Sloane nodded. That all made sense, even if she hated it.

"These are new taxes on old problems," Dominic tried to assure her. "Everything is fine."

"What do you mean?"

"Wentz caught us unaware from the start, and we've been playing catch-up ever since. Security has since been tightened, we're going through all the personnel files again, and we're bringing in our own people to cook. You've had a relationship with Melinda and me long enough to know we never make the same mistakes twice. It's infuriating that we've had so many failure points, and that we've let Wentz get the best of us. But you can be assured it won't happen again."

"What are you going to do?" she asked.

"It doesn't matter what we're going to do. Focus on the production and don't let Wentz distract you any more than he already has."

For every day of the last twenty years.

"Knowing what you're doing will help me feel safe. So I can focus on doing my job."

"Do you want to see the sausage being made or enjoy your breakfast?"

"What are you going to do?" Sloane asked again. "Why won't you tell me?"

Dominic looked at her, his eyes kind but slightly disappointed, telling Sloane without words that she shouldn't be making him say it. "Plausible deniability."

"Oh." She needed to throw up again. He offered his patience while she looked for her next thought. "I just feel like he's been a step ahead of us the entire time …"

"And you feel like that's the way things are going to stay."

She nodded.

"That makes it harder for you to believe that you can nail this project."

Still nodding.

"Right now, you're looking for something you can cling to. You've seen Melinda and me solve enough problems to believe that just knowing what we're up to might inspire you with the confidence required to see this through."

She nodded a final time, looking up at him in appreciation. Something about the Shellys was truly magic.

"Please, allow me to reframe the situation for you." Dominic put his other hand on her other arm and finished his thought. "*Because* you've seen Melinda and me solve so many problems, you should *already have* the confidence needed to see this through."

And abracadabra, Sloane felt suddenly better.

"We need you at your best right now," Dominic told her.

"I know." She nodded harder, still sick enough to keel over, but now a different kind of strength was returning to her body and mind. The one this production needed to live.

"Accusing Wentz without evidence is pointless. He's been scrupulous about using other people and paying them well to keep their mouths shut if they get caught for as long as we've been dealing with the guy. He's been doing this for two decades that we know of and probably a lot longer than that. Like everything else in his life, he gets better at it the longer he does it. Right now, our best course of action is for Melinda and me to handle all things Wentz, while you make your first Oscar-worthy film and we launch Juke. Can you do that for me, Sloane? Can you do that for Melinda? For Miles and Jolie? For the cast and crew and everyone who believes in you?"

"Absolutely." She had never felt more vehement while also needing to vomit.

"We've always been honest with each other, so I'm also going to tell you that despite our excessive padding, we are now concerned about the serious level of budget creep. Extra security, three times the cost on our food going forward, contract disputes and delays. Your indie darling is threatening to balloon past its already admirable allowance."

"I understand." She clutched her stomach. "And I swear on my life that I'm going to start killing it tomorrow. But right now, I'm sick and I need to—"

Chapter Thirteen

Sloane

BARF.

Everywhere.

Sloane was sitting in the driver's seat, taking Jolie home, while reflecting on what had been one of the most humiliating moments of her life.

Sure, Dominic had managed to anticipate the spray a split-second before it spewed from her mouth, dodging to the right and getting only a spatter of mustard-colored chunks on his tie and a couple of specks kissing his cheek.

In a short life filled with long-remembered humiliations, Sloane had never thrown up on anyone. Not until that moment. And of all people to throw up on.

Dominic did his best to soothe her, promising that it wasn't a big deal and that he would be freshened up in no time. He kept extra suits at the office just in case, and was "on his way there now."

It felt like defeat, letting Dominic close things down for the day, even if she needed to go and Lila was already gone. Sloane heard him barking a tidy list of to-dos on her way out, after she had reconnected with Miles.

She felt both better and worse. Confident that the Shellys would protect her from the monster, and eager to prove herself on set the next day.

But she also felt like she was going to die.

It didn't help that Jolie had been talking nonstop ever since Sloane pulled out of the lot. She would have loved to send Jolie off with her father, but Miles was apparently even sicker than she was. While saying goodbye before leaving, he was mostly just mumbles and groans, still laying like a broken comma on the bed, clutching his stomach. She covered him with the comforter that had much richer shades of pink and pistachio than the one that had covered her bed as a pre-adolescent little girl.

He was in no condition to mind Jolie. And besides, Miles was at his worst when ill. He wasn't a baby when sick like other men in her past. But with his immune system down, it also took him longer to think. The second — or fourth — language became thicker on his tongue. He had a harder time expressing himself and understanding the English-speaking people around him as fluidly as he would in peak form. At such times, Jolie's incessant chatter was unbearable.

"RIGHT, MOMMY?" Jolie demanded.

Sloane blinked, then looked over to the passenger seat. "I'm sorry, sweetie. I don't really know what you were saying to me. I feel very sick right now and am having a harder time than I'd like concentrating on the road. Do you mind if we finish talking at home? We could listen to the radio ... or quiet, if that's okay with you."

"Can we listen to JoJo MoJo?"

"Sure." Sloane really hated JoJo Mojo.

Jolie put on her favorite band, then the cabin filled with

caterwauling backup singers teeing up lead singer, JoJo Mojo, for a full-on audio assault.

And then, the sonic equivalent of a dumpster fire.

Sloane should have insisted on silence.

After ten minutes with the soundtrack to her nightmares, she pulled into the driveway of their rental and killed the engine a second after the car was in park.

"You didn't let the song finish!"

"No," Sloane agreed. "I didn't."

She got out of the car and held her stomach on the way to the door. She was hot and cold, full and empty, inside out and upside down and ready to sleep for a week.

"Did you know that JoJo MoJo started singing when she was three years old?" Jolie asked as her mother opened the front door. "She was born in Portugal but moved here when she was seven years old because her parents both knew she would be famous."

To hell with them both, Sloane thought as she held the door open and waited for Jolie to enter.

"It didn't even take her a year!" Jolie kept going. "JoJo was only eight when she made *Castle in the Water.*"

Sloane had loved everything about that movie, except for JoJo, whom she actively hated. Her daughter went gaga on her first viewing while Sloane fell into a shame spiral, feeling guilty for thinking such terrible thoughts about a child who was so obviously trying her best but was little more than marketing sausage in a human casing.

"*Castle in the Water* was the eighteenth highest grossing film of all time!"

That unfortunate fact was the reason JoJo had a career. She had been riding the success of *Castle* — which she had little, or arguably *nothing* to do with — ever since.

"Her next album is called *Brain Candy* and she says it's the BEST ONE EVER!"

Of course she did.

Sloane closed the door then sank down into the sofa.

"Can I make food since you don't feel good?" Jolie asked.

"I'll make something … I just need a minute."

"Okay!" Jolie cried out, then sat on the carpet a few feet away from her mother, prattling on about JoJo while Sloane did her best to try and temporarily tune it out.

Her daughter had a lot to say, and Sloane usually loved that. Jolie was bright and outgoing, always friendly. But she sometimes had a hard time listening to others and was prone to interruption. Miles and Sloane were both aware of the tendency and offered her constant reminders that she had two ears but only one mouth. Jolie tried hard and always wanted to do her best, but she enjoyed talking about a hundred times more than listening.

Miles tuned out her streams of babble much more frequently than Sloane did. As exhausting as it could be, and often was, Sloane also saw their one-sided conversations as a rare opportunity to know her daughter that much better than she already did. It wouldn't always be that way. Jolie would grow up fast. Soon she wouldn't be talking to her mother at all.

Sloane had been there herself not all that long ago. Though that was apples and oranges. Her mother treated her like an employee, so it was natural that Sloane eventually quit. That's why she vowed to do better for her daughter. If Jolie could count on her mom to hear all the little things now, she would be much more likely to share later on, when it actually mattered. Sloane saw listening as an investment.

Just not at the moment.

Right now, she needed her daughter to shut the hell up.

"—so is it okay if we watch *Castle in the Water* together?"

Jolie finished what was surely a well-reasoned and intelligently structured argument.

"Why don't you watch it while I make you something to eat?" Sloane gave her a smile that felt like it weighed a hundred pounds before hoisting herself up from the sofa.

Jolie answered by crawling over to the TV as fast as she could.

Sloane went to the kitchen and dug through the cabinets, looking for something that had zero chance of being there. This wasn't their home in London. It was a rental, stocked only with what they had bought after one trip to Costco and three to Trader Joe's. So a plate filled with jerk flavored plantain chips, mango slices, and a Nature Valley granola bar it was.

She would cook something later. Right now, she needed to lie down.

"Here you go." She kneeled down next to Jolie and offered her the plate with a smile.

Jolie looked down at the spread and gave her mother a grin. "YUMMY! Can I have an ice cream bar when I'm done."

Oh my God. "Help yourself."

She went to her room, closed the door, and climbed into her most comfortable pajamas — cotton bottoms with a battalion of tiny duckies and a cropped matching tee with one giant ducky wearing a trucker's cap.

Anticipating the worst as something rolled over and died in her stomach, she piled her head into a messy bun atop her head to keep it out of her face when she inevitably needed to visit the toilet again.

She plopped onto the bed, buried herself under the covers, then yanked them to her chin.

Sloane closed her eyes. Beautiful sleep was just seconds away …

Jolie knocked on her door. "Mommy!"

She sighed, then swallowed and said, "Yes?"

"Are you going to watch *Castle in the Water* with me?"

"Maybe later. But I'm going to try and nap right now."

"You can nap in front of the movie!" Said like a helpful suggestion.

Fine. As long as she could sleep.

Sloane got out of bed and followed Jolie into the living room, dragging the comforter behind her.

She fell back on the couch, buried herself beneath the blanket, then turned her body so she was facing away from the TV.

"I can wake you up at your favorite part if you tell me what it is," Jolie offered.

"That's okay, honey. Thank you." Sloane's favorite part was every scene without JoJo Mojo in it.

This was stupid. She shouldn't be doing this right now. How many times had Melinda offered to help her with Jolie? Not personally, but with Natural Nurturing, the nanny service used by Shellter Productions. One call and her daughter would be in excellent hands, while Sloane could be sleeping for—

The doorbell rang.

"I'll get it!" Jolie yelled.

"No, you won't," Sloane said, struggling to get up.

That cinched the deal. Sloane wished she had a nanny right now just so she wouldn't have to get up and open the door. She wasn't worried about the monster showing up at her place, although maybe she should be.

Until that moment, Sloane hadn't really considered that as a genuine danger. Appearing at her residence uninvited wouldn't play well in court, whereas a film set was the monster's home, even when it wasn't.

Surely this was a solicitor or someone trying to sell her

on Jesus. Hopefully she looked contagious enough to scare whoever it was away. They didn't have to know that bad mayo had done this to her.

She looked through the peephole and felt her heart fall to the floor.

Sloane wanted to run back to her room and get back in bed. But Jolie would rat her out.

"Who is it?" Jolie was suddenly standing at her side, tugging on her ducky shirt.

"It's Connor and his dad." She opened the door, mortified. "And they brought stuff."

Connor was holding a white plastic bag. Orson was holding two big brown ones. He raised them both, one per hand. "You said yes to dinner."

She looked away, embarrassed, then opened the door all the way so they could both come inside. "I don't know what to say."

"JOLIE!" Connor yelled, delighted to see his friend.

"CONNOR!" She matched his volume and tone.

"This is you?" Orson pointed to the couch and comforter.

She gave him a humiliated little nod.

Orson set his bags on the coffee table, took Sloane by the arm, and gently led her back to the sofa. Then he covered her with the comforter and called for Connor.

"Bag please," he said.

Connor nodded, then marched over and handed his father the bag.

Orson finished getting her situated with saltines, ginger ale, and a bottle of Pepto. He made sure her iPad was within easy reach in case she decided to read the latest *Rummage Report* or article on *Hollywood Hunted*, which he promised would be "surprisingly absorbing if she gave it a chance."

Sloane was still hot and cold, generally miserable and deeply embarrassed, but she also felt thought about and taken care of.

"Thank you," she rasped as her eyes grew heavy.

"This isn't really our dinner date," he told her.

"Okay," Sloane thought she said.

"But I've got Jolie covered. So you can relax and get some rest."

"Thank you … for doing …"

"Stop talking."

She blinked up at Orson, seeing him smile as he set his warm palm against her clammy cheek.

"*Rest.*"

"You …"

Sloane never finished her thought.

Chapter Fourteen

Sloane

SLOANE OPENED her eyes to sunlight streaming through her bedroom blinds.

She inhaled the first moments of her morning, trying to remember how she got here. The fog lifted and she remembered feeling sick. So very, very sick.

Fortunately, she felt much better now. Yesterday's migraine was now gone, her stomach was no longer churning, and Sloane felt ready to tackle the day.

As soon as she took a few seconds to assemble her timeline.

She had been on the couch with Jolie, but she was in her room now.

Sloane looked over to the nightstand and saw a bottle of Pepto sitting next to three cans of ginger ale and a box of saltines. Then it all came back to her at once.

She threw the covers off of her body and bolted out of bed, half of her still mortified that Orson had seen her in such a state, and part of her worried that she had been hallucinating. As relieving as that might be, it would throw her into a panic for something that felt so real to have been thoroughly false.

The living room was empty.

The sofa had been straightened, with every pillow fluffed and neatly arranged. The surrounding area had also been spruced up — surely not by Jolie or Connor.

So the thirty-million dollar man had apparently done a little light housekeeping while Sloane had been sleeping.

She peeked out the window. His Lexus was gone.

Sloane crept down the hallway then quietly opened the door to Jolie's room, where she found her sleeping.

That's when the scent finally found her nostrils and pulled her like a cartoon into the kitchen.

"I'm making eggs," Miles announced when she entered without turning around. "How many do you want?"

Her stomach rumbled with the invitation. "All of them?"

Miles laughed, turning his eggs. "Great. All of them it is."

"You look about a million times better than yesterday," Sloane said.

"Thanks. You too." Another laugh. "Scheisse, that was rough."

Sloane walked over to the cupboard, got a glass, filled it with water from the Brita, then swallowed it in a series of long and uninterrupted gulps. After she set her glass on the counter, she sat on a barstool and rubbed her head. "It might be the dehydration, and it's definitely not yesterday's migraine, but I still have a headache and I feel a little confused. You want to help me fill in the blanks?"

"Sure thing. Like?"

"Like, no offense, but why are you here?"

"That one's easy. I was feeling lousy as merde last

night, but in a misery-loves-company sort of mood. I figured you were probably having a time with Jolie and could maybe use some help."

"That was thoughtful."

"It was only around six or so, but you were already out. And I mean *out*. Snoring like a juggling team full of chainsaws. You know how—"

"I get it, Miles. Thanks."

"Unfortunately for Connor, he had never seen *Castle in the Water* before, so Jolie talked him into watching it."

"Him or Orson?"

"Well, Orson. But he was chill about it."

"He's chill about everything."

"Yeah." Miles nodded, sliding freshly scrambled eggs onto a plate then delivering them to Sloane. "Good guy."

"He is, but what makes you say that?"

"Everything." Miles shrugged and started cracking eggs into a bowl.

"I'm sure you can be a little more specific than that."

"Arbeit ist die beste jacke."

"Are you going to do that for the rest of the time we know each other? You know I'm going to ask for the English translation of your pithy little German saying, so why not just skip to that part next time?"

"You're right." He gave her a playful nod. "I should always try to think in only one language. Preferably yours."

She laughed, wanting to throw a handful of egg at him. "So, what does that mean?"

"It means work is the best jacket."

"So, the best way to warm oneself is by doing something useful."

"Correct." Miles nodded again. "To my surprise, Orson Beck is a man who seems driven to move in the service of others."

"*To your surprise?*" she repeated.

"I'm not trying to insult him. But I've been on a lot of sets with a lot of actors. Many of them come off as humble and professional during the workday, but really it's just another role. There was nothing performative about what I saw with him last night."

"Tell me more," Sloane said. "Also, these eggs are great. You mind making me some pancakes?"

Miles ignored her. "Orson was ready to go around eight or so. Connor's mother needed something or other. Whatever it was seemed to annoy him, but he didn't let his kid know and didn't talk any scheisse about her to me."

"So you're impressed with his character because he didn't talk shit about his ex?"

"No, I'm impressed with his character because he took care of you before leaving. Better than I did, and he wasn't doing it to show me up."

"What do you mean? What was he doing?"

"You were *out*. Snoring like a—"

"We covered that."

"He picked you up and carried you into the bedroom, then got you all set up in there. Granted, I was sick and sprawled in the armchair, but even if I wasn't, I'd have just made sure you were covered up before putting Jolie to bed and getting out of here."

"Who put Jolie to bed?"

"Orson did. He read us both a story." Miles laughed.

"Seriously?"

"Seriously."

"Two different stories?"

"No." Miles poured his eggs into the pan. "One story for Jolie. Connor and I were just listening."

"What was the story?"

"Is it serious?" Miles asked, instead of answering her question.

"There's nothing there."

"There's something there," he disagreed.

"We haven't slept together, if that's what you're asking."

"That's not what I'm asking." Miles shook his head. "I've never cared who you sleep with, chérie. Sex is just sex. But I do care about the most intimate relationships each of us invite into our lives because Jolie is exposed to them."

"I understand that. But seriously, we're not even casually dating. There's nothing there."

He shrugged. "Then there will be. And when there is, I want you to know that I approve."

"Thank you, Daddy."

"You mean *baby daddy*." After a beat, he said, "Don't you want to feel good about the people I'm dating?"

"Sure. Why are we talking about this? And where are those pancakes?"

Sloane had zero difficulties understanding the nature of their discussion, but the topic made her uncomfortable for a few reasons, so of course she was deflecting.

In some ways Miles was the most amazing man she knew. But that occasionally made him infuriating. He was half-French and half-Belgian. He spoke four languages and saw all life as art, which was easy to notice when looking through the lens of his work. In so many ways he seemed fully evolved and had been supportive of Sloane in every iteration of their relationship, from friends, to lovers, to partners, to coparents. Miles had been her rock, all throughout her early twenties, back when she was going through the roughest parts of her therapy and dealing with the realities of what the monster had done to her.

"We are talking about this because our relationship is founded on honesty," Miles said.

"Really? I thought our relationship was founded on good food and wine."

"And the occasional *orgasme*."

"I still love how you say that."

"*Orgasme*," he repeated.

"Fine. You and me, honesty, I hear you. But we hardly get into the details on whoever you or I might or might not be dating. I get the discussion if a relationship is starting to get serious, but—"

"It's a Hollywood relationship," Miles cut her off.

"So? What does that have to do with it?"

He stopped cooking, turned off the stove, then looked at her. "Everything, la mère. Relationships are hard. This industry makes them harder."

"It doesn't have to." But of course, he was right.

"But it is." Miles gave her a patient smile. "Everything is more difficult. Do you remember when I was shooting in Beijing for four months, then in Utah for the next three, before Vancouver for another two? That was hard on you and Jolie, yes?"

"Yes," she agreed.

"Orson is going to go wherever his career takes him, and the same is true for you."

"I'm not asking to marry him, so I seriously have no idea why we're talking about this, other than your occasionally infuriating need to over-plan everything."

"Considering the future is not over-planning," Miles argued.

"My future or yours?"

"Aren't they one and the same?"

"No, Miles. They're not." Sloane felt suddenly

agitated. "You seem to have an awful lot of opinions about something that isn't even happening."

"I don't want to see you get cheated on."

"CHEATED ON?" She laughed. "Are you kidding me?"

"Actors cheat. We both know that. A man like Orson Beck, good as he is, will probably only sleep alone in his hotel room so many times before—"

"I thought you liked him?"

"I do. But sex is a—"

"I'm not in the mood to hear any of your over-enlightened theories on the modern lie of monogamy, Miles. Can we please change the subject?"

"Jolie will be up soon." He nodded. "I'll start the pancakes. What would you like to talk about?"

"How about work?" Sloane sighed. "How do you think today is going to go?"

Miles gave her a reassuring smile. "It's going to go great."

But, of course, it didn't.

Chapter Fifteen

Sloane

SLOANE HAD SUFFERED through many long days in her life, but today felt like one of the longest.

Even with the hardest part now behind her, she couldn't get her brain to slow down. She had learned to accept that self-doubt and second-guessing were both parts of the creative process. It didn't matter whether she was writing, editing, or directing, there came a time in every project where she was sure everything she touched would turn to garbage.

But those feelings had never been so pervasive, especially so early in a project's timeline.

Right now, Sloane was uncertain about *everything*. She didn't know if was her or the work itself, but everything felt flawed.

The cast and crew had all mostly gone home, but Sloane was sticking around on set to evaluate the day's work alone. In peace and quiet without everyone constantly needing something. The burden had been especially heavy since Lila was still out sick. She must have been poisoned something awful — the assistant director wasn't the type to miss a minute of work, let alone two full days.

Despite most of the cast and crew being back on set, no one had been at his or her best.

Except Orson. Apparently he was a Hollywood A-lister for a reason. The dude must never have a bad day. His part of every take was perfect, but that still didn't mean the scenes were good enough.

Sloane didn't know how to make those decisions. It was one thing when she had been making little art films with her micro budgets. She made those cuts fast, and with a confidence born from somewhere deep inside her. But when the budgets were astronomically higher, with livelihoods dependent on her choices, chaos seemed to reign, regardless of how hard she tried to navigate around it. Everything felt wrong, no matter how right it might be.

She didn't want to admit it, but Sloane was at least ninety-percent sure that more than half of Cassidy's work from today would need to be reshot. Her accent had not only returned, it sounded even heavier than before, probably due to her food poisoning and recovery. Worse, her body language now appeared lazy.

It didn't help to cast any blame, but that didn't stop Sloane from spending ample time trying to decide who was at fault more — Cassidy for her shitty performance or her for letting it go without saying anything.

Sloane had watched the footage four times now and found it harder to get through every time. Cassidy's parts seemed worse by the viewing, and by contrast Orson's even better. The actors were in two different movies. Cassidy might as well have been in an after school special while Orson appeared to be angling for his second Oscar.

"How does it look?"

For the second it took her to recognize Orson's voice, Sloane wanted to jump out of her skin. But then she turned with a smile. "Depends who's asking."

"Orson Beck." He jabbed at thumb at his chest, still smiling.

"Your parts are great. The rest of the footage …" Sloane sighed. "I admit to being worried."

"What about?" He cleared his throat. "If you don't mind my asking."

She didn't at all, but it still felt weird if not altogether inappropriate to shit talk an actor's performance without that person being around to defend themselves.

"I'm just not sure I was as on top of things as I should have been today," Sloane admitted.

Orson shrugged. "I don't think anyone was as on top of things as they should have been today."

"You were."

He shook his head. "Today was hardly my best work."

"It was better than anyone else's," Sloane said, only feeling the slightest twinge of future regret for her present honesty. "And no offense, but I'm not sure 'I don't think anyone was on top of things' is good enough. There's a lot of money riding on this."

"Of course there is. But you can't forget it's still a product, same as any other. The best chef in the world still occasionally leaves their meat a minute too long on the grill."

"The Shellys are putting a lot of faith in me."

"Sure they are. And don't think for a second you're not delivering on your promise. Show me one other film on their roster where the director has to worry about sabotage, or—"

"Thanks for saying that." Sloane didn't need to hear

more. She knew how much she had to deal with just fine. "Do you want to see some of what we have?"

Of course he did.

But Orson shook his head. "Not even a little."

"Why not?"

"I hate seeing myself on screen."

"Why?" She hated it too, but only because she was Sloane Alexander.

He was Orson Beck.

"It's never a good idea."

But that wasn't an answer.

"Why?" Sloane asked again. "Does it make you uncomfortable?"

"Not exactly. It's more that if I see something I don't like then I can't get it out of my head. That one sour note gets stuck like a splinter, then that's all I can think about and my performance gets worse and worse going forward." He gave her a self-effacing laugh. "Ask me how I know."

"Seriously, Orson. You have nothing to worry about." It was the first time she had ever said his name like that. The familiarity filled her with chills.

"I'll tell you what. How about I see what I did today at the premier?" He offered Sloane his red-carpet smile that left her with little choice but to acquiesce and surrender.

"Okay," Sloane said in defeat, turning away from the monitor.

"Mind if I ask you something?"

"No, but next time just ask and don't give me a chance to opt out." She laughed.

"Fair enough." He laughed back, light but genuine. "Is it possible that your problems with what you're seeing on the dailies has nothing to do with the work itself?"

"Easy to say when you won't watch them."

But he was probably right. Sloane had too many things

in her head and she wasn't thinking straight. She was thinking about that morning's conversation with Miles and all the many reasons that Orson Beck might be right for her, even if he was also totally wrong.

"Tell me about the worst of it," he suggested.

She shook her head. "It's one thing if you watch it with me, but another if I'm just talking about someone else behind his or her back."

"You're the director, Sloane. *Direct.* What's the worst of it today?"

"Cassidy's accent. And her body language."

"Makes sense." He nodded. "But again, today was off for everyone. Are you worried about today's work or the movie in general?"

Sloane considered her answer, but Orson wouldn't allow it.

"Don't think, respond. *Are you worried about today's work or the movie in general?*"

"The movie in general," she replied.

"Is this a story someone else could tell better than you, or are you the perfect director for this film?"

A slight smile crossed her face. "I'm the perfect director for this film."

Now she had it — Sloane wasn't even letting his questions sit for a second before she was ready with her answer.

"Is *West Hollywood Sunset* an Oscar contender or a box office bomb?"

Proudly, she cried out, "An Oscar contender!"

"And is your problem with the production or Liam Wentz?"

"*Wentz,*" she replied. The word had left her lips before she realized Orson tricked the monster's name right out of her.

"See?" He took her hand. "Now we can focus on the actual problem."

She gave him a reluctant smile, looking into his eyes with an amused strain of defeat. She longed to kiss him, but that wasn't what this was about.

Orson Beck was helping her to see through the haze. "Tell me, *specifically*, what is it you're worried about Liam Wentz doing to you. Or to this production."

"It feels like the calm before the storm."

He nodded. "Okay, keep going."

"Nothing bad happened today because nothing bad *needed to happen today.*" She was explaining things to herself as much as she was explaining them to Orson. "We've been one step behind him ever since we started, and today we were all dealing with the aftermath of his little food poisoning trick. He didn't need to do anything else. But it's only a matter of time before he's back at it and …" She stopped and swallowed, unable to finish.

Orson made an attempt on her behalf. "And you're worried he's going to yank the rug out from under you again. No matter how hard you try, you'll never be able to make the movie in your head because Liam Wentz is like a specter behind—"

"Can we please not say his name?"

"You know that only gives him more power, right?"

"You sound like my therapist."

"My bad," Orson said. "I was quoting Harry Potter."

"You can totally call him Voldemort."

"Fine. What's the very worst thing Voldemort could possibly do?"

Another excellent question.

"It's the unknown that gets me. It's not what he could possibly do so much as the reality that he's capable of doing just about anything." Then she added, "And getting away with it."

Orson kept talking her through it. "And what do you wish you could do to stop him?"

"*Anything.*" And that was her frustration point. "If I could just go to the police or the Academy or ... *someone.* But instead, I'm trapped in silence like I have been ever since I was a little girl."

"No one here wants you to be silent. You understand that, right?"

She nodded.

Orson continued. "Not me or Dominic or Melinda, or anyone working on—"

"Except for the people he has inside the—"

"Yes, except for them. But the Shellys will root those people out and make them sorry. They'll only be able to work with Voldemort from then on. And we all know what happened to the Death Eaters."

"I actually don't remember," Sloane admitted.

"Me neither. But I think most of them were permanently imprisoned in Azkaban or whatever." Orson shrugged. "It wasn't good. My point is that we have to be patient. You're doing all the right things, it's just hard to see that."

"I'm not doing anything!"

"No," he shook his head, "you're waiting for evidence. Right now, you have nothing, so silence is your ally. Speaking too soon will only hurt you, but speaking later could very well destroy him."

"Hopefully," she added.

"It's what we have to believe." Orson offered her another reassuring smile. "You were never wrong to tell the world what he did to you, but accusing Voldemort without having the evidence to back you up is what killed your career the first time, right?"

Yes, that was correct, even if Orson's pointing it out felt like a cold blade between her ribs.

"You're right. Thanks for talking me down. I just hate that he's always winning."

He shook his head. "He's not always winning, but I understand why you feel that way."

Something changed in his face.

"Why are you smiling like that?" Sloane asked.

"Because, I might have a present for you."

"Is it that dinner we were supposed to have?" Not that she could even go right now.

"Better," he said.

"Better than dinner with a box-office dominating, Oscar-winning movie star?"

"I know someone who specializes in getting dirt on people in the industry."

"You mean like a private eye or something?"

"I mean like the guy who writes for *Hollywood Hunted*." He grinned.

"How do you know him? Isn't he a mystery man? And doesn't he hate actors and, you know, like all of Hollywood?"

"He lived a couple doors down from me, before I was …"

"Famous," Sloane finished for him. "You can say it."

"*Famous*," he repeated with a smile. "Anyway, yes, he does hate Hollywood but he has a soft spot for me. Hell, he might already have what we need and not even know it."

"You'll really talk to him?"

"Of course. If I was just name-dropping, I would've mentioned that I met Barack Obama."

"Again, not surprised, but *you have?*"

"I have." He gave her a sheepish yet self-assured grin.

"Thank you." She shook her head with an equal measure of appreciation and disbelief.

"How thankful are you?"

His question got her heart beating faster. "How thankful do you want me to be?"

"Enough to let me finally take you to dinner."

She shook her head again, this time delivering a difficult truth. "I can't. I have Jolie."

"Jolie will understand. I'll have Armando from Natural Nurturing come and pick her and Connor up, then we can all meet up later."

Sloane still hesitated.

He kept talking. "We can take separate cars so it doesn't feel like too much like a date, just in case that's bothering you, and I promise to take you to the second-best restaurant I know, so you can still have another dining experience to look forward to. *Now,* how does that sound?"

She laughed. "Like a dream."

"Well, then …" Orson offered his hand. "Let's make it happen."

Sloane linked her fingers with his. And something inside her whispered—

Chapter Sixteen

Melinda

"You know there's no going back from this, right?" Dominic asked her.

Melinda stopped brushing her hair and turned to her husband. "Victorious warriors win first and then go to war, while defeated warriors go to war first and then seek to win."

"I love a little Sun Tzu before dinner as much as the next mogul, but you didn't really answer my question."

"It's time, Dominic. We played it your way going in, but Wentz is—"

"That wasn't *my way*, love. It was—"

"A little too timid." Melinda smiled at her husband then returned to the mirror and began brushing her hair in the reflection again. "Our efforts now require a much stronger dose."

"No disagreement there. Or anywhere," he amended. "I only question the specific nature of our next move. Danny is dangerous."

"That's why it's time to call him."

"But he's not on our payroll," Dominic argued.

"We're still paying him."

"There's a difference. Ultimately, Danny Whatever His Name Is works for himself."

"That's a good thing. The money is hidden and we have no visible ties. The guy doesn't officially exist, and we don't even know his name. What exactly is it that you're worried about?"

"The things I can't see," Dominic admitted.

Again, Melinda paused her brushing to turn from the mirror and look at him. "Isn't that why we need Danny?"

"I don't want to need anyone but you."

"That's very sweet, but I think we both know you also need to win, especially against Wentz. This is how we do that."

Melinda was right. And Dominic knew it.

She understood his discomfort, but this wasn't the time or place. Not if they wanted to protect Sloane, turn her Hollywood debut into a modern classic good enough to reboot her career that also helped launch their platform, and ultimately obliterate a predator that was swimming around like a shark at the beach that no one had the courage to catch.

Except for them, and this was the way to do it.

Sam, the Treadwells' agent, knew a man who occasionally went by the name Danny ... in addition to several other pseudonyms. Danny, or whomever he was playing at the time, was a fixer. The Shellys had used a few such fixers in their two decades and change in the industry, and Danny was no doubt the best.

Melinda agreed with her husband that it was dangerous to use him. But she also thought at this point, considering how much damage Wentz had managed to level against them in only a week — and their first one in production — it was exponentially more dangerous not to.

Dominic stood from the bed and looked at his watch. "Fifteen minutes?"

"Fifteen minutes," Melinda repeated without turning from the mirror.

Their lives were lived with precision already, but liaisons like this required something extra.

They agreed to meet at a quarter to seven on the back lawn. A terrific spot, where the Shellys had hosted more business conferences than they could count without studying their calendars, but only when meeting with Danny did their guest suddenly appear as if from nowhere. And just like the other four times the three of them had sat out by the pool together speaking of things that should never be said aloud, the fixer brought his own food.

"Good to see you guys again." Danny was already sitting, chowing down on a burger. He gave them a nod as they approached, pointing to the bags. "There's plenty. I didn't know what you wanted, so I ordered a bunch of stuff."

"Sloppy's?" Dominic looked at the bags with utter disgust. "Again?

"You can never go wrong with Sloppy's." Danny took another bite of his burger.

Dominic shook his head. "You always go wrong with Sloppy's."

"Why don't we get started?" Melinda suggested.

She wasn't sure whether it amused or perturbed her that Danny managed to get under Dominic's skin. The guy probably hated Sloppy's every bit as much as her husband.

Danny took another big bite of burger and shoved a handful of fries into his mouth. "Sowhtzthehasz?"

So, what's the haps?

148

"You're a pig," Dominic said, taking a seat. Then to Melinda: "He's a pig."

Danny swallowed, wiped his mouth with the back of his burger hand, then reached for another handful of fries with the other one. "A clean pig makes lean bacon."

Melinda sat. "My husband still doesn't understand that this is all an act on your part."

"What makes you think it's an act?" Danny grinned.

She pointed at his T-shirt and read the caption aloud. "*I suck at apologies, so unfuck you or whatever.* Last time you were wearing a Ted Nugent shirt, and it was Big Johnson the time before that."

"I'm a collector." Danny pointed at the bags, grease stains bleeding through them. Soon they'd look like bullet holes. "You guys should start eating. This stuff is total shit once it gets cold."

"You know how to push Dominic's buttons." Melinda looked at her husband. "He knows better than to let you, but it happens anyway."

"I don't push your buttons?" He shoved the final bit of burger into his mouth.

"We're paying for this?" Dominic shook his head, still not getting it.

"Exactly," Melinda explained. "Our fixer is proving that he can be whoever he needs to be."

"And right now he needs to be a pile of shit who—"

"You never lose your cool, Dominic. And yet, this guy can get you to lose it just by sitting down and eating Sloppy's in front of you."

"That's not all he's doing," Dominic argued.

Melinda turned to Danny, or whatever his name actually was. "No, you don't push my buttons. I like to see what I'm paying for."

"Well then, vamos começar esta festa." He winked at

Dominic. "So, like I said at the start of this little soirée, *what's the haps?*"

"What do you know about Liam Wentz?" Melinda asked.

Danny's body language instantly changed, and for a micro-second she saw him become someone else entirely. The metamorphosis lasted only a moment, then it was mostly gone and Melinda was looking at a man that was both more and less than he'd been just a few blinks before.

He shook his head and stood. "You can keep the Sloppy's."

Dominic looked at Melinda. "Is this part of his act?"

"Sit down." Melinda was commanding enough to nab Danny's attention, but he still didn't sit. "I assume by your reaction that you're more than familiar with him."

"I don't work on that asshole's behalf," Danny said. "And that ain't a part of no act."

"Sit down," she repeated. "I'm sure we have a lot to talk about."

Dominic shifted in his seat, suddenly much more interested in a conversation with their fixer.

"This is my fault," Melinda said. "I apologize for starting out with such an open-ended question without any context. Let me clarify. My husband and I would like to destroy Liam Wentz, and to do that, we need your help."

She almost expected Dominic to chime in with, *She needs your help,* but he was still leaning forward, still interested.

"So, with that in mind," Melinda continued, "What do you know about Liam Wentz?"

"He's a kid fucker who deserves to get a bullet in his dick and a couple in each of his kneecaps. He's also made some really excellent films."

"Do you have any personal experience with him?"

"Not exactly," Danny answered Dominic, the artificial mirth now gone from his voice.

"Are you familiar with Sloane Alexander?" Melinda asked.

"Everyone's seen *Remaking Christmas*, but in the context of this conversation I'm guessing it's more *The Good Daughter*."

"We represented Sloane when she accused Wentz twenty years ago," Dominic said.

Danny nodded, suddenly understanding the edges of whatever this was.

"Sloane has written the script for a film called *West Hollywood Sunset*. She's directed three independent films, but this project has our full backing," Melinda explained. "Sam tells me you know the Treadwells. They're—"

"Sam shouldn't be telling you that."

"—working on a companion memoir. Together, this should spell his downfall. Wentz has mansions full of closets, and most are stuffed with skeletons. We just need to tip the first domino. We tried and failed twenty years ago, and he's been doing it who knows how many times both before and since."

"I'm with you," Danny said. "So, where are we now?"

Dominic responded. "We just started shooting, but it appears Wentz has someone—"

"Or many someones," Melinda cut in.

"—on the inside. We've had a compromised computer code for Shellter Productions' biggest project, actors breaking contracts, a feeble little strike, and a serious bout of food poisoning, plus a crashed light kit so far."

"Also misinformed parents waving their sabers at us," Melinda added.

Danny nodded. "You have any new employees at Shellter?"

"Define *new,*" Dominic said.

"Less than six months."

"No." Melinda shook her head. "Two years is the shortest amount of time we've known anyone involved in the project."

Danny raised his eyebrows. "Good answer. I assume you've already looked into who went home sick, who had access to food, who was around the lighting kit, including all the et ceteras?"

"We have," Dominic said. "But so far none of our leads have amounted to anything."

"That's why you're here," Melinda told him. "We had a plan, but Wentz has forced us into a new one. He needs to go down. So far, he has cost us time, money, and convenience. We've not lost any lives. But at this point, it feels inevitable. Wentz will do anything to dodge his consequences."

"That guy has killed already," Danny said.

"You know that, or you think that?" Dominic had something in his eyes that Melinda couldn't quite interpret — a rarity for sure.

"I know it like I know you two fuck at least five times a week," Danny said.

"He needs to go down," Melinda repeated. "We need to be sure that when it comes down to it, the right people are left standing this time."

"Agreed." Danny nodded again. "We make sure the bastard takes the blame, no matter who pulls the trigger. You already know the good and bad news about this guy. He's been doing his shit for a while. That means there's plenty of dirt to dig up, but doing so is going to be dangerous."

"You know something," Dominic said, and Melinda now understood the look in his eyes. "What is it?"

"I don't *know*, but I've heard a few things." Danny took a moment to finish his thought, and Melinda imagined it was that he was revealing something ahead of schedule. "You two aren't the only people who have been digging into this guy. I've heard talk that Wentz doesn't just like his prey one-on-one. I've heard he's connected to Sprog."

So little gave Melinda gooseflesh, but that word always did.

Sprog: the supposed child porn ring that the Shellys had been hearing about forever, but that no one so far could prove actually existed.

"You think Sprog is real," Dominic said.

"Of course it is." Danny didn't sound like he had a molecule of doubt. "But we need proof."

"How do we get that?" Dominic asked.

"You think you're the first person to wonder?" Danny shrugged, but the gesture seemed far from indifferent. "You know anyone who traffics in underage girls, because I don't, and that would be a great place to start."

Of course he was being sarcastic. But Danny still had an excellent idea.

"Actually," Melinda said, getting what was might be a brilliant idea, "I just might."

Chapter Seventeen

Sloane

"This is *so* not what I expected," Sloane said, looking around the gorgeous restaurant.

"So, I assume you've never been." Orson grinned at her.

"I've been living in London for the last twenty years, so *no*, I've never been here."

But of course she had heard of Arrivé, the Michelin Star restaurant started by world famous pastry chef and host of *Bake it Away,* Amanda Byrd. There were three locations — the flagship in L.A. where they were eating now, a second and supposedly more impressive spot in New York, and the newest location in Austin, Texas which Orson dubbed a "wild experiment" but every bit as amazing as the other two.

Sloane had never eaten paella this full of flavor, including during the three months she spent living in Spain.

"How do you know so much about Arrivé?" Sloane asked him. "Are you an investor or something?"

"Nope. But the Shellys sort of are." Orson looked at her, surprised. "You didn't know that?"

She shook her head. "Dominic and Melinda have way too much going on for me to even try and keep track of it all. I had no idea they were dabbling in the restaurant business."

"They're not … exactly."

"So they're not investors?"

"They're investors in Amanda Byrd. They're the producers of *Bake it Away.* I'm guessing you didn't know that either?"

"Nope." Sloane shook her head again.

"I'm sure you know about Juke."

"Of course. *Sunset* is a launch title."

"Ah, that's right." Orson nodded. "Well, the Shellys have been both acquiring and developing a metric fuck ton of content in anticipation of the launch. They've been planning this for a long time. Years now. They've funded, produced, or somehow finagled their way into a slew of top tier or coveted projects and managed to work eventual Juke rights into all of their contracts, without ever even using the name *Juke.* No one is anticipating that a production studio like Shellter would ever have the ambition to launch their own platform. It's going to take the world by storm when they finally announce it."

"It is a little crazy." Sloane gave herself a chill saying it.

"Oh, yeah," Orson agreed. "It's totally batshit. But I would never bet against the Shellys. I don't know how they've got this, exactly, but I know they do."

"No offense, but …"

"Just say it." He prompted Sloane with a smile.

"I've known them for twenty years. Why do you know so much more than me?"

"You've been living in London. I've had a front row seat for the last five years. I probably have ten-percent of the entire picture, but I imagine that still might be more than anyone other than the Shellys themselves. I've watched Dominic and Melinda predict and invest in the future over and over in the five years I've been working with them. Their track record and execution are impressive." Orson paused then finished his thought. "And by impressive, I mean *impeccable.*"

"For example?"

"You know *F the 90s?*"

"Of course I know *F the 90s.*" Sloane felt her whole body flush. "I love *F the 90s.*"

"When's the last time you saw an episode?"

She thought then said, "I don't know … it's been a while?"

"You haven't seen an episode because the Shellys bought all the rights and have managed to keep most of what's still out there on the Internet — *including the original webisodes* — out of circulation. Why? Because of Juke, of course. They bought *F the 90s* on the cheap, took it off the market to make it scarce, then exploded my career to skyrocket the value of their initial investment. *F the 90s* is a launch series for Juke. There are a hundred titles like that, and that defines the Shellys approach. Their investments work to make something exponential, and all of that is in service of their ambition."

"*In service of their ambition?*" Sloane repeated with a giggle, after she swallowed another exceptional forkful of paella.

"It is serious." He looked sober to prove it. "On the

surface, it looks like they love money more than anything. But there's something else driving them."

"And what's that?" She asked, dying to know.

"I have no idea," Orson admitted.

"You must have *some idea*?"

"Seriously, I think they want to change the world."

"Aren't they doing that already?"

He nodded. "Sure, in a way. But I think maybe they want to remake it."

"How?"

He shrugged. "I don't know. But Juke's just the start of it. And even then, I'm only guessing. You want to ask me something else that maybe I *do* know the answer to?"

Sloane looked down at her empty plate. "Do you know what makes the paella so amazing?"

"I can find out." Orson raised his hand.

A server immediately spotted him — of course — and rushed right over.

"Yes, Mr. Beck? How can I help you?"

"Can you please tell us what makes the paella at Arrivé so throughly delicious?"

"Absolutely." The server smiled. "Our paella uses Mexican oregano instead of the traditional Mediterranean version, and a blend of both sweet and smoked paprika. Plus, Chef Byrd's recipe calls for the onions and garlic to get fried in bacon drippings."

Sloane gushed, "It's better than the paella in Spain."

"I'll make sure to tell the chef." She bowed her head. "Will there be anything else?"

"Can you please bring us two of your favorite desserts?" Orson asked.

"Do you mean my first and second favorite, or my first favorite two times?"

"How about two of each." He grinned at his date. "Just in case."

"I'll have those right out." Another bow of her head then the server was gone.

Her night had been dreamy so far. She had basked in every second at the restaurant with Orson, despite the bombardment of paparazzi on the way inside. Arrivé was a great place for a photographer of the rich and famous to camp out, especially with Cameo just up the street.

But the restaurant staff had been almost supernatural in its ability to keep people away from their table and make it feel as much like an ordinary meal with two regular diners. The food was unforgettable, the wine a delightful lubricant, and the conversation breezier than the night outside.

Sloane put a hand over her stomach. "I'm not sure I can handle dessert."

"Finish your wine. That will settle your tummy."

"My tummy?" She laughed and shook her head. "I'm not sure that's how it works. And besides, I need to drive after our flambe ice cream, or whatever they bring."

"Flambe ice cream isn't a thing."

Maybe it was the wine, or the top finally popping on that insistent something that had been pressing on her mind. "I'm worried that Dominic and Melinda aren't taking things seriously enough."

"You mean with Voldemort as a threat?"

"With Wentz, yeah." She felt the power in claiming his name.

"I promise you, they are."

"Do you know something?" Sloane felt desperate for a *yes*.

"No." He shook his head. "Not specifically about Wentz."

"Then what makes you sure?"

"Plenty. But I'll give you two reasons. First, the Shellys always protect their investments, and they've got a lot wrapped up in this project. Second, and much more compelling, the Shellys always get their way." He blinked, and for a moment he looked lost. "I've literally never seen them lose."

"What do you mean?" Sloane put her hand over his without meaning to.

Orson looked thoughtful as he swallowed. "Dominic and Melinda were willing to interfere with people I loved to keep my career on what they saw as the proper path … meaning, the one they had invested in."

"That sounds … menacing."

He nodded. "That's a word for it. *Effective* is another one."

"Do you trust them?"

Orson smiled. "I trust them to keep their promises. And I trust them to protect their territory." He leaned forward and shook his head. "They're not going to let anyone keep them from succeeding, and right now that includes both of us. So let's go ahead and count ourselves lucky."

"Lucky," she repeated, the words like early dessert on her lips. "Is there anything else I should know about the Shellys? They've been in my life forever and yet they're still so mysterious."

"That's part of their brand." He leaned back and turned his hands so they were now over hers. "But yeah, I'm sure there's plenty you should know. Let me think …" And then he grinned. "Don't ever let them throw a party at your house, unless you're cool with them turning it into an orgy."

She laughed. "You're kidding."

"I absolutely am not." Orson shook his head. "I know you were a kid the last time you were in Hollywood, but this place is sexually rowdy."

Sloane rolled her eyes. "I live in London, not Utah."

"Ha. Utah's probably worse than L.A. — did you know they consume more porn than any other state."

"Makes sense." She shrugged. "It's the *behind closed doors* rule."

Orson laughed. "The Shellys don't need closed doors."

"Are you being serious right now?" She couldn't tell. "What happened?"

"Melinda invited me to join a threesome."

"You're lying."

"I am not." He shook his head, but Orson was definitely smiling.

"You're an actor. You lie for a living. How am I supposed to trust you?"

"Your choice, but I do cross my heart and hope to die." Then he did, ending his gesture with a tap at his right eye to indicate the needle he'd be sticking there in the event of his dishonesty.

"Did you do it?" She had to ask.

"What you be jealous if I did?"

"Yes, I would be." She answered without thinking, then quickly added, "Melinda is *very* attractive."

A pregnant moment stretched between them. Orson stared back at her from across the table, working to determine whether or not she was serious. Then laughter found them in tandem.

As they were settling down, their desserts arrived, alongside a surprise.

"Amanda!" Orson exclaimed and rose to give the celebrity chef an awkward hug as she held a pair of dessert plates slightly askew. "It's great to see you." When he pulled away from her, he reclaimed his seat, then introduced his date. "Amanda, this is Sloane. Sloane, this is Amanda, former owner of Arrivé and present-day host of *Bake it Away* and owner of the bakery behind it."

"It's great to meet you." Then, much lower and said like a secret. "I watch *Remaking Christmas* every December, and *A Prayer for Alice Tremble* is one of my favorite movies."

"Thank you." Sloane looked down, feeling herself blush.

"What are you doing here?" Orson asked.

"Arrive's desserts all come from Bake it Away, but I was here to talk to Harris and he told me you were eating, so I wanted to say hi. And bring you this." She set the pair of plates on their table. "I know you ordered two each of Samantha's favorites, but this is what you really want."

Sloane looked down with a smile at the stunning desserts.

Amanda pointed to the plate on her left. "This one is rose petal panna cotta with damson and lavender Viennese shortbread." Then to the one on her right. "And this one is a prune and Tokaji parfait, prune cake, Tokaji jelly, white chocolate ganache and mascarpone ice cream."

"Thank you!" Sloane was salivating again. "I can't wait to try them."

"Bon appétit." Amanda left.

"So, how do you know her?" Sloane asked.

Over dessert he explained that Dominic and Melinda had asked him to help her out with a bit of publicity after breaking from Arrivé to start Bake it Away. They became casual friends immediately after that.

The dessert was to die for and still remember after death. Even so, Sloane could only eat a few bites. Of each. Same for Orson. Then they were suddenly both all gone.

She felt tipsy on their way outside, and it wasn't from the drink.

"That was the *second best restaurant?*" Sloane asked outside. "When can we eat at the first?"

"Someday." Orson smiled. "Is it okay if I kiss you?"

They were in front of the valet stand, and perhaps a half-dozen photographers. She still nodded, wanting nothing more.

"Even in front of all these people?"

"Just do it," Sloane said.

So he did, and she could hear the shutters snapping.

They said their *goodbyes* and their *see you tomorrows*, then the valet handed Sloane the fob to her RAV4 and she drove away believing that magic really did exist.

The feeling didn't last long.

A quarter hour after leaving the restaurant, her paranoia returned.

Except, it wasn't paranoia.

The driver behind her wasn't just aggressive, he was getting more antagonistic by the second.

She tried to wave him around her, but he refused to take the hint. There was nowhere to pull over and let him pass. So she floored it, going as fast as she could while still feeling safe, but he kept inching closer and closer.

Sloane kept getting more and more scared.

His fender punched at her bumper. She squealed and reached for her purse.

Fumbled inside for her phone.

Cursed herself for not taking the time to program it into the hands-free system of her rental.

She sped up, going even faster.

So did the driver behind her.

And this time when he plowed into Sloane, he sent her careening right off the road and into—

Chapter Eighteen

Sloane

The side of the road. Sloane still couldn't believe it. She was standing on the side of the road, trying not to shatter.

She had been forced off the road around a half hour or so ago. Officers arrived on the scene almost immediately, but not for her benefit. Things started going sideways almost as soon as they got there.

The crowd grew fast. Maybe it was her paranoia, but Sloane was sure that at least a few of the gathered horde had to be plants, there to take photos and make her feel exposed. A quiet stretch of road had made her assault possible, but that stretch was no longer so silent. A passing motorist pulled over just as the police arrived. She never got a chance to converse with the old woman, but the lady looked nice enough, and Sloane was willing to believe that the first person was a Good Samaritan.

But one person turned into three, then ten, and now more than two-dozen lookie-loos were littering the roadside. And her life. The interrogation hadn't left her any time to check, but she could imagine what had happened easily enough. Someone posted her accident on LiveLyfe or some other bullshit social media site, thereby making it open season on Sloane Alexander and her recurring misfortune.

Right now, it was hard not to hate everyone at the scene. But she swallowed her bile, looked Officer Alvarez in his squinty little eyes, then gave him her statement yet again.

"This is the fifth time now, right?" she confirmed, half to let him know that she could tally his crap, and half because Sloane still couldn't believe it herself.

"We just need to make sure that we have an accurate picture of what happened here."

"And you're expecting it to come out of my mouth differently than it has the other four times I told you—"

"You spoke to Officer Jensen, ma'am. I've not yet taken your statement."

"So … what? You don't share information? Did I miss something? Are we in the old west all of a sudden?"

"I'm not sure what you mean by that, ma'am."

"Stop calling me ma'am!"

But then Sloane caught herself.

She couldn't afford to snap. That was exactly what everyone wanted. Her entire life had felt like a trial by media, with people not just willing but actively waiting to turn on her. And not just those working for the monster — *for Liam Wentz* — but regular everyday humans who fed off the misery of others like a vampire bat wading in a pool of blood.

"I'm sorry about that." Sloane gave Officer Alvarez her very best smile. "I'm just a little shaken is all. Go ahead and ask me whatever you need to."

She hated playing the game, but Sloane told herself it

was just another role. She was probably reciting lines before she had been fully potty trained. Her earliest years were fuzzy, and it wasn't like she could ever talk to her mother again to ask any clarifying questions.

Sloane drifted through the interrogation on autopilot, answering every question that came her way with almost the exact same language she'd used before, but now sounding more submissive, more deferential, more like what the officers wanted to hear from her voice, and what the crowd needed to see in her posture.

Her phone buzzed, but Sloane ignored it. She could answer the call in a moment, after she had proved herself to be a cooperative interview subject. *Again.*

The crash had been terrifying, and Sloane spent the first few minutes in the immediate aftermath of her accident scared out of her mind. But now she was pissed, and more so by the second.

Thank God she had dialed Melinda after calling the cops. Sloane had expected the law would respond appropriately to the situation. That they would see her as a victim and try to help. Instead, they were treating her like the cause of it all.

In addition to the inquisition, Sloane had also taken two breathalyzers and had suffered enough flashbulbs to imagine what it might be like to live with permanent damage to her retinas. That was clearly a ridiculous leap in logic, but she didn't know where else to redirect her thoughts. The entire situation was making her feel crazy.

The EMT said nothing was an emergency, including the pain in her neck. He denied doing so when Sloane asked if he was suggesting she was making it up but offered no alternative explanation.

"And how many drinks did you have at dinner?"

Officer Alvarez glared at her like she'd been guzzling at red lights, right from the bottle.

"You asked me that already. Not even five minutes ago."

Alvarez pretended to look back at his notes. "Oh, yeah. Right. How about—"

"How about we finish this up and get me to the hospital." Sloane offered the officer her thinnest smile. "I have an excruciating pain in my neck, and no one is listening to me."

"I understand, ma'am. Just another—"

"Just another nothing!"

Sloane and the officer turned toward the commanding voice in tandem — the Shellys' lawyer, Solomon Tummel.

"Care to explain why you're keeping my client from getting the medical attention she ..."

Sloane let Solomon's tirade fade into the background. She had enough experience with the lawyer to know how the rest of his very short, very terse discussion with Officer Doubt Her Story would go.

"You're going to be okay." Solomon put a gentle hand on Sloane's shoulder and walked her to his car after leaving Alvarez verbally beaten, still dripping metaphorical blood.

He stopped on the passenger side of his big black Mercedes. "Would you rather sit up front or in the back?"

Nice of him to ask. "Up front, please."

Solomon nodded and opened the door for her.

She climbed inside. After he closed her in, she leaned her head against the window.

Solomon was a killer in the courtroom, and apparently the roadside or wherever he needed to be, but a teddy bear of a man as well. The Shellys were his only client.

He was emotionally intelligent enough to ask her no questions, nor leave her to silence.

He turned on the radio and Mozart flooded the cabin.

His "Clarinet Concerto" to drown out the sounds of her crying.

Chapter Nineteen

Sloane

SLOANE WAS IN THE HOSPITAL, dying to go home.

But at least she wasn't alone. By the time Solomon got her to Cedars Sinai, Melinda, Dominic, Miles, and Orson were all there and waiting. As much as she wanted to see Jolie, she was to relieved to hear that she and Connor were with Armando. Her daughter was in good hands. And at least for now, she wouldn't have to see her mommy covered in boo-boos.

"I still don't understand why I can't go," She complained to everyone in the room. "All the tests are done, right?" No one answered, because everyone understood that wasn't what she wanted. Sloane knew perfectly well why she couldn't yet go. "I have mild whiplash and a slight concussion. A few contusions and a blood alcohol level that was well within the legal limits. So why can't I leave?"

Miles gave her the answer she hadn't been looking for. "The doctor has to check you out."

She rolled her eyes. "You're all risk takers. Can't one of you wheel me out of here?"

Part of her wanted to stay in that room forever. Or at least long enough for the crowd outside to lose interest. It was only getting bigger, which gave Sloane an ever-swelling urgency to get the hell out of there. Several online gossip columns were already running stories, none flattering. It would only get worse from here. She needed to be home, with Jolie, even if her home was a rental.

"Just a few more minutes, hon." Melinda gently rubbed her arm.

Orson crouched by the bed and took her hand in his. "I know what you're worried about, and it's going to be okay."

Easy for him to say. Everyone loved Orson Beck.

"And I know you think that's easy for me to say, but believe me, I've weathered some shit. And the Shellys have helped me get through it all." He offered the pair an acknowledging nod. "They'll help you get through this."

"Don't read any of that schiesse online," Miles said. "It will only make everything worse."

Dominic disagreed. "You're wrong about that."

Melinda explained. "You should read whatever you need to get the right kind of angry."

"I saw a few headlines already," she told them.

Orson said, "When we had our moment earlier. She made me give her my phone."

Sloane started quoting headlines from memory. "*Orson Beck's New Lover is a Party Girl. Sloane Alexander Abandons Her Daughter and Wraps Her Car Around a Tree. Sloane Alexander's Life Still Out of Control, Two Decades After Levying False Accusations at Liam Wentz.*"

"We expected this," Dominic said.

"Wait! I didn't get to my favorite one. *Golden Boy Beck*

Always Goes For Damaged Goods. Can He Save Sloane Alexander From Her 20-Year Spiral?"

"Maybe he can." Golden Boy Beck gave her a smile.

"I don't need you to make light of the moment, Orson." Sloane couldn't believe she just said that. "I want to get out of here now. But more than that, I want to have a serious discussion with everyone in this room. We need to acknowledge that Liam Wentz is out of control, and that this situation is—"

"You said his name." Dominic stated the obvious.

"Damn right I said his name." Sloane straightened up in the bed, surprising herself. "Yes, Dominic, we expected this, but that doesn't mean I can ignore what I'm feeling right now. I could have been killed tonight, and yet that's not even what bothers me. What if Jolie had been in the car?"

No one had an answer for that one.

"What if other people — innocent people — had been on the road? What then?"

"What are you actually saying?" Dominic asked.

"Maybe we shouldn't be making this movie." Saying it felt like she was stabbing her own stomach, but Sloane could no longer keep her screaming worry inside. "How much would you lose if we stopped?"

"It's not about how much we would lose." Dominic shook his head. "It's about how many things we would have to—"

"We're making this movie," Melinda interrupted, "and destroying Wentz. Any discussion that runs against that objective is counter-productive to this conversation. You're safe—"

"How am I safe?" Sloane tossed her hands in the air. "I'm in the hospital, and I can't even leave!"

"It's okay, chérie." Miles took her other hand. He and Orson traded a look.

Sloane didn't know if she liked or loathed the exchange. "I couldn't live with myself if anything happened to Jolie."

"No one understands that better than I do." Miles squeezed her hand then turned to the Shellys. "She's right to talk about this. We both believe in you, but how can we make sure that Sloane and Jolie both stay safe? You can't be everywhere at once, and we've already—"

Dominic raised a hand to stop him, redirected the attention back to himself by clearing his throat. "Your fears are real and understandable. Everything you said is fair. But I would ask everyone in this room to remember that Wentz is a producer, and right now his product is fear. He's a lot more careful than it might appear based on what he's allowing us to see. To my mind, Wentz overplayed his hand tonight. We weren't as on top of things as we should have been going into this. That lack of foresight has been acknowledged and compensated for. We're now moving our pieces across the board."

"Aggressively," Melinda added.

"Aggressively," Dominic repeated with a decisive nod. "Neither of us wants you to do anything you don't want to do, but we also both believe that you want to do this and will regret it if you don't. Yes, we have a tremendous amount riding on the project, but Melinda and I will adjust. Shellter Productions will thrive either way. Is that true for Sloane Alexander?"

Melinda spoke into her husband's pause. "We can keep Jolie off set and safe. Removing her from the equation, what is it you're most worried about?"

It was a great question and deserved all of Sloane's

thought. But everyone was staring at her expectantly, waiting for her answer as if she already had it.

When she dug down to the root of it, she had no doubt about the truth. Liam Wentz had her rattled for sure, but it was the trauma of her past experience being smeared by the press that kept drawing the panic like curtains around her.

Memories were a bludgeon, beating Sloane on the back of her head. Those thoughts had been a constant haunting but were now like hail instead of drizzle.

People whispering as she walked past them, tittering and pointing, occasionally hurling insults straight to her face. *The Lolita That No One Wanted* among the worst of them.

The way she had practically collapsed in on herself, like a dying star and a black hole in the making, refusing to go to school and melting down until her mother finally relented and let her stay home — the last place she wanted her daughter to be if she wasn't making money.

How everything about her mother suddenly changed. She made Sloane dye her hair a darker color and hide behind oversized sunglasses, not just in the states, but after they landed in London and she was so much less recognizable. She was living across the pond where people at large didn't know who Sloane Alexander was, let alone what she looked like. But Mom dragged her around shame-faced, anyway.

More than anything it was the inescapable pain of hearing and seeing the worst of herself articulated through layers of poisonous snark. Sloane loathed the judgment of others because it exposed the worst of what she already knew about herself. An unforgiving media had forced her to live with her emotions and vulnerabilities on the outside instead of inside her skin.

"The thing I'm most worried about besides Jolie's physical safety is her emotional security." Sloane finally answered. "The gossip was insufferable the first time, but I expected it again and was ready to deal with it. I just didn't think about how that might affect our daughter." She glanced at Miles, apologizing with her eyes. "Even if we can protect her from danger, she'll know these stories. If this movie is as big as we all want it to be, then that right there is a double-edged sword. This will become part of the permanent pop culture lexicon."

"She's right," Orson said.

Not that he needed to say anything. All four of them were nodding along.

"So again, is getting back at Liam Wentz worth it?"

"This is about a lot more than getting back at him," Dominic said.

"It's about wiping him and his filthy seed from this planet," added Melinda.

"But the cops don't even believe me! They didn't then and they won't now. I'm sure Solomon told you all about that little scene down at the accident. They were blaming *me* for getting run off the road!"

Melinda maneuvered between Orson and Miles. "You're right to worry about all of this, Sloane. Doing so helps us to plot our way out." She turned to Dominic. "Call Karlson."

He replied with a nod, taking out his phone, apparently to dial Karlson, whoever he was.

Melinda explained. "We have a contact in the LAPD, high up enough to give us a straight answer to whatever we need to know. Give him five minutes."

"Karlson," Dominic said with a nod to the room before slipping out into the hallway to make his call.

Miles turned to Melinda the second the door closed. "What's our exit plan?"

"I'm not sure what you mean." Melinda sounded surprisingly terse to Sloane's admittedly sensitive ears.

"Right now, it seems like Wentz is winning. You two are confident that you'll be able to reverse that trend. Like I said, I'm inclined to believe you. But what happens if you're wrong and there's another hard strike that we can't stop? What then?"

"As always, we will respond accordingly. I'm not sure it's constructive to hypothesize about what we should do in scenarios that do not yet exist. Not with our history of adaptive reactions."

"You make it sound like science," Miles said.

"Isn't it?" Melinda looked at him.

The lingering silence was long and uncomfortable, lasting until Dominic's return a few minutes later. "Good news and bad news," he said, closing the door.

He looked around, sensed the unease, then continued.

"Despite the behavior by our officer friendlies on-scene, Sloane's vehicle shows evidence of being hit. But the police have zero leads or any idea who it was. There weren't any cameras on that stretch of road, which might help to prove premeditation, but does nothing in regard to—"

"What about the last place where there was footage," Miles interrupted. "Did you ask about that?"

"Of course he did," Melinda said.

"The last camera footage with Sloane's car shows three possibilities—"

Orson nodded. "That sounds promising."

"An old man, a vehicle full of joyriding teenagers, and a third car that had been reported stolen. "

Orson said, "Definitely that one."

"If it was one of those three and no one turned onto

the road on a blind spot after, it was very likely the stolen car."

"And I'm guessing there's no sign of the stolen car now?" Orson asked.

"It has not yet been recovered. Our friend is sending units to talk to the other two vehicle owners and promises an update as soon as he learns more, no later than tonight, even if his next update is only that they're still working on it." Dominic brightened, then said, "And you're all clear to go home."

"Let me help you," Orson said.

Miles already was.

They helped her out of the hospital bed together. She felt shaky on her feet, but anything was better than staying in that room a minute longer than she had to.

"I'll keep Jolie for the night," Orson offered. "The kids can have a sleepover."

Miles nodded his thanks. "I'll take you home, Sloane."

"That sounds perfect." That was *exactly* what she needed right now.

But before they were even in the car, Sloane realized the opposite was true.

Chapter Twenty

Sloane

MILES AGITATED Sloane the entire way home.

He wasn't trying to, exactly, but he sure as hell wasn't trying not to.

She and Miles had known one another for a long time. Jolie's life, plus nine months of pregnancy and three years before that. Friends with benefits who had an oops and wanted to co-raise their little dose of reality. All that history meant Miles knew how to push her buttons. Every. Goddamned. One. Of them.

While Miles was a gentleman ninety-percent of the time, he had a sommelier level of dexterity with the full galley of varietals in mood. One of her least favorites, and the one he was in now, was having something to say and not saying it. No matter how many *Are you sure there isn't something you'd like to talk about?*'s she tried, he would rebuff every one until he was finally ready to blow his top.

It was exhausting, and infuriating, and now of all times she deserved something better.

Sloane didn't even bother to ask him what was wrong. Instead, she took mental notes. His white knuckles on the steering wheel. His clenched and twitching jaw. His insistence on a silent cabin, even though anything but the quiet would work to twerk his mood.

There was something Miles wasn't saying, and as much as Sloane wanted to ignore it, she was getting increasingly pissed off.

He pulled into the driveway, killed the engine, then turned to her. "Hold on. I'll help you out."

Perfectly nice, but his jaw was still twitching.

He walked around to open her door. After helping her out, he walked her into the house. She didn't want to need his help, but she felt bruised and beaten and downright exhausted. Leaning on him felt nice. It just would have felt better if he wasn't throttling whatever it was he wanted to talk about and pretending the top wouldn't pop on that bottle eventually. Sooner rather than later given the urgency of their life right now.

He helped her to bathroom, then waited outside while she eliminated.

Then he put her to bed and covered her up.

Sloane's animosity melted away. Miles was a perfect gentleman ninety percent of the time, so why couldn't that be good enough? He was trying to protect her by not saying whatever he had on his mind. He didn't want to fight, not when she needed to heal. Problem was, the argument always happened anyway.

And yet, if Sloane understood that, then couldn't she avoid the battle altogether? She'd already done a great job of ignoring his mood instead of falling for the bait like she usually did.

She could let him be tender. Put away her feelings for now. Ease into being taken care of.

Just like she needed.

His phone rang with the *Oh, mama mia, mama mia* part of "Bohemian Rhapsody." He looked at his watch and said, "She must have read something online."

Then he left her bedroom and stepped into the hallway to accept a call from his mother.

Queen fell silent and Sloane heard Miles say hello to his mother in French.

She tried to listen, but the language was too melodic, and Sloane had only a few hundred words worth of fluency. But Miles was talking to his mom, so even a few clues was enough to tell her most if not all of the story.

She was probably chewing on a baguette or baking a croissant, depending on what time it was — Sloane had a harder time tracking or caring about the time difference ever since coming to California — while reading on her le iPad when she saw a news alert for *American train wreck my son narrowly avoided*, but in her words, of course.

Mére then read the article and wanted to know all the gossip, and thus called her son to lavish him with a concern that he pretended to loathe but in truth loved to the point that he didn't know how to live without it. The longer she listened, the heavier her eyelids became.

Elle n'est pas une trollop.

Elle a été chassée de la route!

Un verre, maman! Vous avez plus que cela avant le deuxième apéritif!

Sloane was about to drift off entirely when her bedroom door swung open too fast and too loud, instantly waking her.

She sat up in bed.

"Sorry. I didn't mean to barge in here like that." His eyes said he meant it. "I didn't realize how fast I was moving or how much a conversation with my mother would agitate me."

"Why would this time be any different?"

"It's not always like that," Miles said.

"Okay."

"She was just checking on me."

"On you or me?" Sloane asked.

"On us."

"What about appetizers?"

"I'm sorry?" He looked back at her, confused.

"You said something about 'deluxe appetizers.'"

He laughed. "I think you mean, 'avant le deuxième apéritif.'"

"What does that mean?"

"*Before the second appetizer.* I was telling my mother that you had less to drink before getting behind the wheel than she does before the second appetizer."

"So you were defending me?"

"I always defend you, chérie."

"It doesn't always sound like it," Sloane said, not knowing if she was picking a fight or not, or if she wanted Miles to go. So much of her wanted him to stay, at least until she could see Jolie again.

"That's not fair."

She shook her head. "This is one of my least favorite conversations in the world. So can we please just *not*, right now?"

"Of course." But then he added, "She doesn't hate you."

"Okay."

A long silence lingered between them.

"I'm fine if you want to go," Sloane said.

"I can stay."

"Really. It's fine."

He opened his mouth, paused for a long moment, then *finally* said what was on his mind. "So, are things serious with you and Beck?"

"You already asked me that."

"Sure. Before your romantic-sounding dinner and the accident that brought him to your bedside."

"Are you seriously jealous that he was at the hospital?"

"Not even a little bit." Miles shook his head. "But I do have some concerns."

"About Orson?"

"About all of this."

"All of *what*, Miles?" Dammit. Now she wanted him to go. "And why do you always do this? We could have talked about whatever this is on our way to the car. Or in the car. Or at any point other than when you had to hop on the phone with Le Mama to defend me! So *yay*, we're finally talking. What is it that has you grinding your teeth?"

"I thought our biggest worries would be press who were sympathetic to Wentz, but now it seems like there's a lot more at risk."

"*And?*" Of course there was more.

"And I'm not sure doing this movie is worth the risk."

"Are you thinking about dropping out?"

"This isn't about my involvement, Sloane. It's about the project itself."

"Well, it exists. That's not changing."

"You wrote a lovely script—"

"Thank you!" She clapped. "Your validation in this moment means everything to me!"

"—that's earned a lot of support already. You don't have to direct the film."

"Of course I have to. Who else would bring this story to life better than me?"

"Maybe any great director who isn't so close to the material."

She glared at him, hating that he might be right. "I have to make this movie."

"Fine. But I want to have an honest conversation about the risks."

"Only after stewing on it for an hour first, though, right? We can't ever just get right to it."

Miles ignored her. "Wentz is winning right now."

"And you think he's going to keep winning? Why did you agree to the project if you were just going to back out when things got tough, which we absolutely knew they would?"

"When did things get tough for you? Was it the accident our first day on set? The strike? The—"

"I don't need a list, Miles. It hasn't stopped looping in my head. But thank you for—"

"If Wentz hurts our daughter, it will be because you invited him into our lives."

Sloane felt slapped.

But Miles still didn't stop. "That man would never have bothered with any of this if you weren't feeding your need for revenge or vindication, or whatever it is you think you'll get from this."

"How about a great movie?"

"I'd love to see it. Maybe someone else should make it."

"Why don't I believe your *maybe*, Miles?"

"Maybe because all of your belief is invested in convincing yourself that the risks here are less that they are, and that your fairy godparents are going to make sure that everything turns out okay."

"You're always on me for thinking the worst, now I'm not supposed to have faith?"

"I'm not always on you for thinking the worst, Sloane. But I can't have you putting your head in the sand when our daughter's life is at stake."

"And you don't think that's being dramatic, at all?"

"No, I don't. I think it's much more dramatic to buckle up for the ride without having the conversation."

"Fine, Miles. What do you want me to say? That I need my revenge and vindication more than I need our daughter to be safe? Well, sorry, I'm not going to say that because it isn't true. Don't you think I wish I could move on? And don't you know me well enough to see how much I already hate myself for not being able to?"

"That doesn't mean that plowing forward—"

"It's my turn." She waited for Miles to acknowledge her.

He bowed his head and she continued.

"Yes, I wish I could move on. But I can't." Sloane shook her head, surprisingly in control considering how much she felt like losing it. "Liam Wentz can't win again. He shut me up the last time and it's been eating me alive every day since."

"I understand that, but—"

"BUT no matter how much I might want justice, I would never jeopardize Jolie. And you need to give me more credit than that."

After a long moment, Miles finally sat on her bed. Then he took her hand. "We both want what's best for Jolie. I just need us to keep the conversation going."

"You have my word, Miles. I don't care about her safety or wellbeing any less than you do."

"I understand that." He bowed his head.

"Are you really leaving the project?"

"Of course I don't want to go. And if you're not leaving, then of course I couldn't do that to you. I will absolutely stay and shoot the hell out of your movie. But I want you to promise that we can both drop the film at the first *hint* of direct danger to Jolie. Promise—"

"You have my word. Of course." Sloane was glad that she and Miles made up, but she also now knew that she for sure needed him to leave. "Thank you for helping me tonight. I really appreciate it."

He took her cue, kissing her on the cheek before standing from the bed. "See you on set in the morgen?"

"See you in the morgen," she repeated.

Sloane waited to hear the front door close, then she finally shut her eyes.

She started to play back the best parts of her day, especially all of those delicious moments with Orson. It was too bad, all the stuff that happened after that.

Her head was in the clouds.

Sleep felt like a deep kiss away.

And that brought her thoughts back to Orson.

Sloane wished he was there with her now, even though he would probably agree with Miles, thinking she was reckless, not just with her and Jolie, but with all of them.

Tomorrow she could start to prove everyone wrong.

Chapter Twenty-One

Sloane

SLOANE DIDN'T WANT to get carried away with herself, but so far, the day had been amazing.

She couldn't pack the paranoia away entirely, suspicion kept wanting to pop up out of nowhere to tap her on the shoulder and remind her that Liam Wentz had eyes and ears everywhere. But for most of that time the roiling emotion stayed under control while she stayed in flow.

The cast and crew seemed to be working as a single unit for the first time. Sloane imagined the Shellys gathered everyone around and gave them a good talking to. She didn't care what they did. The results were wonderful. Lila was back and stronger than ever.

Cassidy nailed every take, without showing a hint of her accent.

Orson was amazing, too, which was excellent for both their schedule and the overall production, though Sloane hated the creeping realization that he would be done with his scenes soon, then off to something else. A remake of Metropolis, also for the Shellys and Juke.

Gina, playing Jennifer, was terrific in her first scene, as was Bennett Cole, playing a cinematic version of the man who first destroyed then haunted her life.

Security was tight, the cast was on high alert, and the Shellys were only a phone call away.

Best of all, Jolie was with Jake, still on set with her and Miles, to both parents' relief.

It was lunchtime. The catering was now coming from Arrivé. Sloane made plates for her and Jolie, since Connor was with his mom and she would probably love a break from hanging out with the Kindergarten Cop.

Last night's argument-turned-necessary-conversation with Miles had been a good thing. They were in total agreement about everything, as confirmed by a quick chat before getting going for the day, plus a couple of check-ins along the way.

At first, neither of them wanted Jolie anywhere near the set and were willing to fight hard to get their way on that one. But after each of them thought about it on their own, they arrived to work with matching conclusions — being on set with them was probably the safest place for Jolie right now, relatively. Only pure paranoia would make them believe that Wentz would blow up an entire movie studio just to silence her film. Considering Jolie had all that security — a personal bodyguard, and two parents who were only a page away — having her anywhere else would be silly.

She knocked on the trailer door then opened it without waiting for an answer.

"MOMMY!" Jolie ran to Sloane, overjoyed to see her.

"I thought we could eat lunch together," she said.

"Good to see you, Ms. Alexander."

"You too, Jake." Sloane gave him a nod then showed Jolie the plates, piled with choices for them to share, glad that her daughter was already a foodie, at least when far from places like Pirate Pizza. Fetta-ricotta spinach rolls, a big piece of chicken Florentine, a serving of sole Françoise with lemon butter sauce, broccoli with garlic and oil, penne alla vodka, red potatoes, grilled zucchini, fried zucchini, and shishito peppers.

"Where's the dessert?" Jolie asked, so predictable.

"I'll go back for dessert. This was all I could carry." Sloane turned to Jake. "Why don't you go and grab yourself something to eat."

"You sure? I don't mind—"

"Of course. Please. We're fine."

Jake nodded, then left Sloane and Jolie alone.

She walked to the rear of the trailer then sat on the ground, setting both plates in front of her.

Jolie sat on the other side of their plates, then looked up at her mother while grabbing a napkin and one of the forks. "What do we eat first?"

"Whatever you want!"

Jolie looked down at her choices. "Connor's not here today."

"Connor is with his mom."

"I know. That's what I said!"

"So, what did you do today?"

"I've been working on the Ratatouille puzzle, and Jake played hide and seek with me. I read four chapters of the second Harry Potter and three chapters of the third one."

"You're reading both books at once?"

Jolie nodded, shoving a piece of fried zucchini into her mouth. "I stopped reading the second one because I remembered that I liked the third one better."

"The third one is better ..." Something caught her

attention out the window. She didn't know what, only that it bothered her enough to send her side of the conversation with Jolie into autopilot as she stood and went to look outside. "What do you like better about the third book?"

"Sirius Black!" Jolie exclaimed.

Nothing out the window, at least not beyond the cast and crew milling about, exactly like she would expect them to. But still Sloane kept looking.

"What about Sirius Black?"

"Harry hears about him just before going to Hogwarts. He escaped Azkaban. That's where all the most dangerous wizard criminals are kept. Ron's dad warns Harry that Sirius is looking for him, and that makes Harry really, really scared. But Sirius isn't actually bad, and he was friends with Harry's dad when they were little. Like Harry's age. It also has other new characters like Professor Lupin, even though there are always new professors these ones are better, plus the third book has time travel."

Jolie delivered her Harry Potter soliloquy with barely a breath.

Sloane agreed with every word and one day hoped to have a conversation with her daughter about why the third film was the best among them as well. Right now, Jolie didn't enjoy the Azkaban movie nearly as much as the first two, which broke her mother's storytelling heart, same as it shattered her cinematographer father's.

Sloane sat back down and surveyed what was left of their food. She'd only had a bite of the penne and a forkful of the shishitos before walking to the window, so the dent was especially impressive considering Jolie had been talking almost the entire time.

"You know Becky?" Jolie asked.

"Of course I know Becky."

"I heard her talking to Thomas Meeno that you got in an accident."

Tomosino. Also, to hell with Becky mouthing off in front of Jolie like that.

Except that she probably wasn't mouthing off at all, and any confusion her daughter had about what happened was on Sloane for not telling her.

"I did get in an accident last night." She couldn't help herself from stealing another glance out the window.

"Is that why your face has boo-boos?"

"Yes," she admitted. "I told you that we'd talk about it later when you asked about it this morning because the accident made me sad and I didn't want to think about it."

More than that, Sloane didn't know how to have an honest conversation about what happened. She didn't want her daughter to believe the headlines if she overheard or saw anything, nor did she want to tell Jolie that she'd been run off the road by someone who might have been trying to kill her.

"Are you okay to think about it now?"

NO. "Of course, honey."

"What happened? Were you driving?"

"I was. After having dinner with Orson."

"Connor's Daddy is sooooo nice. Did you know he was in *The Realm Has Fallen?*"

"I did."

"Can I see *The Realm Has Fallen?*"

"You cannot."

"Connor's seen it. Twice."

Sloane didn't believe that he'd seen more than ten minutes of that movie even once, but she wasn't going to argue about it. "I'm glad. You can see *The Realm Has Fallen* when you're old enough."

"How old do I have to be?"

"I don't know, Jolie. Fifteen."

"Promise I can see it when I'm fifteen?"

"Sure."

"So how did you crash the car, Mommy?" She grabbed one of the ricotta spinach rolls.

Sloane glanced out the window again. But this time she saw something. "It was dark, and I lost control of the wheel. I didn't see where I was going, so I crashed into a tree."

Orson and Miles were standing just outside the trailer in the midst of what appeared to be an awkward exchange.

"Were you drinking and driving?"

"I was not," Sloane said, before amending her statement. "I had a little wine with dinner, but even less than I'm allowed to have."

"That's good, Mommy. Because drinking and driving can kill you."

"Yes, it can."

"Same for texting."

"You're absolutely right." Sloane's side of the conversation was still on auto-pilot.

"What do you see, Mommy?"

"Nothing, honey." She didn't know, but it was definitely something.

Sloane returned to her spot on the floor.

The door opened and Jake reentered the room with two plates, same as Sloane had been carrying, but these were clearly both for him.

"I'll be right back," Sloane told him. "I'm going to get us some dessert."

Jake gave her a nod, but was already chewing on something and must not have wanted to speak with his mouth full of food.

Orson was already gone by the time Sloane was

outside. She looked around but didn't see him anywhere, so she approached Miles instead. "What was that about?"

"What was *what* about?" Miles asked.

But her baby daddy was smiling, so of course he knew.

"What were you two talking about?"

"Me and Lila? We were talking about your very picky notes for—"

"What were you and Orson just talking about. Two minutes ago. Right outside—"

"Oh, that!" He laughed. "We were talking about which is better between New York and Chicago Pizza."

"Seriously, Miles …"

"I am serious. Despite the claims of your new boyfriend, New York pizza is insubstantial."

"*Please,* Miles."

"Okay." He laughed then looked at her seriously. "Like I've already said, Orson seems like a great guy, and he keeps on finding new ways to prove it."

"How so? Specifically this time. Nothing about which kind of pizza is better, and I don't want to hear about any imaginary battles about the superior hot sauce or any other such nonsense. I want the vérité, Miles. What did he say?"

"He was trying to get a sense of our relationship … Orson wants to make sure he's not stepping on any toes. He's serious about you, chérie … I think you should make your position clear to him. Assuming you're looking for a boyfriend."

"You make it sound like high school."

"Isn't it, just a little?"

"No," Sloane said, though maybe it was.

She felt embarrassed but happy. Ready for more work, wanting to continue crushing her day. "I'm going to grab some dessert for me and Jolie. You want anything?"

He shook his head. "I'm good. We need to—"

Lila ran toward them, breath heavy, her face flushed with what appeared to be panic.

"What is it?" Sloane asked, trying to sound stronger than she suddenly felt, glad that she had just seen Jolie and knew she was safe in the trailer behind her.

"Maybe you should look at the Rummage Report," Lila said.

"Or maybe you should just tell me," Sloane snapped.

"Wentz has a movie under production …"

"He always has a movie under production. *Many movies*," Sloane said. "What's the real story?"

"The movie is called *All Smoke, No Fire*. It's described as 'an intense drama about a man who is falsely accused of sexual assault.'"

"A bit on the nose, isn't it?" Miles said. "The title, I mean."

"It's well under way, and will almost for sure come out before ours."

"How is that possible?" Sloane exclaimed.

"Because he's scrambling. Throwing spaghetti against the wall." Miles shrugged. "Maybe this is a good thing."

Lila shook her head. "Not with this cast."

"Who's in it?" Sloane shook off a serious chill.

"Some big names."

"I gathered. You mind being specific?"

Lila swallowed and told her. "Gabriel Douglas."

"Goddammit, you've gotta be kidding me." She pinched her temples, trying to think.

Gabriel Douglas had a few stinkers in his catalog, but he hadn't made anything less than phenomenal in years. He had been nominated for an Academy Award three times out of his last five times in front of the camera, and stepped off stage with the Oscar twice.

Like Sloane needed any further proof that she was

going to end up with a legendary disaster. The movie that was supposed to serve as a launching pad for the rest of her life would be a punchline instead. This was her *Cutthroat Island*, her *Hudson Hawk*, her *Adventures of Pluto Nash*.

Her phone buzzed with a text.

She took out her phone and looked the screen.

From Melinda: *You've probably seen the news already. If not, you will soon. Please know that you have nothing to worry about. Just make your movie. Dominic and I will handle the rest.*

Like it was that easy.

Like she could just *not worry.*

Like every part of this production wasn't falling out from under her.

But then Melinda sent another text that helped Sloane to stand a little straighter.

We have a plan, and we're striking tonight.

"Five minutes," Sloane said, looking at Miles before turning to Lila. "I'm taking Jolie her dessert, then it's back to work for all of us."

She couldn't ask Melinda any questions about tonight, especially not over text —plausible deniability and all that.

But Sloane imagined that Dominic was in charge of whatever they were up to, and could only imagine what he was doing right now.

Chapter Twenty-Two

Dominic

DOMINIC LOOKED at the assembled crowd, gathered to celebrate yet another star on the Hollywood Walk of Fame, this one for the Shellys' mortal enemy.

"So just to be clear," Dominic scoffed, "Wentz is putting himself on the same plinth of glory as the great David Spade?"

"What do you have against David Spade?" Melinda asked.

"Nothing. He's fine if you enjoy garbage movies like Joe Dirt. But why him and not Horatio Sanz, or what's his name from Goodburger, the guy who can't stop laughing at his own jokes?"

"Keenan Thompson."

"Right. Keenan Thompson. Fuck that guy."

"There are better targets," Melinda said. "Did you know the Rugrats have a star?"

"You can't be serious. That's not even a person. It's a cartoon."

"Mickey Mouse, Bugs Bunny, Woody Woodpecker … there are plenty of—"

"Those are all individuals. Rugrats is a show."

"Fine. How about the Simpsons?"

"How do you know so much about who has stars on the Walk of Fame?"

"The same reason you should."

It wasn't much of an answer, but same as always, Dominic knew exactly what Melinda meant. "I'm a lot more interested in who *doesn't* have a star. Clooney. Roberts. Eastwood. You know what all three of them have in common?"

"They all knew they were too good for it."

"Exactly," Dominic said with a satisfied grunt. "The 50K it costs is a drip of piss for any of them, but they sure as hell aren't paying into the scam. George Lucas and Jim Carrey." Two more as he thought of them, followed immediately by another pair. "Brad Pitt and Angelina Jolie."

"How do *you* know so much about celebrities who *don't* have stars?"

"Like I said, much more interesting. They all understand that respect is more important than money, and that respect can never be bought."

Melinda shook her head, knowing what was next. "You're going to start talking about Samuel Jackson again."

"Damn right I'm going to start talking about Frozone again. The man goes from playing Jules to doing Citibank commercials? He should be ashamed of himself."

"You're awfully judgmental for a man who talks about money when he climaxes."

"That's for you more than me," Dominic said.

"He's here." Melinda nodded to Wentz, now visible at the lip of a quickly growing crowd. "Do you want to keep telling me about how your ways of making ridiculous sums of money are superior to Samuel Jackson's, or do you think we should maybe take care of business?"

Dominic wanted to take her hand and start brushing her skin with his thumb as they walked over to face Wentz in front of his growing horde of well-wishers and outright admirers. But they would appear more powerful as two separate people. Though, that was only an illusion, the Shellys' true strength was in their union.

The sidewalk was littered with people and media. Dominic and Melinda had investigated every open opportunity to hit Wentz in their immediate horizon, and the Walk of Fame was their best chance to make a hard strike, by far.

"It's the Shellys!" One of the photographers yelled, prompting Wentz to instinctively look their way, then twist his face into a mockery of benevolence.

"Dominic! Melinda!" Wentz waved them over as if he had invited the couple to the ceremony himself. "It's great to see you two. I can't believe you came to see my star."

"I wouldn't come to your funeral, but I figured this was more embarrassing." Dominic laughed and waved to the crowd, showing them that this was all in good fun — just two Hollywood moguls mugging and teasing each other in front of the cameras.

Wentz glanced at the assembly of handlers around him, waited for them to scatter, then spoke in a voice low enough that only the Shellys could hear. "I'm surprised you could make the time. Don't you have a pet project to look after? I heard you were having some serious problems."

"Our announced projects are all running on or ahead of schedule," Melinda said.

"Is there a particular film or show you're talking about?" Dominic asked. "We're not sure what you mean."

"The one with the publicity stunt of a director who's always getting herself into trouble, and might eventually take things too far and find herself in a situation the media and public at large won't even think to question."

"And that's when they find all the little girls in your closet," Melinda spit.

"Isn't this entertaining?" Wentz bellowed, raising his arms to the crowd. Then back to the Shellys with more of a murmur. "It's entertaining for now. But I'm sure you know my history in this industry. I've no problem pulling the plug on a project once it stops being profitable, or starts becoming a pain in my ass. Right now, your little pet project feeds my little pet project. I just hope it doesn't bite me."

Dominic stepped closer, until his exhales were kissing the bastard's clammy skin. "You've had a few misses lately. *A Day to Die For* is what … sixteen percent on Rotten Tomatoes?"

"So kind of you to read up on my reviews before your little chance encounter with me. *A Day to Die For* is a piece of shit, but that piece of shit still netted out in all the ways I needed it to."

Wentz gave them a serpentine smile and Dominic wondered what demonic thing he had done behind the scenes of that particular film.

Dominic continued, "There's also *The Alone Syndrome* and your laughably bad Oscar bait from last year, *Appreciation*. Point is, you prehistoric pile of shit, your judgment isn't what it used to be, and you're one wrong move from spending the rest of your life playing Chinese finger cuffs in prison."

"Ha." Wentz affected a laugh. "And I thought we were making veiled threats."

Melinda laughed for the crowd to fuel their little facade.

His phone double buzzed to signal an urgent call, but Dominic ignored it. "You're the one with the secrets and everything to lose. Back off."

"Or what?" More laughing and smiling for the assembly. "What are you going to do? Sure, the two of you have done a couple of impressive things. But you're slow to learn when it comes to the big stuff. Like the fact that you will *never* be able to touch me. You missed that lesson the last time, which brings us to now. You have nothing, and you can do nothing. The best you have is a piece of fiction that if you're lucky will end up as a footnote in cinematic history — a former child star and attention whore's failed attempt to stomp her foot and demand one final grasp at the spotlight."

"Or it's the film that finally brings you down," Dominic said, still inches away from his face.

Melinda waved to the crowd one last time, then turned to Wentz and whispered. "We're going to enjoy destroying you."

Then they turned around and walked side by side to their limo.

Dominic took out his phone to see what that double buzz had been all about as he sat. Roberto pulled away from the curb as he looked down at the screen, scrolling to absorb the news.

He looked up from his phone to find Melinda looking at him expectantly.

"Good or bad?"

"A bit of both," Dominic told her. "Juke's dirty code

has all been found and eradicated. And — you're going to love this — Parvati says she's glad this happened. The attack apparently illuminated a few issues that would have been big problems eventually. Best of all, again according to Parvati, is that she also found the back door where the hacker got in. She sealed it, along with several other vulnerabilities. So, in some respects, Juke is looking better than ever."

"I imagine the bad has something to do with budget."

"Both of them — time and money have taken a hit. We told Parvati to spare no expense in solving this problem, and she didn't. Even used Bishop to—"

"Christ." Melinda shook her head.

"It had to be done." Bishop — B15H0P — was the best hacker either of them knew. Maybe the best hacker *anyone* knew. Dominic didn't know how much this particular problem had run them, but it was a fortune and a half for sure. The initial engagement with Bishop cost 100K, plus the cost of any work. They had used the hacker three times so far, and each of those times it would have been much cheaper to have the problem permanently eliminated, including the price of bulletproof alibis. They took the much more expensive route in the past, not because they were concerned about the law, or about the consequences of getting caught — they wouldn't be — but because the Shellys were only ruthless in the ways that felt right to them.

"So we've paid through the nose to keep Juke on track while running consistent overages on virtually every part of the Sunset Project. Any idea what our total damages are?"

Dominic shrugged. "Again, we don't know the total number on Juke yet, though I'm sure it's bad. We can *probably* still hit our launch date, but the taxes on doing so are monumental. We might need to move a few other projects around to make that happen, in addition to the outright expense. We'll need to investigate the ripple effect of all that. Run a couple of models."

"And Juke's the smaller problem. This *All Smoke, No Fire* bullshit could fuck us."

"We won't let it," Dominic said.

"That's not enough." Melinda shook her head, much more agitated than Dominic ever wanted to see her. "His movie will come out first, discredit ours, and we'll lose millions."

"No." He shook his head. "*Fire* will come out and garner a lot of conversation, which will only fuel interest in our film. This is his first big mistake. Wentz is seeing this as *Armageddon* vs. *Deep Impact*, *Ants* vs. *A Bugs Life*, or *Capote* vs. *Infamous*. But this isn't the twin film phenomenon, this is two sides of the same story. We'll turn our entire marketing engine on using his movie to promote ours."

"I like that." Melinda nodded, giving him that look that said, *This is why I married you.*

"But that strategy is contingent on us having the movie and the platform to leverage, so the question remains, *What do we do now?* We'll need to spend substantially more on both projects to keep them safe and make their deadlines. An upfront cost, but at least we'll release on time."

"If we miss our target, we'll lose a lot more later."

"So, we're agreed? We'll do whatever it takes."

Melinda scooted closer to him. All that room in the limo, and they were pressed together like always. "That's barely a choice. It's our turn. His time is over, whatever that costs."

She leaned her head against Dominic's chest as he stroked her hair, settling into the moment, enjoying the inevitable downfall of their first collective enemy. When the Shellys stood up to Wentz for the first time on Sloane's behalf, the predator did everything in his ample power to ruin them. But that hadn't been enough and it never would be. Despite the uber producer's many connections he had managed to mangle or burn, the Shellys made it bigger than anyone ever expected.

Ten long, hard years of climbing one permanent rung at a time — no matter how long ascension from one to the next might take, they never allowed themselves to lose a rung once gained — chased by a decade of remarkable, unprecedented, and now exponential growth.

Melinda was absolutely right. His time was over. Now it was their turn.

Another double buzz in his pocket.

Melinda pulled away as Dominic went to answer it.

He looked at the screen and said, "Danny."

"Be nice."

"What do you have for us?" Dominic asked as he answered.

"Plenty. There's an envelope in your mailbox with more than you need, but I figured you'd like some of the pancakes and syrup over the phone."

"Can you please pick one of your personas that talks like a real person?"

"The rumors aren't rumors. Sprog is a fact."

"Proof?" Dominic said.

"I'm working on it. So far, no one's willing to go on record, and we don't have any hard evidence, but I'm confident we'll get it, given time. But that's not the big thing."

"Well, shit." He glanced at Amanda. "What's the big thing?"

"He's putting together a kid's show."

"*A kid's show?*"

"A kid's show?" Melinda repeated.

"Yeah," Danny said. "Something called Replay for one of the streamers. He's shooting ten episodes for the first season. They're taking classic movies and casting kids in all the roles for forty to sixty minute child-friendly remakes."

"Probably remakes to content he already owns," Dominic muttered, mostly to himself, but also for Melinda's benefit.

"Sprog is a long-term project. It'll take a while before I can find anyone willing to testify, but I've got a few eyes and ears inside his staff already. There's a lot in the envelope on Replay and a few other projects at your place. I'll keep you updated on anything else I find out."

"Thank you, Danny." Dominic was surprised to realize how much he genuinely meant it.

Melinda held out her hand.

Dominic dropped his phone into it.

"It's possible we'll need to stop our client in a more permanent way. Are you prepared to do that?" Melinda asked.

"Is that something I should do now?"

"No," Melinda said. "Let's call that Plan C."

"Plan C," Danny said.

Then he was gone.

Melinda handed the phone back to Dominic.

"You're sure about this?" he asked, knowing she was but feeling the need to send a silent reminder that this was the one line they could never uncross.

She turned to him, her eyes sad but insistent. "I'm sure he threatened Sloane tonight. His life is worth nothing to me, hers is worth everything." She took his hand. "There's nothing we won't do to protect her."

"Agreed."

. . .

Sloane

DAISY LOOKED up at Oliver as if she didn't believe him, her eyebrows dramatically raised. "How do I know you're telling me the truth?"

"I don't even know how to lie." Oliver beamed down at her, radiating warmth and honesty.

"You lie about some things." Daisy crossed her arms in defiance, petulant instead of precocious.

"What do you think I would lie about?" His face filled with wonder and concern for her answer.

Daisy thought — really pondered it over a what felt like an overly chin-strokey moment — then said, "I bet you've lied about Santa Claus. All the grownups do."

Oliver kneeled down and met her eyes. In the gentle voice of a man who could never break the truth, no matter how hard he tried, he said, "You are absolutely right, Daisy. I have lied. To protect a child from the sadness of never knowing Santa, I have stretched the truth. But I would also argue that Santa Claus lives inside us all." He smiled and tickled her on the arm. "Am I right?"

Daisy laughed way too hard.

"I love how much older you are than your years," Oliver told her, still kneeling, still looking into her eyes, still radiating warmth and honesty, and the best kind of genuine affection. "A question like that about Santa ..." He shook his head in admiration and awe. "*So smart.*" He pet her on the back of her head as he stood.

"So what did you want to show me?" Daisy asked with only a shadow of interest.

"CUT!" Sloane called.

"What now?" Cassidy replied, sounding more like a

brat than the unknown yet seasoned young actress she had hired.

"It's just … let's take ten," she finished, instead of hurling a flurry of unprofessional insults Cassidy's way. Three days of this constant nonsense had Sloane's confidence in herself and the project at an all-time low.

She expected at least a few of the cast and crew to come over and ask her if everything was okay after pouting so noticeably, not that she wanted them to. But even Lila was giving her a surprisingly wide berth.

Fine. She needed the space. That last scene had given her a lot to process. More than chewing through Cassidy's stilted performance, it was the flashbacks and triggers returning her to the memory of Liam Wentz luring a little twelve-year-old version of Sloane Alexander into his trailer to grope her.

It filled her with fury to see how obvious the path to her personal danger had been in retrospect. That reality shined a light on how many grownups had failed her. And none more than her very own mother.

The way Liam Wentz had made Sloane a target from the very beginning, measuring her vulnerability, like a tailor fitting her for a dress. Choosing a child with a needy mother willing to maybe look the other way on a thing or two if it led to a big enough break — a child who thrived on compliments and could eventually be left alone with him, so that he could do as he wished.

The way Liam Wentz had slowly gained her trust. Constantly watching her. Learning more about her. Understanding her emotional needs well enough to naturally meet them. A warm and gooey intrusiveness that remained mostly invisible, sometimes even to those who were looking.

The way his well calibrated attention once made

Sloane feel so very important. Not just like a big girl, but like the biggest and most important girl in the world. For a few fleeting moments, he made her feel essential to the future. Back when his extra attention still felt like a gift instead of the tax that would break her.

The way Liam Wentz kept trying to get her alone. And what happened once he finally did.

Today's scene dragged her back into that moment. Because the nightmare of her worst day not only lived, but still thrived, inside her. Despite the years, despite the therapy. And because Bennet's performance was dead on.

But Cassidy had done nothing to sell it.

Her inexperience was starting to show. Sloane had insisted on a no-name actress, strongly feeling that someone without any track record in Hollywood whatsoever would sell the story best.

But now she was starting to regret her decision, wondering if she had made a colossal mistake. Cassidy might not have the chops to pull it off. Her work on stage and smaller productions might not be anywhere near enough. Sloane couldn't rid herself of the feeling that despite all of her available resources, some of the scenes she had already shot would eventually play like marginal, or even worse, *forgettable* TV.

Sloane deserved more, and so did the Shellys. She just needed to figure out the source of the problem so she could then make the best possible decision.

Because this was about more than the performance. Cassidy's moods were becoming erratic. Her acting could be tweaked, the Shellys would hire world class coaches if that's what was needed. But this ran deeper than that. Sloane wasn't sure about anything, and didn't know where to dig.

The Shellys kept checking in, wanting to know if Cassidy was delivering what their director needed her to. Sloane kept delaying a definitive answer. Now they were pressing her, needing to know.

Before it's too late. Melinda, still in her head.

Sloane had narrowed the reasons for Cassidy's crap-acting into a short list of three distinct possibilities, in order of how damaging each would be to the production.

Maybe this all started when Sloane corrected her accent. She had worked with a coach for three months before shooting and likely had a difficult time accepting that her hard work wasn't enough. Feedback had been a grind to deliver, because Cassidy was taking everything personally. If that was the case, she needed to understand that they were all in this together. Sloane could tell her about the time she had to do the bridge scene in *Remaking Christmas* a staggering forty-seven times, spread over two days and a gallon of tears.

Maybe this was all because Cassidy was a temperamental pre-teen and being a brat was par for the course. That could go two ways. If it was the obvious start of a downward spiral, then Sloane would have no choice but to sever the head before it gobbled through her production. The Shellys would hate to scrap what they had and start over with another actress, but they were heavily invested in the film's success, and the buzz of a big up and comer attached to the project would surely light them up.

But maybe Liam Wentz had gotten to Cassidy, and this was another arrow from the quiver of her nightmares thunking into the heart of her dream.

In any event, it had been three days. Sloane kept falling further and further behind schedule. She wasn't willing to move on without nailing this scene. Maybe she had learned that from her two days of torture on *Christmas*. She had been so upset during the shoot, but that scene was the one strangers had commented on most. People she had never met and would never see again, stopping her on the street to gush about how much they cried or laughed or thought hard about that scene.

Those three and a half minutes on the bridge said everything *Remaking Christmas* needed to say. The sequence of scenes in *Sunset*, from Daisy and Oliver just outside his trailer, to the one where she's sobbing in her mother's arms, *were the movie*.

It needed to be perfect, or it was sundown on *Sunset's* potential.

Her ten minutes must have expired, because the cast and crew were crowding back around her, with Cassidy wearing a scowl.

She marched up to her director and cranked her accent up to eleven. "Are you going to let me do my job or keep opening your mush to stop me every ten seconds?"

"If you can go ten seconds without making me feel like we're filming a Hallmark movie, then yes, Cassidy, I'd be happy to keep my 'mush' shut."

Sloane caught sight of Cassidy's parents standing near the exit and put two and two together. Clearly they were egging her on. Not that it proved anything. The girl was their meal ticket — the Cavallis complicity could neatly fit into any of Sloane's three proposed scenarios.

Cassidy's accent somehow grew even thicker. "Not my fault you spent all week cheesed off."

"I'm not upset, Cassidy. But there are certain things I need you to be doing, and it's your job to take my direction. *Literally*. That's what we're paying you for."

"I'm getting dosh to act. Not get yelled at."

"I haven't been yelling at you," Sloane said, picturing

herself slapping Cassidy then feeling immediately guilty for the image. "I've been *directing you*. That's literally *my* job."

"Ronnie Borman made *Full of Beans* without yelling at me once." Cassidy crossed her arms like a petulant little brat, failing to mention that *Full of Beans* was a tone-deaf message movie that was universally panned and came off like unintentional parody.

"This isn't Ronnie Borman's set, and I'm not apologizing for doing my job when you should be apologizing for not doing yours. I suggest—"

"That'll be enough." Cassidy's dad was suddenly three feet away, with Mom just one step behind him, clutching her purse. "Come on, Cass, we're going home."

"We're not finished." Sloane couldn't have heard them right. "You can't leave."

"Like hell we can't." Dad was already turning around, Mom now in the lead, Cassidy brushing past Sloane to trail her parents.

Dammit. She should not have to do this.

Sloane looked around, but everyone looked lost, including Miles and Lila.

After a heavy exhale, she gave chase and caught up to the Cavallis outside as they were approaching their car.

"Wait! Please."

Dad turned first. Then the other two, Mom impatient and Cassidy smirking.

"What do you want?" Dad asked.

To replace your brat of a daughter with someone who can act. "To work this out."

"Seems like you're not happy with Cass's performance. That makes the three of us" — he nodded to his wife and daughter on either side of him — "question whether this project is right for her brand."

"And how is that?" Sloane asked, wishing she didn't feel the need to.

Dad said, "There's plenty of rumors that this film's a sinking ship."

Your daughter is both the hole and the anchor. "Not at all. We just need to work on a few things."

"Good luck with that." Dad nodded and turned around.

"You don't want to break your contract, Mr. Cavalli."

In a blink, Dad was back to facing her.

He took a step forward. "That a threat, Ms. Alexander?"

"Not at all." She shook her head but kept her eyes boring into his. "But this town works on reputation. Cassidy doesn't want to be known as the kind of performer who doesn't perform."

"Maybe we already have other places to go, in the event of things not working out here."

"I'm sure you do, Mr. Cavalli. But some of those places might be dangerous. And being involved with this project in particular should—"

"And maybe there are two sides to that story too, eh?" Cassidy widened her smirk.

Sloane imagined slapping her again, but this time the pictures arrived in her mind without any guilt.

"Look." Sloane took a bold step forward, closing the narrow gap between them. "We're already invested with each other. Why don't the three of you enjoy a long weekend. I'll use that time to figure out exactly what's wrong, and exactly how to fix this scene and everything else. No more guesswork. If we're not all happy after that, then we'll—"

"Fine, Ms. Alexander. See you on Monday."

Then they all turned and finished their short jaunt to the family sedan.

Sloane turned around and started walking back to the set, trying not to shake her head in defeat or face the truth that she had probably just given the three of them — and Liam Wentz — exactly what they, meaning he, wanted.

Everyone was standing around, looking expectant. She mustered her strength to announce the three-day break for Cassidy, a shuffling of their shooting schedule, and the day's remainder, needed to determine how they could best leverage the final day of what was turning out to be a wasted week.

Sloane had five minutes of alone time on her little couch before she heard a knock on her trailer door. Unless it was God wanting to prove His existence or grant her some wishes, she wasn't interested in company from anyone. She was ashamed of her behavior and her performance. She needed to be left alone.

Curiosity did get her glancing at the window, but even Orson Beck didn't stand a chance right now.

Still, he knocked again, less insistent, almost in surrender, then one last time before Orson made an about-face on her steps and walked away.

Great. She was ruining everything good because she couldn't deal with her shit.

Miles was right. So was everyone who doubted her.

What was she doing? Why did she have to dredge all of this up?

Perhaps proximity to her pain was the problem. Her first three movies were all straightforward to make, rewarding on set, and critical darlings once finished.

Maybe she was too close to this story. Maybe Miles had a point, and another director should finish what she started. Maybe her sticking with the project would only let everyone down.

Sloane closed her eyes and sank down into the couch, thinking. She would spend the rest of today getting tomorrow on track. One more day to prove herself.

She kept thinking the same thing on repeat. *Tomorrow is going to be a great day.*

But Sloane's roiling gut kept insisting it wouldn't be.

Chapter Twenty-Three

Sloane

IT WAS GOING to be an amazing day.

Sloane inhaled the crisp morning air and wondered why she didn't get up early more often as she walked back inside.

She closed the door behind her, still enjoying the silence, same as she had all morning.

Yesterday had sent her home in defeat, but this morning Sloane woke up in triumph, ready to conquer a day without Cassidy. Though she didn't really want to see Orson or anyone else last night, she did allow him to help her, responding *yes* to his friendly text request asking if he could please take Jolie for the night and bring her to set in the morning, since Connor had been dying to play with her.

Sloane knew a pity invite when she saw one, but was still willing to take advantage of his offer.

The morning quiet had centered her. She knew exactly what to shoot, how to use every member of the available cast and crew, and precisely how to best leverage their entire day.

She couldn't wait to see the look on Lila's face. Not that it was Sloane's job to impress her AD, but she felt proud of her work and hoped Lila was, too.

Maybe Cassidy really was the problem. Because for the first time, Sloane felt the creative flow behind the camera she had been expecting to feel on her fourth film, especially since the material was coming from a place of personal significance and fiery passion.

Every project had taught her plenty, but the lessons with *Sunset* so far were numerous and ultimately elusive. Sloane needed to see the work through to understand how it had changed her.

Her first film, *A Quiet Compass* taught Sloane what she would ultimately need to get her fourth film financed by the Shellys. Rookie directors were deadly attachments and risky by definition. Financiers were sometimes willing to roll the dice, but only after a list of substantial concessions. Absolutely fair, it was their money after all, but Sloane's goal was to find herself from one film to the next in pursuit of steady personal and professional growth. So *A Quiet Compass* was shot on the cheap, or cheap enough, with a quarter-million dollar budget Sloane could afford from her own dwindling funds. The Shellys taught her that it was always smarter to use other people's money, but in this instance the risk had been her reward, netting Sloane Alexander a decent amount of buzz for her directorial debut, and just over four-million dollars by the time her first film finished its initial run.

Her next feature, *Blossom,* taught her that the wrong background actors could upset the balance of an otherwise wonderfully calibrated film. She could have her shot list memorized and clearly see the emotional arcs required to anchor each and every scene, yet the wrong extra could ruin everything. *Blossom* was her "coming of age" film, or at least the first of them, and the twenty-one-year-old she cast to play the seventeen-year-old lead was perfect. So was the actor who played her best friend, the entire family cast, and every teacher at school. But three kids shaking their fists and over-emoting in the background of an elaborately staged playground scene had Sloane reshooting the whole thing. For her next film, Sloane gave every character on screen a name and backstory. *Kid #1* was no longer enough.

Her best lesson on *Capsized* — a tidy little two-person disaster flick, still self-financed, but now with the six-million dollars in profit she'd accumulated from her first two features, and built to prove that Sloane Alexander had an eye for cinema, regardless of genre — was an understanding that she liked to shoot long and that too much footage was something that should be expected. Cutting each of her first two films to under two hours had been hard. With *Capsized,* coming anywhere close was impossible. The story was small, but there were still so many notes it needed to hit. Sloane ended up with three hours and twenty-minutes that got painstakingly whittled down, until it was only two hours and twenty-one minutes. Critics enjoyed the visuals, but found the runtime a slog. The clear lesson was for Sloane to wrangle more control over her movie's length, but the more important bit of wisdom suggested the opposite, that maybe she should have let her story sprawl and saved it for TV.

All three films taught Sloane that she *needed* to work. That she lived to express herself through story. That for the rest of her life, when one project ended, a new one would need to be born. She almost wanted to get a tattoo after the wrap party to commemorate the film, but the reality of doing so might turn Sloane into the Painted Woman by the end of her career.

All three films also taught her the lesson she most needed to learn. She didn't need Liam Wentz — or *him* back then — to be successful.

That little bit of the monster's brainwashing had lasted the longest. There were days when Sloane could forget it, but she spent too much of her childhood with the predator stuck in her head, repeating his refrain that she would never be anything without him. That he could close every door, same as he could open them.

A choice that was never a choice.

Each of those first three films had prepared her for the fourth. Until she wrote *West Hollywood Sunset*, Sloane didn't know which part of her story to tell, or even how to eventually tell it. Only that she had to. There was the truth, and the truth as it should be delivered. Finding the beating heart between them took her years to figure out.

There were the things she knew and the things she didn't. The things she needed to say and the things she never would. The things she deeply felt but had so far failed to articulate.

This film was supposed to change her life.

Today it would finally live up to that promise. In another—

The door exploded open, and Sloane embarrassed herself with a yelp.

She looked over toward the sound and saw her worst nightmare confirmed — Liam Wentz marching right toward her.

He stopped a few feet away, looming over Sloane, making her feel like a teeny tiny little girl as he bellowed, "You have some nerve!"

"Get out," she ordered, ignoring her aggressively stoked curiosity.

"You're done. Ruined. TOTALLY FUCKING FINISHED!" Spittle rained from his mouth. Then Liam Wentz leaned forward and lowered his voice. "I hope you understand what you've done."

Despite her best intentions, Sloane fell prey to the bait. "I have no idea what you're talking about."

"Like hell you don't!" He raised his clenched fist and for a moment she seriously thought that Liam Wentz was going to strike her. "You know exactly what you're doing." Then he growled, *"You're doing whatever the mother fucking Shellys tell you to do."* Then he straightened. "Same as you have for the last twenty years."

"Jake!" Even if the Kindergarten Cop wasn't on set yet, calling for him might give the monster pause. "Security!" There were at least two guards around here somewhere. "I need help!"

Liam Wentz fell a step back, raising his hands in pacification, but his tone remained violent. "I know all about your little memoir and—"

"You need to leave. NOW!" Her fists were clenched even tighter than her jaw.

Where the hell was security?

"—if you don't pull the plug on that project, I'll sue you for libel, for defamation, the works. *I will ruin you.*"

"That's not a new threat. It's how you said good morning. SECURITY!" In another second, Sloane would start screaming her throat raw.

"You can tell the Shellys that they've made their last mistake."

The cast and crew had started to arrive, along with both guards. Maybe eight or nine people total, it was hard to tally them all in a glance. But the crowd was pregnant with nerves, waiting to see what would happen.

And Sloane was in a nightmare, trying to claw her way up from the bottom.

Everything had been going great just a few minutes ago. But same as he'd been able to do for the last twenty years, Liam Wentz had managed to completely unseat her.

She saw him offering her attention and presents, promising that she was as talented as they came and there was nothing she couldn't do.

She saw him leading her into his trailer.

She saw him sitting next to her on his couch beneath the window.

And then she heard his filthy words. *I want to know what you taste like.*

She screamed, long and guttural.

He stood a safe distance away from her, his hands back up, still in pacification, looking around the room with a bemused smile as if to say, *I know, right? Isn't she crazy?*

The guards approached Liam Wentz from either side.

"You need to leave the premises immediately," one of them said.

"Of course," he nodded, perfectly compliant. "I absolutely understand. There's no need for any of us to get hysterical."

Then he turned to her with a leering smile.

And Sloane totally lost it, bellowing again as she shoved him with all of her might toward the door.

He was smart enough to slacken his body and allow her to push him into a cumbersome stumble. Then Liam Wentz walked the rest of the way to the door on his own, turning back at the threshold to address her with a smile. "Just a fair warning … I will be filing assault charges."

Then he was gone.

The guards were suddenly by her side.

So were Lila, Becky, Sasha, Bennett, and Tomosino.

But no Jolie, Miles, or Orson.

And then in a flash all three of her saviors appeared, along with little Connor.

Leaning down, Orson said something to his son, then passed them both off to Miles, who looked over to Sloane with understanding eyes as he led the children away, probably taking them to Jake.

Orson marched over, pulled her into an embrace, then he held her while she broke down, petting the back of her head and promising that everything would still be okay.

Once she was calm enough, he kissed her, turning Sloane's screaming mind into something blissfully blank until she finally pulled away with a shake of her head.

"I need to work."

"Not yet." He took her hand and started walking toward the door.

"Where are you taking me?"

"We're not shooting anything else," Orson told her. "Not without talking to the Shellys first."

Chapter Twenty-Four

Sloane

SLOANE LEANED CLOSER to Orson and said, "We should have called."

"It doesn't matter how many times you mention it, we didn't, and it's too late to call now."

They were sitting outside the Shellys' office, waiting for the receptionist to invite them inside. Sloane hadn't wanted to barge in unannounced, but Orson assured her that this issue wasn't a text exchange, or even a phone call. Some things needed to be settled face-to-face, hopefully once and for all.

"We're not just here for Dominic and Melinda," Orson said.

"Then why are we here?"

"Because we needed to get you away from the set."

"You mean away from my job. The Shellys will be pissed at me."

"They're not going to be pissed at you."

"Do you have any idea how many times they've told

me I just need to 'make the movie' or 'stick to the sched-ule,' or … never mind." She shook her head, the bluster now gone from her argument.

She pulled out her phone.

"Put that away." A gentle hand on her wrist. "There's nothing there you need to see."

Sloane had seen plenty already. Photos from that morning's altercation, and all the artificial stories to go with them. Of course the Shellys must have already seen them.

Pictures of Sloane Alexander shoving Liam Wentz — her face irate and his hands raised in surrender. Pictures of Sloane Alexander in the loving arms of Orson Beck — just another example of a home wrecking Mr. & Mrs. Smith situation. Pictures of Sloane Alexander acting unstable in public, yet again.

She stared at the dark screen, tempted to turn it on and look, even if doing so made Orson disappointed in her. But she put the phone back in her pocket instead, then looked at the receptionist and asked a question she already knew the answer to.

"Any updates?"

"Sorry, Ms. Alexander." She shook her head. "I'm sure it'll just be another few minutes."

"*Sloane,*" she reminded her, not that it would make any difference. The receptionist still referred to Orson as "Mr. Beck."

"They're lying about me." Sloane stated the obvious.

"I know." He nodded and took her hand.

"Everything is being misconstrued."

"You're absolutely right."

"They're acting like I'm having an affair with you right in front of Miles!"

"Only the haters are acting like that, but yes, they are."

Orson continued to nod with the disaffected air of someone who had seen it all before.

"Like I'm flaunting my movie star boyfriend in front of my daughter's father, just to hurt him, and Jolie. When I bother to remember being a mother at all, of course. And you just know the Shellys are going to hit me with their *all publicity is good publicity* line. I bet they're actually happy about this."

"I'm sure they're the opposite. But I do agree that—"

"Dominic and Melinda can see you now," said the receptionist said, cutting him off.

They stood, and Sloane tried not to feel irritated that Dominic and Melinda both got first names while she would apparently always be Ms. Alexander.

"Sorry about the wait," Melinda said before either of them had taken a seat. "We've been swamped all morning and weren't expecting you."

"Though it is understandable that you're here," Dominic added.

The Shellys traded a glance.

Sloane got the distinct feeling that she and Orson were interrupting something important.

"So, you've already heard?" Orson asked them.

"Of course," Melinda said.

"I should have kept shooting." Sloane shook her head, unable to look at either Dominic or Melinda for fear of witnessing their disappointment. "The whole thing just really caught me off guard and—"

"It's understandable," Dominic said for the second time. "Wentz should never have appeared on our set — *again.* It's disconcerting that he did, and you have every right to a genuine reaction."

"Thank you." Sloane felt like a baby, wanting to cry.

"What are you guys doing to take care of this?" Orson

was more to the point. "No offense, but it seems like more than a few—"

"Do ever actually mean *no offense* when you say those words?" Melinda asked him.

"He's just protecting me."

"Obviously," Dominic said.

Melinda gave a slight shake of her head. "There's only so much we can do as a direct response to what happened today. The encounter was designed to encourage this exact result. *No offense*, Orson, but Sloane played into his little plan perfectly."

"I'm sorry," she said.

"Don't be," Orson told her.

"She should be," Dominic disagreed. Then directly to Sloane. "You know better."

"Dominic ..." Melinda said.

But she was only playing Good Cop. Of course he was right.

"Just tell us you have a plan and we'll believe you," Orson said.

Dominic turned to him. "You already know we have a plan."

Orson tried again. "Then tell us what it is."

Melinda shook her head. "You know we can't do that."

"He's hitting us hard, and in unexpected places, but we're dealing with it."

Sloane didn't want to feel weak, but the words of defeat left her anyway. "Do you know how much it hurts to see all that gossip online?"

"Melinda and I have both seen plenty of—"

"And worse than none of it being true—" Sloane cut Dominic off for the first time in her life "—is that a tiny circle of people who were all hired by someone in this room can't be trusted."

Someone was betraying them, and that someone had been brought into the fold by either the Shellys or her.

"You're absolutely right," Melinda said, but offered no solution.

"People from your studio or my crew were taking pictures and video on their phones and selling them, either to make a quick buck with no regard to whether the stories were even true, or because they've been bought and paid for by Liam Wentz and that was part of their jobs — despite your constant assurances that this has all been taken care of."

The Shellys traded another look, then Dominic delivered some expected yet still devastating news. "This is a good thing, Sloane. People are talking about you, and about—"

"How crazy I am? That I'm picking fights and throwing tantrums and having affairs and doing all kinds of—"

"It's okay," Dominic said, his voice still soft. "Calm down."

"Don't tell me to calm down!"

"Dominic's right. We understand how you feel, but this isn't as bad as it might seem," Melinda said. "Wentz has no case when it comes to libel, or anything else, and any footage out there can and will be used to fuel interest in our film."

"It looks like the feud might be starting to work for us," Dominic added.

"THE FEUD?" Sloane repeated. "*Starting to work for us?*"

This was infuriating.

Dominic explained. "Our crews record happenings on set and leak them to the press all the time. It's—"

"On this production?" Orson asked.

"No," Melinda said. "Of course not."

"Then it *is* a problem, right?" Orson looked right in her eyes.

"A problem we're dealing with," she told him.

Somehow, Sloane's nightmare had decayed into something even worse. She had always imagined that as bad as things got, the Shellys would put her first. But sitting on the other side of their desk right now, with the two of them staring back at her, the truth had never felt more obvious.

Sloane Alexander was just another pawn to them. Just another tool.

She couldn't trust them, which meant she might not be able to trust anyone.

Including Orson. Sure, it *seemed* like he was on her side. But how long would that last? Everyone who had ever professed to love her, or promised to care for Sloane had failed her eventually.

"But *how* are you dealing with it?" She shook her head. "And I don't want to hear anything more about plausible deniability."

She got silence from the Shellys. And from Orson, who sat there waiting to see what might happen next.

Sloane nursed her thoughts before spewing any more words. She was angry, sure, but the Shellys deserved more benefit of the doubt than anyone else in her life.

She took a breath then made her argument. "Liam Wentz came to the studio this morning to provoke me, hoping to catch me in a vulnerable moment, which he did. And if he hadn't, I'm sure he would have had someone PhotoShop the needed scene and the 'evidence' would be online, anyway."

Dominic nodded. "That's all been established."

"But you still won't tell me what you're doing to make sure it doesn't happen again!"

"And we're not going to," Melinda said with a shake of her head. "I know that's not what you want to hear, but it's all we have for you this morning. Now, you'll have to excuse me, I have an appointment in just under a half-hour from now, and at this time of morning, it's a forty-minute drive."

The Shellys stood in tandem.

Sloane and Orson left their seats a beat later.

"I promise we're looking out for you," Melinda made a vow as they walked toward the door.

"Okay," Sloane said as she opened it, wanting to believe.

Orson was quiet on their way to the car, then on the drive, and as they walked onto set. His disposition reminded her of Miles nursing something he both did and did not want to say.

He stopped and turned to her just before they went back inside. "I know you don't want to hear it, but I've seen the Shellys pull through enough—"

"That's not what's on your mind right now," she said. "What are you thinking?"

Orson exhaled, then after a long moment he answered. "I've been through this before, and I don't want to see you crucified in the media."

"What are you saying, Orson?"

"That I think we should be more careful about how we treat each other in public ... for now."

"I understand." But it hurt so, so much.

"*For now*," he repeated.

"Of course." His qualifier didn't make her injury hurt any less. "We should probably go inside."

Sloane entered and Orson followed.

It was fine. She could deal with the pain. She would keep taking whatever this production or the world at large kept trying to pile on her. She would finish the movie and reap the rewards of her blockbuster art. Sloane had been through hell and come out the other side, so she could handle whatever Wentz or anyone else threw at her.

So long as nothing happened to Jolie.

Chapter Twenty-Five

Melinda

ONCE UPON A TIME, there was a stunning young housewife who got in over her head and had to break a little bad to save her family.

Instead of meth, she dabbled in prostitution. Her success was immediate, at least in the ways that matter, as she proved to have a sixth sense not for sex, but for human behavior itself.

This made her an interesting asset for a married pair of up-and-coming moguls, in love with each other and with mission-based capitalism. Sex was one of their causes, and this wonderful MILF promised a way they could thread many of their initiatives together.

Natalie Monroe secretly ran Blush, the most exclusive escort service in Hollywood and arguably the world. The Shellys secretly ran Natalie Monroe.

Melinda was on her way to their opulent brothel for a much-needed discussion with Nat.

They had started with twenty-nine escorts a few year

ago and ran twice that number now. Women with an array of interests and looks, specialties and availabilities. Melinda had helped Natalie design a training program. These weren't trick-turning college girls looking for a fast buck. This was a career for women who knew how to play *best in the world.*

Blush was more than a mansion nestled in the hills where some of the world's most expensive dreams could come true. The place served as a goldmine of information when the Shellys needed it. This was the dirtiest they played, but Dominic and Melinda were both smart enough to embrace holding history's strongest hand.

Sex had driven the planet for all recorded time, and surely eons before that. Sex was currency, and the blood in everyone's veins. That simple understanding had fueled their ascension in Hollywood and business in general. *Everything* was about sex, not just the movies they made — all of them, in one way or another, even if there wasn't so much as the barest hint of a coital suggestion. Sex had been a core component of filmmaking since long before the Hays Code because sex was core to humanity.

In-call or out-call, their brothel was absurdly profitable in more ways than one. At Blush, sex was a secret weapon. Women were paid to listen as much if not more than they were paid to fuck. Sometimes the Shellys used sex to ply specific information out of an unassuming and overly vulnerable decision-maker's hands. Knowing which emotional levers to pull or physical buttons to push or perhaps intimate areas to massage in exactly the right way could get an unwitting informant to spew like a fountain. The Shellys had sixty or so spigots at their everlasting disposal.

Melinda pulled up to the mansion, handed her keys to the valet, then took her appointment card. A *just in case* given to every visitor coming to Blush — or the Hollywood Hill Center For Emotional Wellness, so far as the permits were concerned — including the big boss.

She looked down at her card. Bianca would be her on-call therapist for the day. Melinda wouldn't really be using her services, but given more time she would love to indulge in the Playboy cover model, also Italy's Playmate of the year in 2010. Bianca spoke three languages and had used two of them to write bestselling books under a male pseudonym.

Twenty-thousand square feet worth of estate, insulated by acres of land. Melinda ascended the front steps with pride. Nat ran things here, but she and Dominic had built this, just as they had built so many other things together.

Things that were now coalescing. Separate pieces finally becoming one. And ultimately whole.

"Mrs. Shelly." Elsa stood to greet Melinda as she entered.

"Don't get up." She offered Elsa friendly wave as she passed. "Natalie is expecting me."

"Of course." Elsa sat back down.

Elsa's real name was Andrea White. Melinda usually made a suggestion or two when a new girl joined the roster — so far none had left — but Nat had final call and always came up with excellent names. Elsa had platinum hair and Nordic features. Once she finished her training, she would surely have a waiting list.

The door was open, so Melinda entered Nat's office without knocking.

She looked up from her computer screen, brightening at the sight of her. "Melinda, hi. I lost track of time. Please, sit." Melinda was already taking her seat. Nat's eyes were back on her computer screen. "Sorry … I'm just … okay, all done."

"Everything okay?"

"I was just finishing the one-pagers. Here—" Nat clicked something with her mouse, apparently sent the one-pagers to an iPad on her desk, then slid the tablet over to Melinda. "You tell me."

Nat had started making the "one-pagers" for Melinda about a year ago. All Nat's idea, and Melinda couldn't love them any more. Blush was looking for lifelong clients, not random encounters, so first times were everything when it came to establishing potential lifetime value. Nat compiled all the pertinent information about a potential pairing when a new client contacted Blush, not just their interests and specialties, but those interests and specialties in specific relation to the client, as defined after an exhaustive background search.

So far, the only new clients who hadn't returned to Blush within ninety days of their first visit both had that first visit less than a month ago.

Melinda swiped from the first one-pager to the next then back twice before setting Nat's tablet back on the desk and pushing it ever so slightly toward her.

"You decide."

"But—"

"I trust you." Melinda shook her head. "When was the last time I disagreed with any of your choices? This is an inefficiency we should move past, anyway. I enjoy being involved with this, but I certainly don't need to be. You know the girls and the clients better than me, and my earlier concerns about security are now non-existent. I marvel at what you do, Nat, so hopefully the next time I drop by, it'll be so us girls can open a bottle and have a little chat. But today I need—"

"I know. A couple of girls, plus some hard candy if I can manage it." Nat sighed. This was just as ugly for her.

"I do have leads on some girls, and the hard candy if it comes to that."

"Tell me about the girls first."

"We have three."

Melinda raised her eyebrows. That was excellent news. "Three of them?"

"Yes." She nodded. "But none are willing to testify."

"What would they be testifying against?"

"All three women say he either seduced or assaulted them. The exact language depends on the victim, but their stories are still remarkably similar, and each one has at least two verification points."

"Do you have names for me?" Melinda asked.

"Not yet." She shook her head. "I mean, I do, but that's part of the problem. All three of our potential witnesses are of age now, but they were all minors at the time of their assault."

"Can you tell me how they originally came into contact with him?"

"No surprise, each of the girls was acting in a Wentz production."

"Are any of these girls working now?" Melinda asked.

"I see what you're doing, narrowing the field of options, but I'll answer you anyway. *No*, none of them. And one is an escort for Minx."

Blush's biggest competitor.

"How do we know these girls, and how did we get their stories?"

"Through the planet's most intimate grapevine."

"Come on, Nat. Can you please not feed my lines back to me? It's insulting."

"Your orders." She shrugged, following her pre-established directive but clearly having a good time doing so, or at least as much mirth as this ugly situation might allow. "Plausible deniability."

"Fine. I guess for now I'll be grateful that we have two verification points per account. So what's next? You said none of the girls is willing to testify."

Nat nodded. "Seems each of them will need a different sort of encouragement. One seems like it's a cash payout or bust, but the other two probably just need assurances of protection. They've all seen what he's done to Sloane and others. They're all terrified of becoming his next target."

"Again, who are these girls? One works for Minx. Do the other two work for you? Friend of a friend of one of your girls? I can't protect what I don't—"

"I have my eye on things for now. But—"

"What about the hard candy?"

"I found someone." Nat nodded. "I'm not sure she'll work, and I'll keep looking in the meantime, but for now she's the best I can do."

"Why the hesitation?"

"She's two months from turning nineteen, but still looks fourteen or fifteen. That's still a bit too old for Wentz from what I'm understanding, but I seriously don't think we're going to do better than that. But more concerning, I don't think she'll be able to pull it off. Despite her looks, there's nothing really innocent about this girl. Even if she's acting ..."

Melinda finished the thought. "Claiming that innocence for himself is the main draw for a monster like Wentz, and it's something he can probably sense more than see."

"Right. We're talking about a core trait, and those are the hardest to fake, especially if we're talking about pairing an artificial trait with a genuine need."

"Hopefully, we can do this without her. Right now

we're trying to cover our bases so that when the time comes, a jury won't even blink before sending that child rapist to jail for the rest of his life."

Melinda stood.

The women hugged and said their goodbyes. Then she left, feeling grateful for Blush.

Melinda made the first of her two calls while waiting for the valet to bring her Tesla around.

"Orson," she said when he answered. "I need a favor."

"Of course. What is it?"

"I need you to call your friend at *Hollywood Hunted*."

"Who do you mean?"

"You can play coy or dumb or whatever you need to," Melinda said. "I respect that there are boundaries and privacy issues at play. But I still need you to make the call. Ask Ellis to dig up everything he can find, or deliver everything he already has, on Liam Wentz."

"Oh," Orson said.

"Exactly. Call me when you have a yes." Then she hung up and dialed her favorite number. "I'll text you when I'm five minutes away. I want you to meet me out front."

"Sounds like an adventure," Dominic said. "Where are we going?"

"To solve our problems."

Chapter Twenty-Six

Sloane

THE DAY WAS *ALMOST* DONE.

Sloane felt productive but hollow.

Just that morning she had felt so in control, so ready for anything.

But that anything hadn't included Liam Wentz. He'd liquified her bones the second she saw him. It was as if her skin itself needed to scream. Too many demons stirred into the front of her mind. Sloane spent the rest of her morning and all afternoon slaying them, down from an unrelenting horde to a restless minority — few enough to no longer feel like she was actively dying.

The Shellys usually made everything better, but today she left their office feeling worse.

The little girl in her wanted to believe that Orson was her knight in shining armor. But that was an unfair expectation, and this morning had already proved otherwise.

Regardless of her inner misery, the day was still productive. *Sunset's* best so far, and by quite a margin. It didn't matter that Cassidy wasn't on set. Either because of that morning's incident or despite it, the cast and crew were all fully present and at peak performance. A beautiful thing to see when they were only now getting started. All that prep work really made a difference. Not just during her moment of quiet, but every accumulated day from the three projects leading into this one.

And yet, Sloane felt no joy in her work.

She missed Jolie something fierce and wanted nothing more than to slip away with her for a Mother-Daughter Day of Fun. At least a hundred times both before and after lunch she imagined calling fifteen minutes then breaking her baby girl out of her trailer and spiriting them away for a game of miniature golf. Maybe a movie, or a picnic, or whatever Jolie wanted to do.

Too many elements of the project so far had revolved around keeping Jolie safe. It was hard to think about anything else. The nature of this gig gave her no choice, and it felt like repeatedly stabbing herself in an open wound.

But at least the work was getting done.

Sloane had an hour or so before she could finally go home. The day was done, but she wanted to prepare for tomorrow. *Needed to*, if she expected another successful run. The production wasn't supposed to shoot on Saturdays, but there was a lot she could do without Cassidy around, and she intended to claw back some of *Sunset's* battered schedule.

She considered checking in with Jolie to let her know they would be going home soon — *she promised no more than an hour!* — but Miles told her he'd relieve Jake a few minutes ago. He knew what Sloane was up to and would tell Jolie without her even asking him to. An hour with her father was a good thing.

"That was a great day!" Lila walked toward her, beaming like a blue-ribbon winner. "You must be exhausted!"

Sloane nodded. "I could sleep standing up."

"I already want to take a nap mañana. I can't imagine how you must feel."

"I'll be going soon. I just have a few more things."

"Anything I can help with?" Lila asked.

"No. I'm—" Sloane stopped.

99 Red Balloons bleated on her phone. Miles calling, even though he was somewhere on set … with Jolie. The song kept on playing.

"Are you going to answer that?"

Sloane looked down at the phone. Of course she was going to answer.

They were on their way to get dinner and wanted to know what she wanted. Miles was calling instead of texting despite knowing that she was trying to finish up and didn't want any delays because Jolie had wanted to talk to her.

In fact, it was probably — almost for sure — Jolie using his phone to call her mommy right now.

"Hello?" Sloane answered, trying not to sound frantic.

"Is Jolie with you?" Miles asked, sounding frantic enough for both of them.

"I thought she was with you!"

"She's not in the trailer and neither is Jake."

"Where have you looked?" She asked with a lump in her throat.

"Just in and around the trailer. That's why I'm calling, in case you know something."

"I don't know any—" She stopped talking and hung up the phone when she saw Miles walking toward her, phone to his ear.

He dropped the phone in his pocket and continued his approach.

"What's going on?" Lila asked. "Is this about Jolie?"

OF COURSE IT'S ABOUT JOLIE!

But this wasn't Lila's fault.

"Yes," Sloane said, the word like a brick. "Lila, I need you to gather anyone still around. I'm sure Jake and Jolie are somewhere close and we'll all be laughing at ourselves in a couple of minutes, but—"

"Got it." Lila nodded and skirted away, more sober than Sloane had ever seen her. "I'll start by checking the security footage."

But there wasn't anything to look at because the cameras had been turned off.

Not that they needed the footage to find Jake. One of the grips who had still been hanging out just because found him stuffed in the far stall of the men's room. Beaten to hell, naked, and thoroughly unconscious.

"Call the cops," Sloane said to Miles. "And have them bring an ambulance."

"What are you going to do?" he asked.

"I'm calling Melinda."

Chapter Twenty-Seven

Sloane

SLOANE WAS GOING TOTALLY out of her gourd.

She wanted to believe Miles that everything would be all right, but that was impossible. He had comforting words in a quartet of languages, but that didn't make a single one of them true. He was just guessing, same as she was. Their daughter could be in mortal danger and there wasn't a single goddamned thing they could do about.

Sloane had dialed Melinda three times already, but there was no point in even trying a fourth. Melinda always answered when she could and got back to her when she couldn't. Same for Dominic, and he wasn't answering either. Right now, Sloane had to do the hardest thing in the world — exhibit patience and try to believe that Miles was right.

Everything would be fine.

The police would arrive in a minute or two, then the manhunt would begin. She could hear Dominic in her mind, promising Sloane that this was a good thing. That

Liam Wentz had made his final mistake. That they would find Jolie, and thanks to this overly aggressive blunder, Liam Wentz would spend the rest of his life publicly shamed and getting raped behind bars.

Her phone rang and she was flooded with relief, despite hearing the generic chime of a private caller rather than Beyonce's *Run the World* she used for Melinda.

"Hello?"

"Good. You answered." The voice of Liam Wentz poisoned her cells. "Are you in a place you can talk?"

"Where's my daughter?" she asked through gritted teeth.

Miles put a hand on her shoulder, looking furious as the concerned stragglers gathered around her.

"I'm not referring to privacy when I ask if you're in 'a place you can talk.' I mean are you in the proper mental state to hear what's good for you."

"The police are on their way, asshole! *Where's my daughter?*"

"You're going to start listening like a good little girl, do you understand me?" He paused for her response, but since he apparently wanted to hear her voice, she wouldn't even use it to ask her question again.

He cleared his throat and continued. "I'll assume that's a yes. Of course it is. You've always been smart enough. Surely you understand what's going to happen if you don't start behaving."

Another chance for Sloane to respond.

More silence as she looked to the people around her for support, her gaze fixed on Miles longest of all.

"I suppose I'll have to spell it out." Liam Wentz gave her a long sigh that sounded a little too gleeful. "If you don't start acting like a good little girl, then your Jolie will have to become one of my good little girls instead. Do we understand each other?"

"No," she whimpered.

"I think we do." He laughed, sounding angelically natured, as if he had just finished delivering the punchline to a perfectly wholesome joke. "You're going to shut down the movie, abandon the book, and scurry back to London. You do that and I'll leave you and your little girl for good. You do that" — his voice turned lecherous — "and she never becomes *my* little girl."

A pair of officers walked side-by-side through the door. Lila ran to greet them.

Miles tightened his hand on her shoulder.

Sloane said, "The police are here."

"Tell them I said *Hi*."

"Where. Is. My. Daughter?"

"She's at the Pirate Pizza in Burbank." Liam Wentz insulted her with an insidious sounding laugh. "She loves that place. Says she wishes she could go there more often."

"You're done," Sloane said. Then covering the receiver and whispering to Miles, "She's at Pirate Pizza."

"Likewise, kitten. You've been warned."

Then Liam Wentz was gone.

Sloane was already pocketing her phone and running toward the exit with Miles right beside her.

"Ma'am!" One of the officers called out to her. "We're going to need—"

"Lila's got it! I'll be back!"

"Want me to drive?" Miles asked as they ran.

"Absolutely."

Either one of them would drive like a maniac right now, but Miles might manage to do so while still getting them to Pirate Pizza alive.

Neither of them spoke, but the cabin was thick with Beethoven and heavy breathing.

Nineteen minutes that felt like an hour, with most of it spent wondering if Liam Wentz had sent them to the right place or on a goose chase. Maybe a few minutes from now they would find men in white coats waiting in the Pirate Pizza Parking lot, ready to drag her away in hysterics.

Miles pulled up to the curb and Sloane bolted out of the car without waiting for him to kill the engine. She exploded through the double-barreled entrance to find herself lost and looking around, hoping for the best but dreading the worst.

She was supposed to check in up front and would be called out by some pimply faced kid for not doing so, but there was zero chance that she would even stop at the line, let alone wait in it. Instead, she plowed her way past the front and marched into the general area, ignoring a shouted reprimand from the eyepatch-wearing cashier up front, feeling a sweltering panic as she raced from one area to the next without seeing her daughter.

Jolie loved both the ball pit and skee-ball, but she wasn't in either place. Ticket games always captured her attention, but Sloane didn't see her at any of the machines, including the ones that always spit easy easier payouts.

Miles burst through the entrance just as Sloane was making her way back.

"I'll keep looking around. Can you stand in line and ask if anyone's seen her?"

He nodded and got in line without a word. She wanted to yell at him to cut his way to the front — THIS WAS AN EMERGENCY! — but instead she dashed back into the general area.

The ball pit and skee-ball were still a bust, same for the

party rooms. But rounding the corner back toward the game area, Sloane finally saw her daughter.

She wasn't alone.

But it wasn't Liam Wentz or some other adult male or obvious danger.

"Hey there, Mom," Jolie said, in a voice her mother had never heard, surrounded by a trio of girls she had also never seen.

"Jolie." Sloane didn't know what to say. She had been disarmed without warning. There was something happening here that she didn't yet understand. The other girls were all slightly older, twelve or thirteen, all standing slightly behind her. She had to say something fast, wrestle control of this suddenly delicate situation. "Who are your friends?"

Another unexpected slap as Jolie rolled her eyes, tipping her head an inch, apparently to indicate the mystery trio, before she delivered her response in a disaffected mumble. "Hailee, Pipa, and Chloe."

"Nice to meet you." It absolutely was not, but Sloane smiled at the girls anyway.

All three of them giggled. Their makeup made everything worse. So did the fact that they were all holding phones, two of them staring down at their screens, while one appeared to be mindlessly scrolling.

Sloane didn't know them, so yes, she was being judgmental, but Jolie had gone missing and in that context, she was handling things damn well. She couldn't help thinking these three girls were *exactly* what she hated about this town, and the number one reason she hadn't felt like returning. Of course London had its share of the same behavior, and much of it worse for the blood being bluer at Jolie's private school, but what was considered exclusive in the UK felt more pervasive in the States, and downright permeating in Southern California.

It wasn't that the girls were older, it was that they were dressed in designer clothes and carrying absurdly priced handbags. Unless they were knockoffs, which would somehow make the situation even worse, because then the girls were only pretending to have money while living in the shallows of life. Sloane had made millions with her first three movies, but she'd poured almost all of that back into her art, and carried a two-year-old phone because that was more than she needed. All three of the teenagers hovering over Jolie were carrying this year's iPhone.

In other words, they were exactly the sort of girls she and Miles had insisted Jolie never become.

"What are you guys doing?" Sloane asked, still holding her smile.

"Having fun," Jolie grunted.

Who was this girl?

"How did you get here?"

Another grunt. "In a car."

The girls behind her laughed.

Miles had his back to them, now in front of the line.

Sloane fought to keep her voice patient and the smile on her face. "More specifically, who brought you here?"

"Mendes."

"And who is Mendes?"

"The guy who brought me here, duh." Jolie snorted laughter.

So did the girls.

Sloane wanted to grab her daughter by the wrist and drag her out of Pirate Pizza, screaming if she had to. Instead she tried again. "Why aren't you with Jake?"

"He had to go, so Mendes came to replace him."

"Where did he go?" She needed her heart to stop beating so fast.

Jolie was being obnoxious, but the crisis was over.

"Home, I guess." Jolie shrugged. "Mendes showed him something, then he left."

"Why would you just trust someone you've never met before?"

"Jeez. Chill out, Mom. He was dressed exactly the same, in that black polo shirt with the little red logo."

Jolie's new friends were all leaning ever so slightly forward, now more interested in what was developing in real time in front of them than whatever had been happening on their phones.

"Why would you get in a car with him?"

"Because you and Dad were both working late. Connor wasn't there, and I was *booooooored*. Mendes said you guys would meet me here. He gave me a bunch of tokens and money for pizza and ice cream. I had fun. And now you're here. So what's the big?"

Miles joined them before she could answer.

"Great. You found her." He was beaming, the poor guy had no idea. "Who are your friends?"

"I can't believe you left the set!" Sloane yelled, nice and shrill before Jolie could deliver another one of her snotty little answers. "You're not supposed to leave with *anyone, under any circumstances!* What don't you understand about that?"

"I left with the bodyguard, Mom." Then to her friends, "They think I need a bodyguard."

Miles looked ready to intervene, but Sloane shook her head and kept going.

"What have we taught you about talking to strangers?"

"I'm not five years old!" Jolie exclaimed, a different strain of immaturity now seeping through.

"We're going, Jolie," Miles said. "Tell your friends goodbye."

"I don't want to go."

"Last chance to say good—"

"I DON'T WANT TO GO!" She took a breath. The next bit was calmer, but still irate. "We never have any fun. You and Mom are always busy! Connor's mom picks him up early sometimes. And Jake isn't as much fun as Tiffany was." Then back to screaming. "I HATE IT HERE AND I WANT TO GO HOME!"

Sloane was about to reply with something she would for sure one day regret, but Miles grabbed her by the wrist before she could assemble the proper order of words, let alone push them out of her mouth.

Dad had his daughter in one hand and her mom in the other.

"Nice to meet you." Miles tipped his head toward the trio of girls it had absolutely *not* been nice to meet, then led them both out of Pirate Pizza while Jolie thrashed and her "friends" twittered behind them.

She was quiet by the time Miles put her in the backseat.

Then he turned to Sloane and said, "I know exactly what you're thinking."

But really, Miles had no idea.

Chapter Twenty-Eight

Sloane

SLOANE COULDN'T STOP THINKING about Nicole.

Same as their frantic trip to Pirate Pizza, Sloane was grateful that Miles took the wheel on their way back. Jolie was still acting like a brat, but doing it quietly in the back. She muttered under her breath, kicked the seat, and rolled her windows up and down until Dad killed the ability for her to do so.

Sloane sank down in the passenger seat, settling into her thoughts as she remembered all those old struggles with Nicole.

No matter what anyone thought or said or printed or lied about, Sloane had never wanted anything but the best for Nicole. They were best friends before they were enemies. Even all these years later, the disintegration of their relationship was one of Sloane's biggest regrets. They didn't need to know or like each other, especially now with both women in their thirties, but the unknown had felt like an open wound for two decades now.

Did Nicole really hate her? Or was that just another role her mother had forced the poor girl into? If so, that was something she could understand.

Once Sloane understood what Liam Wentz was trying to do, at least on some primitive level, *of course* she had to warn her best friend. She and Nicole had met on *The Explorers Club* and even after that show ended, they DMd each other on LiveLyfe every day, back when the platform was still relatively new and they felt so grownup for using it.

But Nicole didn't want to hear what her friend had to say. Sloane might as well have been speaking in tongues. She listened at first, with what seemed to Sloane like a blend of mild curiosity and even milder fear, followed by pure indifference after that.

Nicole never wanted to hear that Liam Wentz was dangerous, so she never really listened. And when Sloane pressed her friend — begged her to tell a grownup about what was happening — Nicole lashed out at her. Accused her of being jealous that Mr. Liam liked her more than Sloane.

Their last fight was the worst. Too bad that one hadn't been caught on camera. Sloane could only remember a little of what Nicole had said, but she could still hear the discordant notes in her tone.

You should do whatever he says anyway, because you don't have enough talent to make it otherwise.

Sloane did remember that one, yet she was alone in the memory. Unfortunately, the whole world had heard what she had bellowed at Nicole in a flurry of hurt and anger.

You'll never ever be as good as me at anything! And yes, of course I'll lie if I have to!

An absurdly unfair quote when taken out of context. The first part was fueled by anger, and understandable given the circumstances, even if it wasn't acceptable. The second part was in reference to something Sloane had said before someone on set decided to turn the camera on their little dispute. If the scene had happened a few years later, everyone would have been capturing the exchange on their phones.

When discussing whether she would be willing to say she had seen things Nicole had only told her about, Sloane said that of course she would lie to protect her friend. But out of context, the callback sounded like she would do anything to win.

Losing her friendship with Nicole was part of what made that time of Sloane's life feel like she had been living at the end of any world that mattered. It felt like a failure. She couldn't get through to her friend and thus couldn't protect her. The majority of Sloane's nightmares featured her and the monster — *Liam Wentz* — alone. Most of the rest starred Nicole, tiny and shattered in a parade of escalating atrocities from the time Sloane left for London, and abandoned her best friend to an unspeakable fate, at least until Nicole was far enough on the opposite end of adolescence for him to finally stop fawning all over her.

But this was even worse.

Now it wasn't a "rival" actress Sloane would be failing to protect, it was her daughter.

At least Jolie had finally stopped kicking the back of her seat.

"Moonlight Sonata" reached its conclusion with perfect timing as Miles pulled back into the parking lot of Shellter Productions.

He killed the engine. Sloane had no idea what might happen next.

But then he turned to the back seat and in a stern voice she rarely heard from him, Miles said, "Don't even think about opening that door."

Then he got out of the car and waited for Sloane to meet him outside.

He ran a hand through his mess of hair as she closed her door, looking around. The cars were all gone, the place was deserted.

"So, what do you think we should—"

"We never should have brought her here," Miles said, cutting her off.

"Where were we going to bring her?"

"We should have sent her back to Bruges?"

"*Back?* That's never been her home, Miles."

"Maybe it should have been."

"Of course it shouldn't have been. Jolie should be with her parents."

"Then maybe both of her parents shouldn't have agreed to this project."

"Miles …"

"We talked about this. It's time for a change. I'm bowing out. You should, too. Jolie was happy in London. So that's—"

"I'm finishing this film." She shook her head, turning so her back was facing their daughter, doing her best to study the conversation from the back seat.

"You promised to drop the film at the first hint of direct and genuine danger to Jolie. I strongly feel that this situation right now fits that definition."

"You're right, I gave you my word. And I'm not trying to take it back. Of course, Jolie needs to be safe. And yes, she can stay with your parents, that's a great idea. I'll head to Bruges after the shoot. I can do the editing there. Or maybe we'll go back to London before we figure out what's next. But I can't run, Miles. *West Hollywood Sunset* will ruin Liam Wentz and give me a new life. We can't let him win."

"*Us* a new life." Miles gave her a nod, finally getting it.

"I love you as a human. And as an artist. I will truly, deeply miss you on this project. But I'm also sure that the Shellys will be able to nab me someone amazing, even at the last minute."

"I'm sure they can." He waited a beat. "Mind if I ask you something?"

"Ask me anything."

"Are you really staying for the movie? If I'm dropping out of the project and taking Jolie with me, then I deserve to know."

"What are you actually asking me?"

"Are you staying for him? For Orson, I mean?"

The unexpected laughter felt good. "I truly hadn't even thought about that. But yes, I suppose I'd be lying if I said a small part of me didn't want to see what might happen there. Still, that's a slice of the pie. Mostly, I can't let *him* silence me a second time. And besides, I owe it to the Shellys. After all they've done for me? And after all they've poured into this—"

"Well, sure, chérie, but all they've done for you with this film has been for them, too. They want this to be a blockbuster as much as you do. And they also want their revenge."

"Does any of that matter? Even taking away the fact that Dominic and Melinda have always been there for me, I made my three movies so I could finally play with a real budget. It's not just their money, it's mine. One successful project leads rights into the next. And I need that in a way you don't. You'll shoot the hell out of whatever you're hired for, whether that movie tanks with the critics or not. No one will ever shit on your cinematography, and you'll always be in demand."

"It's not that easy," he argued.

"It's easy enough. At the very least, it's *easier.* I need this movie, Miles, and I know you understand that there's more than one reason why."

"I do." A little bow of his head. "I'll miss it. And you."

"You too, Belgie." She gave him a hug.

"Belgie? So you do know I'm not German."

"Of course I know."

"I don't like the nickname."

"I'll work on another one," she said, pulling away.

Each of them pretended not to notice that the other one was crying as they parted. Miles opened the rear door, told Jolie that they would talk in the morning and to stop giving her mother such a hard time, then got into the driver's seat and closed the door.

He gave a final wave to his partner in parenting.

Sloane waved back then started walking toward her new rental, expecting Jolie to follow.

She got into RAV4 Number Two and started the engine.

Jolie climbed in the passenger side, slammed her door, then got right to it. "Did you have fun talking about me?"

"We absolutely did."

"What did you talk about?"

Sloane ignored Jolie's question and grabbed her phone before backing out of the parking space, feeling dumb if not downright negligent when she saw three missed calls from Melinda.

She returned the call hands-free while backing out of her parking space.

"Sloane," Melinda answered.

"Sorry I missed all your calls. I was—"

"Is Jolie with you?"

"Yes. Liam Wentz had some goon pick her up and take her to Pirate Pizza. Unfortunately, Jolie was dumb enough to go right along with him. He didn't even have to entice her with candy."

"I can hear you, Mom!" Jolie informed her, clearly missing the point.

"Everyone is gone." She pulled out of the studio lot and turned right onto the street. "Do you know what happened with the police? Has anyone talked to Jake?"

"He woke up with a concussion. He was told that we wanted two people on Jolie. Wentz's guy apparently showed him a phony work order then prompted him into taking a bathroom break. Jake says he was attacked in the bathroom."

"*Apparently*," Sloane repeated. "*He says*. Am I sensing that you don't believe him?"

"We don't know what to believe. Dominic is furious and looking into it right now. Jake better pray he doesn't find anything."

"How is Jolie?"

"Awful."

"Did he hurt her?"

"Not like that," Sloane said. "I think this is all too much for her. Miles is taking her to Belgium. His parents have a farm not too far outside Bruges. They'll stay there until I'm finished with the shoot."

"NO WAY!" Jolie bellowed. "YOU CAN'T DO THAT!"

"So you haven't told her?" Melinda asked.

"I just did."

Jolie kept screaming, but by now it was just nonsense words and almost curses.

"I'm sorry to lose Miles, but it sounds like this is what's best for your family. I assume you'd like us to curate a few possible choices for his replacement."

"When can I see them?"

"First thing int he morning will be best."

"Your office or the house?"

"The house. We're up early."

Of course they were.

"I'm sorry about all this," Sloane said.

"Don't be. You can't risk him going after Jolie again. Getting her a continent away is the smart thing to do, the *right thing* to do. If one of her parents needs to be with her, then this is the most appropriate choice."

Melinda, always the pragmatist.

"Thanks," Sloane said.

"See you in the morning." Then Melinda was gone, leaving Sloane and her daughter alone.

"I hate you," Jolie said.

"I'm sure you do."

Chapter Twenty-Nine

Sloane

"Can you play Alejandro's reel one more time?" Sloane asked.

"Of course." Dominic pressed *play*.

She felt guilty for making the request, even though Dominic would never want her to. There were so many things to do and Sloane couldn't help but feel the time incessantly ticking. She didn't want to pick up her phone to check the time, but she must have been looking at the reels with Dominic for a few hours already. After last night's disaster with Jolie, and losing Miles as a result, yet another day on *Sunset* had been scrapped. Dominic had five choices for her to look through, and she'd had her eyes glued to sample work ever since two minutes after sitting down.

She hated that she was choosing her cinematographer this way. She preferred to fall in love with someone's perspective in one film, then get lost in their catalog. Sloane had a list of her favorites, but none were available. All five of Dominic's choices were award winners who could drop everything to help her. Sloane felt fortunate for the opportunity and resentful of the reality in unison.

Alejandro's reel finished with one piece of an incredible long take from *Soldier Boy* that reminded her a lot of the one in Brian DePalma's *Snake Eyes*. That scene had wowed her in the original film when she saw it in a Notting Hill theater, and it did its work here.

"It's between Alejandro and Baxter," she finally announced. "Is there a reason to go with one more than the other?"

"Alejandro is probably better overall. But Baxter is probably better at taking direction."

"You decide, I don't care." Sloane sighed and shook her head, hating that she wanted to cry. Then a sudden change of topic, more fitting to her state of mind. "To hell with plausible deniability — what are you doing to go after him?"

Dominic had been kind all morning. Somehow his voice managed to sound even gentler. "We've made progress, but I still can't tell you anything more than that until the details are locked down. I'm sorry."

"You don't have to be." Sloane shook her head, knowing she shouldn't have asked. "Thanks for everything you and Melinda have done for me."

"Of course." Another kind smile, followed by a nod.

"You're bailing me out again ... I owe you everything."

"No," Dominic said. "The only debt that's being paid back is the one Melinda and I owe Wentz for the underhanded tactics that asshole has used to compete with Shellter productions over the years. Soon, we'll have that paid off, and with an absurd amount of interest. In the meantime, I need you to promise that you'll finish the film."

"Shellter is about to have another Oscar-winning film

in its catalog," Sloane said, sitting up straighter to prove her faith.

"I absolutely believe that," Dominic said.

"I just wish ..." She shook her head.

"What?"

"Never mind."

"Sloane, we have a tremendous amount invested in you. If I can do something to make your job easier, tell me."

"I just wish I knew what you were doing. I know, I know—" She waved her hands "—plausible deniability. I get it. It's just hard for me to understand your commitment to bringing *him* down when these horrible things keep happening and I don't know what your plans are to stop it. But I appreciate all you're doing for me, and now that Jolie's safe, I'll be more focused. And when *Hollywood* is finished, *he'll* be finished, too."

His usual charming smile morphed into something predatory. When he spoke, his typical measured tone took a sudden and rather severe shift. "You take care of the movie. Melinda and I will take care of the rest. And if I can take a shit on Wentz's rotting corpse when it's all said and done, then all the better."

Sloane wasn't sure how to respond. She appreciated the faith, but Dominic's brutal addendum caught her by surprise. She was grateful to have lived for so long on his good side. The ruthlessness in his words and expression when discussing Wentz was downright terrifying.

But isn't that what she wanted and needed right now? Someone to hate that monster as much as she did? The Shellys had struck without mercy in front of her a few times before. They didn't obscure their intentions or actions because neither of them ever viewed their behavior as worthy of hiding. Melinda and Dominic hadn't always told Sloane everything, plausible deniability and all that, but they struck her as honest about who they were overall, even when it came to behaviors that might otherwise leave her with chills.

"Alejandro, please," Sloane said to fill the silence.

"Alejandro it is." Dominic offered Sloane his regular smile, followed by a change of subject. "How is it going with Orson?"

"Oh." The question caught her off guard. "Things are going ... good. I guess."

"There's nothing to be embarrassed about."

"I'm not embarrassed." Sloane was totally embarrassed.

"Of course we knew it was happening," Dominic said, not making her feel any better.

"He told you?"

"Orson would never do that, so no, but it's fair to say he knew we'd be aware. Beck is one of our biggest assets. You, and this film, are one of our biggest investments. Shellter Productions can't afford to be surprised by a romance between its top talent and its newest director, can we?"

"No ... I suppose not."

"You don't have to look like that." His voice was still so gentle. "Staying on top of the information doesn't mean we don't care about you or your feelings, Sloane. Nor does it mean Melinda or I see either of you as props. But you are both Shellter assets, and given the numbers involved, I'm sure we can all agree that the investments are substantial."

"Seems like you've made plenty on Orson."

"We have," Dominic agreed. "But not nearly as much as we're going to. And so far, nothing on you. The point is, staying ahead of the information helps us to manage it."

"You mean manage us."

"No." He shook his head. "I mean manage the perception. You've been through a trial by media before. You of all people should understand that controlling the story is everything. I didn't caution you against a relationship with Orson, nor did I force one upon you. But I do appreciate the development and can already see how we'll want to leverage this romance for—"

"You're always thinking about publicity." Sloane wasn't even sure if she meant that as an insult.

"Of course I am. That's my job. Isn't that what you want me to do? Isn't that my role in this, to make *West Hollywood Sunset* a CGI free blockbuster?"

"Yes, absolutely. I understand what you're saying, and I appreciate all the creative ways you and Melinda have to grab a ton of attention and make different parts of the business work together. I guess I just don't want my relationship with Orson to be part of the press junket."

His tone shifted, ever so slightly yet more than enough. "I'm sure I don't need to remind you about the night of your accident. The two of you got caught having dinner together. So you *already* decided this was going to happen. I had nothing to do with that, but you can bet I'll have something to do with how that reality is handled. Your relationship with Orson will be part of the *Sunset* press because whether or not that was your intention, *you* made that happen. And now, we might as well use it to our advantage."

"So I should just get over it." A statement instead of a question.

"There are consequences to dating one of the most famous men in the world." Dominic smiled, not saying the words, but yes, it was time for her to get over it.

Even if she couldn't argue with his logic, Sloane didn't

like the feeling that the Shellys were using her ... at least not more than she was using them.

"Thanks again." She stood.

"You'll love Alejandro."

"I'm looking forward to it."

"Monday. We'll get this right." Dominic walked Sloane to the door, then brightened thanks to whatever he saw on the other side. "Selena! Are you here to see Melinda?"

As Sloane got closer to the door, she saw a woman who appeared to be in her early fifties. She had a wide smile, pleasant wrinkles, and a big head of healthy blonde hair. Selena Nash. Sloane was a fan.

"I'm early," Selena said, her voice carrying the slightest hint of a Texas drawl. "I drove down from Almond Park, but there was zero traffic until I hit LA, so I have like half an hour before we're supposed to meet. Don't worry about me, though, I've been reading." She held up her phone to show them.

"Selena, meet Sloane Alexander. She's working on one of our marquee projects. Sloane, meet Selena Nash. She's been invaluable as a consultant for us, and host of—"

"I watch your show," Sloane said, surprised to feel a little embarrassed. "I love it."

"Thank you." Then, looking every bit as abashed as Sloane felt, Selena added, "*Remaking Christmas* is the best."

"I'll let Melinda know you're here, but she might not be able to—"

"Really, don't worry about me." Selena held up her phone again. "I'll be fine."

"I can keep her company," Sloane offered, surprising herself again.

"Well, then, I'll leave you ladies to it." Then Dominic closed the door with yet another smile.

Sloane sat next to her. "So, do you—"

"I'm sorry, but I gotta ask," Selena said, cutting her off. "You don't have to tell me, and I know all about the Shellys' NDAs and whatever, but I'm also involved in several of their projects, and you just have to tell me …" She leaned in and whispered, "Are you making a movie about Liam Wentz?"

"I am." Sloane nodded, proud to tell her.

"I hope you bury him alive. He's a quintessential predator. There's nothing you can do to that man that he doesn't deserve."

"What makes you say that? I mean, of course I agree, but do you have … first-hand knowledge? Have you talked to someone he hurt?"

"Nothing first hand, no. But I've read a few anonymous accounts. And I've seen hours of interviews. Glib, full of superficial charm, a grandiose sense of self-worth." Selena seemed to get angrier as she spoke. "Pathological lying, the manipulation of others, a total lack of empathy or remorse." She shook her head. "And zero ability to accept personal responsibility."

Selena seemed equally fascinated and engaged.

Sloane was both acutely uncomfortable and rooted to her seat.

She wanted to stay as long as Selena kept talking, while also feeling the need to flee immediately.

"That all sounds a lot like Liam Wentz," Sloane replied.

"The problem is that we don't know enough about his childhood to figure out what broke him."

"Does it have to be something from his childhood?"

"It doesn't *have to be*, but it usually is. With men like him, anti-social behaviors and poor impulse control are usually present during or prior to adolescence. That's also the period in their lives when they first learn to obscure their nature and deflect the sort of investigative attention that might promote the wrong kind of question."

"You mean that's when they learn to manipulate everything and everyone around them?"

"Yes, that's absolutely right," Selena agreed. "That's when they learn to operate."

"Like how?" Sloane had heard a lot of this from her childhood therapist, but it sounded more direct, and somehow more valuable, coming from Selena. Maybe she was better at this than Dr. Diana had been, or maybe Sloane was simply more able to hear it now.

"Like, all the stuff you lived through. The quiet little horrors Wentz used to manipulate you and Nicole and who knows how many other little girls before or since."

"So, gaining our trust."

"Not just your trust, but your mothers'."

"He might have been able to write a check for that," Sloane bitterly replied. "At least in my case."

"Do you really believe that?"

"No." Selena's question made their exchange feel a little too much like therapy for her comfort, but Sloane knew it was her fault for saying that. She shook her head. "Not really."

"What you really mean is that your mother didn't make you feel protected."

"No. She didn't."

"And yet, that's what you needed from her more than anything else."

"Yes. It was."

"I'm sorry about that." Selena nodded and gently touched Sloane on the arm. "Do you feel that on some subconscious level your mom knew what was happening?"

She nodded, now wanting to cry. None of this was new, but it had been a while since she'd said any of it out loud.

"He would always give me presents, and I never wanted his presents, but Mom said I had to take them because it would be rude to refuse them."

"Presents like what?"

"Like jewelry or clothes … one time underwear."

"Underwear?" Selena repeated. "That's … bold."

"They weren't lacy or sexy or anything, just a pack of multicolored underwear in there with a bunch of other clothes and stuff. But I told her that it made me uncomfortable, and she said I was making too big a deal about it. Just like when he wanted to talk about sex."

Selena shifted in her seat, appearing bothered, though not at all surprised. "What did he want to talk about."

"*Sex,*" Sloane repeated, before she explained. "I don't even remember the specifics. I was too young to have the context for what he was saying, or really understand any of it, which looking back now I can see what he was trying to do. Those exchanges were wildly inappropriate, but that was the point. He was trying to make sex sound normal, or even fun, despite how young I was."

"Right." Selena nodded. "It wasn't just the actions, he was making an effort to desensitize you to the vocabulary around sex. How often did he touch you — casually, I mean?"

"All the time. He used to hug me a lot, then he started kissing me on the top of my head all the time, before he moved to my cheek."

Selena was shaking her head. "Like I said, Liam Wentz is the quintessential predator. It's horrifying what we do know about him. I don't even want to consider the worst possibilities."

"What do you mean?"

"That man has a *lot* of power, and he also has a lot of property, meaning he can do whatever he wants if he finds the right place to do it. What if he's abducted some poor young girl? Not even an actress, but maybe someone from another country that no one is even looking for?"

Sloane hated every part of this conversation, but that didn't mean it was one she had any ability to stop. "What kind of places?"

Selena rattled off her response, apparently thrilled to have an answer ready. "If he had such a place, it would need to be close enough to his home base that he could come and go without a lot of fuss. Easy in, easy out, and no one watching. It could be a red-light area where most people are almost professionally minding their own business. Maybe the basement or back room of a night club or bar. An isolated landscape, or derelict area of the city where people are used to looking the other way."

"What about—"

Sloane stopped as two things happened in unison. One, her phone sounded with a newly installed ringtone for Orson — the Gorillaz' *Clint Eastwood,* a choice she still wasn't sure of — and two, Melinda appeared on the other side of an opening door.

"Selena! It's great to see you." She glanced at Sloane. "Dominic told me the two of you were out here. I'm glad you had the chance to meet."

Sloane silenced her still ringing phone, then looked up at her new friend with a smile. "Well, I guess that's time."

Selena pulled a business card from her purse then handed it over to Sloane. "If you need anything at all, just give me a call. Anytime. I'm happy to help however I can."

"I will." She probably wouldn't. "Thank you."

Sloane wanted to stick around and hear all the things Selena might say, especially now that Melinda was joining the party. But she didn't want to overstay her welcome, and she was suddenly very interested in what Orson might have to say.

So she said her goodbyes then excused herself, returning his call on her way to the car.

"You mind meeting me somewhere?" Orson asked without much of a hello.

"You sure we're allowed to do that?" Sloane asked, sounding a lot snippier than she meant to. "We should really be more careful about how we treat each other in public."

"This won't be in public." Orson's reply felt like an arrow. "This is important."

"Of course," she said, ashamed of her attitude. "Just tell me where."

She hated the answer, but that wasn't about to stop her.

"I'm on my way."

Chapter Thirty

Sloane

SLOANE TOOK the pipe when Orson passed it her way, finally no longer embarrassed, then took a long drag of some truly delicious weed.

"I know, right?" Ellis grinned at her.

She nodded, holding the smoke, amused by Ellis and, surprisingly, this entire situation.

Sloane had been sitting on his ancient couch for more than an hour now, and she still wasn't sure what intrigued her most — The Brick, the weed, or Ellis Hunt Himself.

Orson had asked her to meet him in his old neighborhood so he could introduce her to the "guy who might know more about Hollywood grime than anyone else in the world." Sloane wasn't sure if that was even remotely close to true and didn't think she wanted to be anywhere near to such a person if so. But he texted her the address to The Brick and she started her drive from the Shellys to Orson's old dump immediately.

The building was six stories and looked more than a

century old, with at least half of those decades having forgotten the place enough to make it look like a crack den. The Brick was surrounded by newer buildings that appeared superior in every conceivable way, and according to the plaque out front, was actually called *The Regency*.

Orson was waiting outside when she arrived. He took her by the arm then gently led her up the steps, past a pair of what Sloane assumed had to be prostitutes — one male and the other female — judging by the way they were dressed, and their offer of for a little on-the-clock stress relief, then past a man who might have been the oldest person she had ever seen.

"How are you this fine afternoon?" the old man had wanted to know as Orson ushered her by.

"That's Angus," Orson said, as if that explained everything.

Up six flights of stairs because the elevator apparently only worked every other leap year, then Ellis was waiting outside his door, perhaps to make sure his friends weren't accosted on their way up from the lobby.

Ellis was a large man with a big red beard and intense yet friendly eyes. His presence, in a word, felt *honest.* And as deeply uncomfortable as Sloane had felt a few seconds before seeing him, despite having Orson by her side, something about the guy put her at immediate ease.

And that was before the Green Unicorn.

Though Ellis didn't grow the weed himself, he might as well have considering how proud he was of the strain. It was "practically magic," he said, and Orson agreed. Green Unicorn came from Humboldt, and there was only one farm in the world that grew it, though copycats were becoming a cottage industry. Sloane's Hollywood child-hood had permanently scared her off of drinking and drugs. That included weed, but after a little eye rolling from Orson and Ellis, she finally surrendered to a curiosity she'd been carrying for the last fifteen years by deciding to partake.

Ellis took another drag, still shaking his head in mild bewilderment. To Orson, he said, "I still can't believe that her first time riding is on a unicorn."

"Now she understands." Orson took the pipe then a hit of his own.

"What do I understand?"

"That cannabis is the remedy," Ellis answered, pulling a hit before passing to Sloane.

"To what?" Sloane asked, taking the pipe.

Ellis grinned. "What'dya got?"

She considered her answer while holding the smoke in her lungs, then used the prompt to recover their earlier, and much more pertinent, conversation. "Is it the remedy to pedophile predators in Hollywood?"

Ellis took the pipe from her then set it on the coffee table with a sad little shake of his head. "No. Alas, it is not. But fortunately, we do have a few ways to hit back. Thanks to Cary Grant here."

"I see myself as more of a Paul Newman," Orson said.

"You wish." Ellis snorted.

"Liam Wentz." Sloane returning them to center again, though she wanted to laugh, long and completely out of control. "Ways to hit back?"

Ellis abruptly guffawed, and given what he'd said a few minutes earlier regarding his tolerance, she didn't think it had anything to do with the weed. "It's sort of an embarrassment of riches."

"I've never smoked before, so maybe I'm missing something obvious, but I don't understand."

Ellis glanced at the coffee table and Sloane felt sure he would reach for the pipe, but then he laughed again. "I've been after that creep as long as I've worked on *Hunted*. But I've never had enough to nail the guy. And with his resources, it's best to stay invisible until—"

"Oh, I understand." Then she laughed, even though it wasn't remotely funny.

"I did have a little, though," he continued, "and when combined with the what I got after talking to Melinda, then her friend, Elle, we now have a lot."

He laughed again, this time with a self-satisfied shake of his head.

"Is he always such a cock tease?" Sloane asked her new boyfriend.

Was he her new boyfriend?

Orson exploded with laughter, but only partly from the weed. "I'm not sure I've ever heard you swear!"

"I swear." Sloane said *damn* every once in a while but never included a deity.

"I don't know anything about Elle, or even if she was using her real name. But I believed everything she said, and—"

"What makes you believe her?" Orson asked.

"We talked about this. I—"

"Not for me." Orson tipped his head at Sloane. "For her."

"Oh. Well, you talk to enough people and you get a sixth sense for bullshit, but it's more that the lead came from Melinda Shelly. I'm getting pulled into an *enemy of my enemy is my friend* situation here, so I'd be an idiot to not ride this gift horse as hard as I can."

"You don't have to convince me. I've known Melinda for most of my life."

Ellis looked at Sloane like he had something to say, then opened his mouth and quite obviously said something else. "Elle, or whatever her name was, put me in touch with three different women, all with distinct yet echoing stories about Liam Wentz from when they were little girls."

"No way," Sloane said in awe.

"A swearer would've said *no shit*," Orson told her.

Ellis kept going. "*Way.* None of them will go on record *yet*, but I'm sure that at least two of the three will once the appropriate protections are in place. And the third …" He gave it a moment's thought then eventually nodded, "Yeah, I'm gonna say she's an eventual lock as well."

"If there are three, there's probably thirty," Orson added.

"Agreed." Ellis nodded then finally reached for the pipe. "We just need the dam to burst." He took a hit, passed it to Sloane, then blew a plume of smoke into the air. "One of Elle's three girls ended up leading me to a fourth that I don't even think Elle knows about."

"Have you told her?" Sloane asked, passing to Orson. "Or Melinda?"

"Not yet." Ellis shook his head.

Sloane laughed, in euphoria and delight. "I'm not sure I've ever known anything before the Shellys, except for maybe when I might need to use the restroom."

"Seriously." His face turned sober before Ellis continued. "I spoke to that fourth girl's mother."

"Oh, no …" Sloane could feel something terrible lurking on the other side of his thought. "What happened to the girl?"

Ellis glanced at the carpet before looking at Sloane. "She killed herself. A few months ago."

"Eight years after Wentz paid her mother off," Orson said, apparently having heard the story already. He returned the pipe to the coffee table.

"Shit." Sloane sank down into the couch. "I guess you can't tell me who it is?"

"No." He shook his head. "Sorry. But I'm sure you'll know eventually. This story is coming out. The mom was just … that was a rough conversation, man. The girl never made it as an actress. Her mom thinks she didn't have a chance. Wentz never even intended to give her a role. He just wanted something to play with. She did what he asked, but nothing ever happened for her."

"Shit," Sloane said again.

"Much better." Orson nodded approval.

"The layers of guilt in her voice were hard to handle. It's possible she had a hand in things, not directly, but sin of omission stuff. I'm not really sure, people are capable of telling themselves all sorts of stories as a means to live with their mistakes. She did explain her guilt, though, saying she ignored all the signs, even the ones that seemed so obvious in retrospect. Even worse, she didn't speak out on her daughter's behalf when she found out what was happening. Not until it already happened. This was about a year before your story hit the tabloids. She saw that and it made her wonder how many other girls there were."

"So that's when she contacted Wentz and got the payout?"

"Right." Ellis nodded. "According to Mom, the money never helped. Her daughter never got better. The depression came and went, but mostly stuck around until she couldn't take it anymore. Now, all of that is terrible, but there is some great news."

"She's willing to tell her story on the record?" Sloane guessed.

"She's willing to tell her story on the record," Ellis confirmed with a satisfied shake of his head. "Best of all, she's believable. I really think this is all just the first bellow to bring down the avalanche." He shook his head. "I seriously can't believe we have the Shellys to thank for it."

Sloane said, "The Shellys aren't who you think they are."

"The Shellys are *exactly* who I think they are," Ellis replied.

"Orson?" She said, expecting him to defend them.

He shrugged. "He's harsher than we are about the Shellys, but not unfair."

"You act like they're terrible people, and yet they're helping to put an end—"

"They're doing whatever it takes to protect, preserve, and promote their empire." Ellis glanced at the coffee table, but ignored his impulse. "Look, I get it, and I swear, there's no judgment coming from me. The Shellys are morally flexible. They've been responsible for some terrible shit, including things done to friends of mine, like that smug looking Paul Newman wannabe sitting right beside you, but they all benefit from what the Shellys have done for them, and I suppose the same is true for you."

Ellis gave her a shrug, looking seriously confused about his feelings on the topic, then went on with his rant. "They are also geniuses who have done some remarkable things, and the more I learn about them, the more interested I am in what their future holds, not just for them, but for all of us." Another shrug. "In an industry as dirty and corrupt as this one, I guess the Shellys understand that they have to live their lives in battle, and never lower their sword or shield. Not my life, but like I said, I get it."

"Enough of your monologuing about the Shellys." Orson looked from Sloane to Ellis. "Maybe she hasn't heard your tirades on repeat, but I have. We've been sitting too long, I'm going to need a walk soon. Can we please get back to—"

"Sorry Newman. I forgot how much my sedentary life-style offended you." Ellis turned from Orson to Sloane.

"We put these new leads with the ones I already had, and now have a half-dozen girls who've been victimized by Wentz in the past and are now willing to come forward, so long as they're not alone. Considering the issue, we'll need a surgical level of media manipulation. And *that* is something I'd trust the Shellys on, more than just about anyone else in the world."

"You do realize that's not a compliment, right?" Orson asked.

Sloane was apparently still laughing at things that weren't funny. She looked at Ellis, trying to decipher his strange expression, then turned to Orson and saw that he was doing the same thing thing.

"What is it?" Orson asked. "Why do you look like that?"

"Because I said, 'We now have a half-dozen girls who have been victimized in the past.' But we *also* have two girls he's currently molesting. One of them even has a video of 'Wentz at his worst.' I've not seen the recording yet, but the evidence has just started coming in, and there's already enough that there's no way he'll never be able to bury it all."

"You might be surprised," Sloane said.

"No." He shook his head. "I wouldn't be."

"He wouldn't be," Orson agreed.

"But you are right that even if the evidence is enough to finish him off in court, doing so will take years, and he's a master at manipulating public opinion. For this all to work, Hollywood needs to turn against Wentz in a way that would will make it impossible for him to fight back with money. People need to see the suffering he's caused in these girls' lives. Again, that's where your Shellys come in."

"They're not *our* Shellys," Orson said.

Sloane's head was swimming.

And it had nothing to do with the Green Unicorn.

But everything to do with what was surely the best idea of her entire life.

Orson pointed to her. "Now it's on her face."

She barked laughter. Again, nothing to do with the Unicorn.

"What is it?" Ellis asked.

So she told them.

Chapter Thirty-One

Sloane

THE SHELLYS KEPT LOOKING at Sloane, but so far neither had spoken.

That was fine, she could wait. For the first time in her entire history with the Shellys, she wasn't going to break. She presented her idea and dropped the mic. Now it was their turn to talk, however long that might take them.

They traded a glance, and in their mostly masked expressions Sloane could see the faintest trace of a smile on each of their faces. Melinda and Dominic both liked her new idea, so far as she could tell, and they might even love it. She was surely seeing a lot of mental math and writing on the backs of imaginary napkins happening without any words passed between husband and wife.

It was surreal to see the Shellys communicating with only a glance, or a brushed knuckle against an arm, like Dominic was doing to Melinda right now.

She looked up at her husband. Nodded and smiled

with the tiniest shake of her head. But still, neither of them said a word.

The anticipation filled Sloane with a new kind of anxiety. But this one she didn't mind. The temptation was ever-present, but she managed to stay in front of it.

So … thoughts?

But she wouldn't — *she couldn't* — ask.

She folded her hands and crossed her legs instead.

"It's an excellent idea," Dominic finally said.

"There are a few particulars to work out, but I agree, this is very interesting," Melinda added.

"I'm surprised we didn't think of it our—"

"We couldn't have, darling. The pieces wouldn't have fit if we were forcing them together. This only works *because* it's Sloane's idea."

"True." He nodded, looking from Melinda to Sloane, still apparently over the moon.

She was flooded with relief. Of course there would be particulars to work out — there were *always* particulars to work out. It only mattered that the Shellys appreciated what she wanted to do.

Now that she knew they did, everything else could finally fall into place.

And so much simpler than ever before.

"It's a big shift, even if it's the right one," Dominic said.

"Mind if we ask what made you want to change directions?"

Sloane nodded. "I guess I finally saw *West Hollywood Sunset* for what it really was.*"*

"And what's that?" Melinda asked.

"Something that's all about me."

Dominic nodded. "Go on …"

"It's a fantasy. A film about how I *wished* things had

ended up after Liam Wentz flipped my life upside down and turned what felt like the entire world against me. But that makes the movie about *me*, which means it can't really affect change the way we all want it to." She shook her head. "I don't want to shoot a film that focuses on the past, or even the present. I want to make a movie that works for a better future instead."

"And thus," Melinda said, "a documentary."

"Exactly. If we make a movie about the current generation of Liam Wentz's victims then we'll be giving them a voice, and talking about something that's *happening* instead of something that's *already happened.*"

"It's an excellent idea," Dominic repeated, wrapping a bow around his earlier thought.

"So, what now? What should I be doing next?"

"There's a lot for us to work out," Melinda replied.

"But we no longer have to worry about being over budget with either time or money, right?" Sloane asked.

"Right." Melinda nodded. "This is a more straightforward project in every way. Let's get Lila in here and the four of us can cut our crew to the essentials."

"I'm not sure we even need that," Sloane said. "We'll need a few locations and a basic setup. But I'd prefer to interview the girls myself."

"That's a non-negotiable," Dominic said.

"The kill fees will be substantial," Melinda seemed to be talking mostly to herself, "but this is still a much more cost-efficient film all of a sudden."

Orson already knew, having been present at the birth of her idea, but Sloane couldn't wait to tell Miles or dig into the details.

She didn't have to wait long. The Shellys were hammered for the rest of the day, but they told Sloane not to worry about a thing. They would take care of communicating everything to the cast and crew, then everyone could reconvene in the morning to make a plan.

Three days later, Sloane was working on an entirely new project and over the moon to be doing so. Miles was relieved at the change in direction but still wanted to take Jolie to Belgium until the project was finished and was planning to leave in a week or so.

Orson was on set, but only because he wanted to be, sticking around for emotional support and probably to feed his own sense of curiosity.

John and Vicky were there as well. When not the subject of their well-meaning interrogations, Sloane found that she liked them a lot. They were full of storytelling insights, always taking notes or making suggestions, telling her which questions to ask each interviewee, along with those to avoid. She was using her own story as a general framing device, and her experience to deliver a sympathetic interview with each and every girl.

Individual accounts were full of expected yet devastating narratives, even hearing a fraction of each story was enough to flood her with chills.

Adrianna Womak: "I was auditioning for a role and Liam Wentz asked me to pose for him, promising that the pictures would never go anywhere. He said that Pierre, the director, needed to see more of me. It was only a small job, but I was on the way to having my dream career. But then Liam wanted more, threatening to send those pics around or release them on the web to destroy my reputation. I didn't know what to do, so I said okay, and that's when things went from photos to sex. When I finally stood up to him and told Liam I was going to the police, he told me my parents had some tax issues that could get them into big trouble. I have no idea how he knew that, but he was right. He told me my parents would either be going to jail or not, it all depended on me. So I stayed quiet and did everything he asked until he finally lost interest."

Cori Long: "Liam Wentz brought me to a party to meet a director that supposedly thought I was perfect for a role. But I never got to meet Reginald Mank. That didn't matter all that much, at first. Liam was still charming and made me look like a star to everybody there. Then someone handed me a drink. I woke up naked in a bed and knew something bad had happened, but I didn't know who did it. I went to Liam, upset as I'm sure you can imagine, but he said I got drunk and kept coming onto a bunch of guys at the party. Liam also said he was pretty sure they had filmed it, and that it would be in my best interests to 'drop it immediately and never think about it again.' Things got worse after that. I still don't even know if that supposed movie ever existed, but I was scared enough to do whatever he wanted me to for a while. I should have just gone to the authorities, but I'd heard the old stories, of course, and figured everyone would think I was lying. Besides, and *believe me*, I know how stupid this sounds, Liam convinced me he actually cared for me."

Eva Bankes: "It started innocently enough. I had a drunk mother who was your typical stage mom monster, and I had zero freedom in my life. As my career took off, she kept more and more of my money. Liam Wentz was the only one who listened to me. He offered me ways to keep my money and reclaim control over my life. He helped me to get emancipated, and then he put me up in a nice place. I finally had freedom and was living my dream, even though I was still just a little girl. But then Liam also offered me escape, in the form of drugs. Which of course I got addicted to. He used that addiction to get me in bed. He made me fuck him and his friends until I wound up overdosing one night and waking up in rehab two days later. I told the people there, but they were all scared of him. Even the ones who believed me said it was best just to drop it, especially since he didn't "technically" force me into anything. I always had a choice, an option. I know that was bullshit, and that regardless of my emancipation I still wasn't old enough to consent, but I sure as hell *felt* like an adult, and was scared that if I did anything, Liam would destroy all that I had. He threatened to do exactly that, every single day."

The stories went on and on and on. Sloane worried that they had "too much footage" and was ready to wrap well ahead of the deadline.

"There is no such thing as too much footage," Dominic told her, already planning on turning the feature into an eventual series, assuming its legs were as long as he and Melinda kept thinking.

Sloane was finished with her final interview for the day when Ellis walked on-set with yet another and all the breath left her body. Despite the subject matter of her interviews, it was still the last person she expected to see.

"Nicole," she whispered.

"Sloane," Nicole whispered back.

And then, quite suddenly, they were sobbing in each other's arms.

Both of their faces were wet when they pulled away from one another, but so were others in the room, including Ellis and Orson.

"I heard you were looking for victims of Liam Wentz …" Nicole gave the room a tiny, awkward laugh as she raised a hand and gave it a wave. "I'm here."

Nicole's interview was long and exhausting for everyone, not only covering the nightmare of what Liam Wentz had done to her, but the horror of dealing with the media aftermath as well. The questions were hard for Sloane to ask, and often seemed even harder for Nicole to answer, but together they made it through every one, her former rival now on a mission to tell the world that Sloane had never been lying.

"So, how are you feeling today?" she asked Nicole as they neared the end of her interview.

"Better than I ever have." She wiped a tear. "But I'm still trying to work through the psychological damage with MDMA-therapy, after years of numbing myself with alcohol and drugs ... and whatever."

"Isn't MDMA a drug?"

"Sure, but it's not for numbing out," Nicole said. "MDMA is the opposite."

"That's molly, right?"

"Not exactly. Molly and ecstasy can have MDMA in them, but they're often mixed with other fillers. And it's not like I'm taking the drug at a rave. MDMA-therapy is just more direct than talk therapy, for me, because I'm forced to digest my experiences."

"How so?"

"The drug quiets the amygdala."

"The fear center," Sloane said.

"Right. Meaning I can explore the trauma without being overwhelmed by it."

"Sounds a lot like this conversation." Sloane wiped a tear from each side of her face.

"I'm glad we're finally talking ..." Nicole had been stoic throughout the entire interview, only needing to break twice. Once for water and a second time to use the restroom. But now she finally lost it. Both of them did.

Then they stood from their chairs, crossed the narrow distance between, and fell into another embrace.

"I was so sure that you hated me," Nicole blubbered through her tears.

"I thought you hated me …" Sloane worked to gain control of her breath and voice so she could say what she needed to. "I always felt so terrible that I couldn't make anyone believe me, and I was always weighed down by the guilt that I couldn't convince you to stay away from him … before it was too late. I escaped, but you never did—"

"No." Nicole sounded suddenly sharp, and was looking right into her old friend's eyes, the pair of them seemingly oblivious to all the spectators still in the room. "You can ask me again and I'll say it for the interview — not that it matters since we're no longer speaking — but this was all my mother's fault. She encouraged me to do whatever Liam wanted for the sake of my career. There was nothing you could have ever said to convince me. I'm *glad* you escaped, and I loved that you thrived despite all the negative publicity. I've always been your biggest fan."

"Let's take him down—" Sloane started, still sobbing, but now with the best kind of tears.

"*Together,*" her oldest friend finished.

The moment would have made her day perfect.

If it hadn't been for the next one that came just ten seconds later.

Chapter Thirty-Two

Sloane

SLOANE WOULD NORMALLY IGNORE her phone entirely at a time like this.

But it wasn't on *Do Not Disturb* because Miles was leaving with Jolie in the morning and despite having lived most of his life as a nomad, he was still a nervous traveler.

So she glanced at the device.

She didn't usually answer calls from unlisted or private numbers. Too many solicitors, journalists, and emotional scars from dealing with both of them, the second much more than the first.

But this was a text. From an unknown number.

Then she was staring down at the screen with a heart that quite suddenly wanted to pound right out of her chest.

She clicked the text and the pounding stopped.

For the most frightening moment of Sloane Alexander's life, her heart was no longer beating, and she couldn't draw a breath at all.

She pressed *Play* on the video, then watched in horror

as a camera panned over Miles, tied to a chair and beaten to a pulp, then over to their cowering daughter.

A disembodied voice added an audible disease to the video. The sound was disguised with distortion, but Sloane had zero difficulty identifying its source.

"It's time for us to play, little kitten," said the nightmare.

A second before the video cut to black.

Sloane looked up from the video and into a dozen dumbfounded stares.

Orson broke the silence. "Call the cops right—"

"I can't call the cops! They never do—"

"They will this time. He's gone too far, given you proof."

Sloane shook her head, feeling like she might melt right into the floor. "They couldn't see that he was behind the sabotage on set or the hit and run. They never even found the guy who attacked Jake." Her voice kept rising in pitch and her arms were wild. She felt like she might have a seizure. "Don't you realize that he *owns* the police!"

It wasn't even a question. But Orson didn't argue. Instead, he held her, investing ten long seconds into calming her down. Then he said, "I'm not suggesting that's our only move, but we should call the—"

"Wait!" Sloane suddenly had an idea.

She remembered talking to Selena outside Dominic's office.

That man has a lot of power, and he also has a lot of property.

Meaning he can do whatever he wants if he finds the right place to do it.

"What is it?" Orson asked.

But Sloane didn't know how to say what she was thinking. Not yet.

Close enough to his home base that he could come and go without a lot of fuss.

Easy in, easy out, and no one watching.

It could be a red-light area where most people are almost professionally minding their own business.

Maybe the basement or back room of a night club or bar. An isolated landscape or derelict area of the city where people are used to looking the other way.

Another question from Orson. "What are you doing?"

Sloane ignored him. She was thinking too many things at once and couldn't afford to sacrifice even a splinter of her attention to answer. Instead, she dialed the phone.

It was answered after one ring. "Hello."

"Melinda!"

"What's wrong?"

"Can you get a list of all the property Liam Wentz owns in or around LA?"

"Of course," Melinda said. "Why?"

"He has Miles and Jolie." Normally Sloane would have been on the verge of tears, but right now she felt only outrage and an unrelenting, savage fury. "Selena said he might have a place that's isolated, where he could—"

"He has property down off Wall, by the flower market. It's a three-story building. An old hotel from like a hundred years ago, from back when the Southern Pacific stopped on Central Avenue. He uses it as a place to shoot every once in a while, but I understand he's holding onto it as a legitimate investment for when the city's zoning adjustment allows for units smaller than 450 square feet in size. That might be what you're looking for. I'll text you the address."

Sloane hung up with Melinda to find everyone still staring at her.

She turned to Ellis. "I need you to call the cops. Tell

them anything you think they might need to know and make sure they're aware that this is a hostage situation."

"On it."

Orson was heading toward the door as she dashed right past him. "Wait, Sloane. I'm coming with you."

"With me?" she called over her shoulder. "No. You're driving me. Now!"

Chapter Thirty-Three

Sloane

SLOANE WASN'T sure if she preferred the quiet or not.

Orson had been dead silent ever since leaving Shellter, and her eyes were closed through most of the trip as she focused on her breath, working not to lose her goddamned mind.

She was trapped in her nightmare, fingers digging into her knee, finally opening her eyes only to see how close they might be to finding Jolie.

"Three more minutes, I'm guessing," he said.

"Go faster!"

"I'm going dangerously fast already. Just another—"

"GO FASTER! Maybe a cop will start following you."

Orson floored it. Turned a corner. And then another one.

"Half a mile," he said.

Sloane's heart was beating out of her chest.

This was all her fault. If she was going to play with fire, then she should have left Jolie in a place where she couldn't get burned. It was selfish of her to have ever wanted — *needed*, she had told him — Miles for this project. Sloane could have found another cinematographer, but Jolie needed her father around, if her mother was determined to live on a tightrope between skyscrapers.

If anything happened to Jolie, she would never forgive herself.

"That's it." Orson nodded at a three-story structure that made The Brick look like an *Architectural Digest* centerfold. Its last paint job had been white, but the entire building was now peeling and gray, with the top two floors full of broken windows and — from what she could see through the holes where windows used to be — the bottom floor decorated with sleeping homeless, shopping carts, and an untold number of thirty-two-gallon bags of trash.

A man with a beard that reached past his nipples was dropping trou and squatting as they slammed the doors to Orson's car then ran across the street.

She set her phone to record, then dropped it into the front pocket of her flannel shirt, just in case.

They tried all the doors and found every one of them locked.

Onlookers outside were staring — no one seemed to notice that one of the two people attempting a break-in of this derelict building was a world-famous actor. So, no subscribers to Variety.

"They got in." Sloane gestured to the people inside. "How do we?"

Orson answered by bashing his foot against the door, next to the keyhole where the lock was mounted, four times until it finally crashed out of the frame.

"I learned to do that while I was making *First Watch*," he explained.

She wasn't thrilled to lose the element of surprise, or in any position to complain.

"Thank you," she tried not to whimper, much too frightened to say anything else.

Orson didn't answer. He *couldn't* answer.

Either they had made enough noise to announce their presence or they'd been expected. Either way, there was a Shaq-sized goon pointing a Dirty Harry-sized pistol in their faces.

"I loved you in *F the 90s*," said the goon.

"Please. I just—"

"You can shut up." He waved the gun in her face. "I can't stand Christmas movies."

Shaq waved the gun again, this time with purpose, ushering them out of a filthy lobby that reeked of urine and feces and worse. Surely someone had died in this place.

Maybe more deaths would be coming.

Orson tried to take her hand but the goon ordered him to stop. "None of that."

Then he led them out of the lobby, up two ancient flights of stairs, then down a long grimy hallway to an open door at the end. Shaq waved his gun yet again, this time at the entrance. "Both of you. Inside."

Orson went first.

Sloane followed him into the next part of her nightmare.

Shaq stood slightly off to the side, in between them and the hideous scene.

She felt a flicker of relief then the feeling faded to black. Sloane was glad to see Miles alive, but he was tied to his chair, badly beaten and apparently unconscious. Jolie looked fresh-faced but terrified, which filled her mother with a raw fear that somehow felt even worse than the uncertainty of a moment ago.

Liam Wentz was standing behind Jolie with his hands on the little girl's shoulders.

"Mommy …" she whimpered.

The monster smiled at Orson and Sloane, but instead of greeting the newcomers, he bent down and whispered something in Jolie's ear.

Her lip quivered and she said nothing else.

Sloane didn't need to know what it was. Gravity sent her straight to the floor. Needing to vomit and down on her knees, she started to beg.

"Take me. I'll do whatever you want. Just—"

He silenced her pleas with his laughter, slowly approaching her, apparently not realizing that he was partially blocking the goon's shot if Sloane were to make any sudden moves.

Maybe he knew that she would never have the courage.

She tried again. "Please … whatever you like … I can …"

But Sloane couldn't even finish her thought.

And Liam Wentz was back laughing again. "You're not the fresh-faced little thing you used to be."

"I can try!" What a worthless thing to say.

And he knew it. "Sorry. Not interested." Then he looked down at Jolie with a vile little smile and said, "I have what I need now."

"PLEASE!" She begged, louder and harder. "I'm sorry I never let you touch me — you were right, maybe I would have liked it if I'd given it a chance. I'm sorry I told on you. I'm sorry I talked to Nicole. And I'm sorry about my movie."

"*Movies*," he snarled.

"Movies," she repeated with a vigorous nod. "I won't make any of them. Please, just let us go. Let *her* go."

"It's too late for any of that." He squeezed Jolie's shoulders then walked away from her, slowly approaching Sloane instead.

"It's not too late, Wentz." Orson, making his best attempt. "We can still figure this out. We're both too high profile — this whole thing is too high profile. Everyone knows where we were going and why. The police will be here any minute now. You can't just make us disappear."

"Can't I?" He looked at Orson as though the actor was only a boy who didn't understand a thing.

"I forgive you for everything. Please can we—"

"There's nothing to forgive ..." He smiled as he stood over Sloane, plucked the phone from the breast pocket, then looked down at the screen to see she had been actively recording. He shook the phone in front of her but smiled again. "This hardly seems like the act of someone in a forgiving mood."

Liam Wentz didn't seem like a man who was even the least bit afraid of the police.

And right now, that was the most horrifying thing in the world.

She glanced at Orson. He was looking around, clearly searching for some means of either attack or escape, probably both.

"Face front," Shaq ordered him, with yet another little shake of his gun.

Her heart felt bruised, pounding hard as it was against her ribcage. But Sloane didn't care if Liam Wentz killed her, so long as Jolie got away.

Her gaze locked on her daughter. She screamed, "RUN!"

Jolie darted for the door.

Wentz grabbed a handful of Sloane's hair. She clawed at his hand, but she couldn't break free of his grasp.

"Get the girl!" Then he slammed Sloane into the wall.

Pain exploded in her head. Her vision grayed.

Shaq turned toward them, angling for a clear shot.

Wentz pounded her into the wall again.

Sloane fought to remain conscious. Struggled against Wentz's grip. Flung her body back just enough to obscure Shaq's shot as the monster kept trying to shove her against the brick on repeat.

Orson ran over to the goon and attempted to tackle him, but that was a suicide mission.

"The girl!" Wentz bellowed.

Shaq swatted Orson back onto the ground where he landed with a heavy THUD.

There was a terrible cacophony from somewhere downstairs, followed almost immediately by an inhuman sounding howl from Jolie.

Miles's eyelids fluttered then snapped open wide.

"NO!" Sloane cried out, sure the monster's reinforcements had arrived and her daughter was dead.

But that was when the police rushed into the room.

Chapter Thirty-Four

Melinda

ENDINGS WERE USUALLY Melinda's favorite part of anything.

She loved the closure, but even more than that, endings were often the precursor to a new beginning, and a better something else. So much of this particular story was over, but it had paved the way for a future that was brighter than anything the Shellys had imagined twenty years ago.

"Satisfied?" Dominic asked.

She took her husband's hand as they looked out at their party. "*Satisfied* is such a relative term."

"Fair enough," he nodded. "In that case, how about *satisfied for now?*"

Melinda couldn't have smiled any wider. "Yes, for now I am deeply content. You?"

"Couldn't be happier." Dominic looked around their sprawling back lawn again, appearing even more self-satisfied than she probably did. "It's almost as if we planned this all from the start."

Maybe not *all of it*, but they did plan much if not most of what had happened, in one way or another, and the celebration was certainly earned.

Fade to Black was one hell of a documentary. Possibly Shellter Production's finest work so far, and the start of a new era for the studio. The picture of Liam Wentz being led out of that shithole skid row tenement while someone took a massive crap in the background was the most memed image in years, and the parody song "Good King Wentz A Loss" was climbing toward a billion views.

The Shellys had fueled the frenzy and fed the media with all the chum they could manage. Then they pulled a Beyonce, dropping the doc without any warning or fanfare. There were rumors it was on its way, and that it would be out of this world when it finally premiered, but few saw the shockwaves coming. Dominic and Melinda had always intended to make *West Hollywood Sunset* a launch title for Juke. Initially, they had assumed the same would hold true for *Black*. But Juke wasn't coming out for another year and the doc could not have been hotter.

Dollar for dollar, *Fade to Black* was the cheapest publicity the Shellys had ever bought. The film was free to stream on every platform. They would yank those rights back once their new platform was ready, but until then they wanted the documentary on everyone's lips. Unless an exposé on real life aliens dropped some time in between now and the Oscar noms, Sloane Alexander would be taking home her first Academy Award.

Fade to Black centered on allegations of child rape levied against founder of Wentz Studios, Liam Wentz, featuring interviews with twenty-three women and girls, accusing the predator of everything from inappropriate touching to forced oral sex and anal rape.

Wentz had been caught red-handed with Jolie and his thug. The trial was coming up, and word was Wentz would be singing on Sprog, the pedophile ring the Shellys were currently throwing a substantial amount of internal resources to rooting out, thanks in part to some hard candy from Nat.

The Rotten Tomatoes score for *Fade to Black* was at 98%, with only two asshole critics either approving of child rape or living their unfortunate lives without any clue. The audience score was two drops lower at 96%, but Melinda figured that was because some moviegoers were either too dumb or easily bored.

A brutally self-aware film.

Fade to Black is the first masterpiece this year.

Heartbreaking and infuriating in equal measure.

Necessary like no other documentary I've ever seen.

This film moves us past the media cycles of accusation and denial to bring us fireside with some brave victims of unimaginable trauma.

It's not like she needed the critics' approval, but—

"What are you happiest about?" Dominic asked, pulling Melinda from her thoughts.

"I'm happiest for Sloane. Not just for all of this." Melinda waved her hand around the room. "But because her gift is now evident to everyone, and the worst of this nightmare's behind her. How about you?"

"Same." Dominic nodded. "Orson, too. Just look at them."

Marquee star and wunderkind director, pressed together like they always were.

"My favorite part is that we had nothing to do with it," Melinda said.

Dominic nodded again. "It is nice to not do all the work for once."

The Shellys held hands, observing the couple in silence. They were standing too far away to hear what they saying over by the pool. But Orson had clearly started a story that Sloane was now finishing. There was something beautiful about that.

"Hanks and Wilson or Baldwin and Basinger?" Dominic asked.

"Hanks and Wilson," Melinda smiled, "No doubt in my mind."

"Because he just became the highest paid star on the planet and she doesn't even swear?" He chuckled.

"Good analogy, but no. I meant their relationship. They'll go the distance."

He scanned the lawn again. "We've done a lot of great work."

"We sure have."

Miles was there with his plus one, a stunning Nicole Everett, who had a slew of offers coming in and was actively refusing every one. Nicole had no desire to be anywhere near Hollywood, but was perfectly fine leveraging her smile and relative fame into a lucrative real estate career in Cielo Del Mar.

The Shellys might have little if anything to do with Miles and Nicole, but they had everything to do with Selena Nash, standing over by the bar laughing with her husband, Adam. She was retiring from her juggernaut of a series to become a producer for another six shows, all in development for Juke.

And the Shellys had everything to do with Amanda Byrd, there with her husband, Mike. Bake it Away was a whopper of a brand, and she too had several shows on the way, including *Vegan Cooking for Carnivores* and *Get Baked*, which adapted Bake it Away recipes with cannabis.

They also had everything to do with John and Vicky. The Shellys found the couple shortly after the Treadwells' marriage had crashed on the rocks. Still divorced, the partner writers were now two of the biggest names in publishing and had a dozen adaptations on the way for Juke, a new one every month for the streaming platform's first year. There would for sure be more after that, but nothing would be green lit for the second year until the Shellys could look at the data. The Treadwells were happy to write anything, "so long as it moves."

And finally, they had everything to do with Natalie, there with her steady yet unofficial boyfriend, Bennett Cole. Considering everything that needed to happen for Juke's second phase — the one that would change the world — Nat might be more important to their empire than anyone else.

Soon she would know. Right now, she had no idea.

"Are we being too standoffish?" Dominic asked.

This was their party, and yet they hadn't really spoken to anyone.

"Not at all," Melinda said. "We're here for anyone who wants an audience, but sometimes it's nice to stand in the back and survey all we've accomplished. In some ways, tonight feels like the culmination of everything we've done so far."

He squeezed her hand. "And a peek at all we're still going to do."

That was true. It wasn't just John and Vicky, Selena and Adam, Orson Beck, Natalie Monroe, or Amanda Byrd — it was seeing so many of the fruits of their labor all in one place. And, of course, Sloane Alexander. It made sense that she would be both their first and their newest. There was only so much they could do to help her all those years ago, when they first stood up to Wentz and he declared war on their futures.

It was a lava cake of revenge. Not only was their part of the story a blockbuster, with Wentz waiting for a trial he would never be able to buy his way out of, his downfall hadn't been entirely personal. The Shellys had been moving things around for a while, maneuvering every possible piece in place so they would be ready to sign on the dotted line when Wentz Studios suddenly became available for slightly less than a song. They were even making the kids show Replay, now with access to Shellter productions as well.

They cleaned house, fired anyone questionable while keeping any possible gems and putting the entire staff on probation. The end result was a goldmine of a back catalog the Shellys would know exactly how to leverage, starting with a massive boost to Juke's launch library, and a content machine they could immediately use to keep their production line producing some of the best television and film in the world. And they got their hands on *Replay*, the hour-long kids' remakes that prick had been developing, so they knew the next generation in the industry would be safe from predators of Wentz's ilk. At least, the actors who signed with them.

And it was still just the beginning.

After a little housecleaning of their own, Melinda felt more than satisfied. With Wentz out of the way and Shellter now the biggest name in town, it was easy enough to find out who on their staff had once been on the enemy's payroll or even taken a too-good-to-pass-up payoff. Their house was now in order, too. All was finally right with the world.

"Do you think we can do it?" Dominic asked, referring to the next phase of what might be the planet's most ambitious strategy. "Can we pull off the impossible, right in front of everyone?"

"It's only impossible until it's all done," Melinda said, still looking out on a swelling crowd of their accomplishments.

"Well then," Dominic met her eyes. "Let's get started."

Chapter Thirty-Five

Sloane

EVERYTHING WAS PERFECT.

Or at least as it could be for now.

"So," Orson smiled at Sloane from across the table. "Was I right?"

"No doubt about it," she beamed, "this is definitely the best restaurant in the world."

"*That I've been to,*" Orson corrected. "There's a place in the Maldives that's underwater. That might be better."

"Maybe the atmosphere, but not the food." Sloane looked down at their empty plates with a shake of her head. "No way."

Bella by the Sea was unlike any other restaurant Sloane had ever seen, or even heard about. The place was small, but not tiny. Still, it only hosted a small handful of diners each night. The bistro was owned and run by a father and son team from Italy. Five-star food that thanks to the ambiance and attention managed to deliver an experience that felt more like ten. The restaurant was located in the

Palms Couture shopping center in Cielo Del Mar. Orson managed to snag a reservation for the two of them a week ago, despite the months long waiting list.

This was Sloane's favorite kind of date — dinner and a movie.

And not just any movie. They had gone to see *Fade to Black* with a crowd, slipping in after the theater was full and taking seats in back because she was determined to see it anonymously in front of a paying audience at least once.

Sloane wondered if she would be as addicted to reading all the reviews if they weren't so overwhelmingly positive. Most agreed that a viewer had to be dead inside if they didn't shed a tear or several while watching the film. She was eager to see if that was true. But instead of sitting in the back row counting how many members of the audience were shedding tears, Orson spent a hundred and sixteen minutes holding her while she quietly sobbed with relief, validation, and victory.

The Shellys were proud of her, Orson was proud of her — hell, the world at large seemed proud of her. But mostly, Sloane was proud of herself.

The poison was finally out of her.

She was no longer living a rented life. She and Jolie had picked out a house and a car together. Sloane paid cash for the car and could have done the same for their new home if she'd wanted to.

Now there would be nothing standing in her way.

And if there was, then she would stand firm with rooted feet and fight off whatever attempted to stop her. *Fade to Black* had given her everything she needed, despite the project ultimately depriving Sloane of what she initially thought that she wanted.

Ever since leaving what was clearly the wrong side of the camera for her, she had longed to make movies in a different way. Sloane had imagined herself becoming a full-time director and pictured all the cinematic boundaries her career would eventually push, especially once she employed the Shellys to help her. She saw herself making the kinds of movies that got eager audiences wanting to hug their tubs of popcorn, delighted by the pure joy of cinema.

But *Fade to Black* had taught Sloane Alexander exactly what kind of filmmaker she actually was — a proud documentarian. No longer the broccoli of movies in her mind, she now saw the medium for what it was — an unparalleled opportunity for her to tell evocative, emotional storytelling that might not change the world on its own but could at least inspire the change makers to rattle and hum.

She'd hit it out of the park with her first swing, thanks in large part to her personal history with the material. Sloane was now looking forward to all the future projects that would have nothing whatsoever to do with her past.

Black had been nominated for a slew of smaller awards already and was still playing in a few theaters in cities like Cielo Del Mar, despite it having been available to stream for free on day one. Even the few critics who didn't care for the doc or didn't think it deserved the Oscar had zero doubt that a nomination was coming.

Sloane wanted to win but didn't care if the award went to someone else. The real victories belonged to her already. Liam Wentz was serving several life sentences — way too much time for him to ever get out on parole for good behavior. She would never have to see the monster again.

More and more girls kept coming forward with stories, not just about Liam Wentz, but about a few other notable men in Hollywood. Ellis was aggressively peeling the edges back on the Sprog story, and Sloane could still hear his chilling words in her head.

If this goes where I'm thinking, the story won't just be big. It might be the biggest story ever.

She didn't want to know the details.

But of course she would, and of course she would throw herself behind the camera and deliver the truth if that's what was required of her. Sloane didn't have much choice about her next project, seeing as she promised the Shellys that she'd deal with the flood of fresh accusations and follow this Sprog thing wherever it went. *Fade to Black* would be turned into a true crime docuseries with at least one season scheduled for Juke, and probably more, even if Sloane only shot the first one.

After this last round of adventures with the Shellys, Sloane now had zero doubts about Juke's eventual success, not that she had much before. There was something much bigger than what they had told her so far. Maybe that was due to the usual plausible deniability, and maybe it was something else. Sloane would be ready for whatever, whenever she needed to be.

"Are you in a food coma?" Orson asked, after she hadn't spoken for what had to be at least a minute. "You're not fading away on me, are you?"

Sloane Alexander had spent the last twenty years of her life terrified of losing herself to the darkness, but now she was no longer scared.

Because she had faded to black, and that was a blessing.

What to read next

Revenge is served ... Twelve people bound by a secret arrive for an exclusive dinner to find the other guests familiar in the most troubling ways. Their host is a star with glamour to spare and all the money in the world to spend on revenge.

Get Pretty Killer Today!

A Quick Favor ...

If you enjoyed this book, please take a moment to write a review on your favorite bookselling platform so other readers can enjoy it too. It would mean a lot to me.

Thank you,
Nolon King

About the Author

Nolon King writes fast-paced psychological thrillers set in the glitzy world of entertainment's power players with a bold, insightful voice. He's not afraid to explore the darker side of human nature through stories featuring families torn apart by secrets and lies.

Nolon loves to write about big questions and moral quandaries. How far would you go to cover up an honest mistake? Would you destroy your career to protect your family? How much of your soul would you sell to get the life of your dreams? Would you cheat on your husband to keep your children safe? Would you give in to a stalker's demands to save your marriage?

Also By Nolon King

Cold Vengeance

Cold Vengeance

Cold Reckoning

Hidden Justice

Hidden Justice

Hidden Honor

Hidden Shame

Hidden Virtue

No Justice

No Justice

No Escape

No Hope

No Return

No Stopping

No Fear

Once Upon A Crime

Once Upon A Crime

Twice Upon A Lie

Three Times a Murder

Dead For Good

Dead For Good

Left For Dead

Dead Of Night

Wake The Dead

Dead For Life

Stand Alone Novels

Pretty Killer

12

Blown

Miserable Lies

The Target

Secrets We Keep

Close To Home

Heat To Obsession

A Simple Kill

Tell Me No Lies

Red Carpet Black

Fade To Black

Victim